MOIST

MOIST

mark haskell smith

AN LA WEEKLY BOOK FOR
ST. MARTIN'S PRESS
NEW YORK

ISBN 0-312-30364-5

First Edition: October 2002

10 9 8 7 6 5 4 3 2 1

For Olivia and Jules

MOIST

1

"**T**HIS IS SO fuckin' cool, man."

Morris burst through the doors of the lab carrying what looked like a log wrapped in black plastic. His white cotton smock, bearing the name United Pathology, flapped around his bony frame as he rushed forward. Morris was excited, breathless. He had something really good. His sneakers squeaked on the tile floor as he skidded to a stop in front of a young man with tall black hair.

"Bob. Dude. Check this out."

Bob didn't look up from the computer. He slouched his skateboarder-lanky body in a stylish black chair designed to improve his posture, draping one of his legs across the desk so that one scuffy black shoe touched the side of the monitor while his other foot twitched to some unheard autonomic beat on the floor. He kept his eyes on the screen, thoughtfully stroking his trim goatee, as he scrolled through a digital gallery of young Canadian virgins on the Internet. He eyed the young blondes intently, staring at their pert breasts, ice-cream-scoop butts, and spread patches of pink surrounded by wisps of blond curls. They could have been Swedish or maybe Norwegian, but they were definitely from some frosty part of the world. Cold and clean and young. Their bodies promising sex fresh as mountain air, clear as spring water, and as pure as new-fallen snow. Like a beer ad. Bob twisted in his seat, his pants suddenly too small.

Morris cleared his throat.

"Dude, it's totally grisly."

"Can't you see I'm busy?"

Undaunted by Bob's lack of enthusiasm, Morris put the package down on the desk in front of him and began to unwrap it.

"It smells a little."

"Then don't open it."

"I thought you liked tattoos."

Bob heaved a sigh and moused his way out of the porn site.

"Put it in a tray, all right?"

Morris nodded and crossed the lab to the sink. He pulled out a large stainless steel examining tray and carried it back.

"Good idea, Bob. These things are always seepin' a little."

Morris gently plopped the package in the tray and pulled the plastic away, unveiling his prize. Bob recoiled at the sight, instinctively covering his mouth and nose. Morris looked at him, surprised.

"You gonna puke?"

Bob shook his head.

"Check out the tattoos, dude. Check 'em out."

Morris picked up the severed arm and rolled it over. Congealing blood oozed out and smeared the surgical tray. It was a tough-looking arm. Muscular and hairy. Tattoos were scattered up and down, inside and out. The letters *H-O-L-A* etched into the knuckles. Morris rotated the arm again and Bob saw an exceptionally beautiful tattoo of a woman laying naked on her back with her legs in the air. A man lay with her, his head buried between her thighs.

"What'dya think, man?"

Bob covered his nostrils and leaned in close. The tattoo was skillfully drawn, with real flair. The woman's body seemed to quiver, as if she were coming.

"Good, isn't it?"

Bob looked up at Morris.

"It's amazing."

Bob opened the bottom drawer of his desk and pulled out a Polaroid camera.

"Rotate the arm a couple of inches up."

"Like this?"

"Up."

Morris complied. Bob got close to the arm and then pushed the button. Flash, whir, ding. The camera spit out a photo. Bob stuck the picture in his pocket and put the camera back in the drawer. He looked at Morris.

"I'm thinking about making a coffee run. You want some?"

"Let me go. I've spent too much time with the arm. I need a break."

Bob looked at the arm.

"What are we supposed to do with it anyway?"

Morris wrapped the appendage in the plastic.

"I gotta take it to the lab at Parker Center tomorrow morning after they drain it or whatever."

Bob shot Morris a look of disbelief.

"This is evidence?"

Morris shifted his weight from foot to foot, something he did when he was nervous or really had to pee. He took his sunglasses out of his pocket and stuck them on his nose so he wouldn't have to look Bob in the eye.

"Bob. Dude. I don't know that it's evidence for sure."

"Is it from a crime scene?"

Morris finished wrapping the arm.

"Double latte, right?"

Bob shook his head.

"Whatever, man."

Morris spun on his heel and left. Bob sighed, picked up the

arm, and walked it over to a large freezer. He swung the big silver door open and slid the arm onto a shelf filled with hundreds of other lumps, bumps, cysts, clippings, cuttings, kibbles, and bits. Bob sat back down in front of the computer, but the blondes had lost their allure.

He pulled the Polaroid out of his pocket and watched it slowly finish developing. It was a clear picture of the tattoo. The artist was obviously very talented. Bob looked closer, studying the woman. Intricately drawn, her breasts hung voluptuously, spreading across her chest and swinging down just a little toward her armpits. She had a full head of long black hair that flowed away from her body. Her legs, arms, and ass were perfectly proportioned, not thin or skinny; there was nothing girly about her, she had a womanly weight. A sensual mass. Her mouth was a half smile, half grimace, as her body bucked and kicked in the throws of orgasm. Her eyes wide open as if surprised by the sensation.

Bob looked at her and felt a strange sensation of his own. It was as if he knew her. Or maybe, closer to the truth, as if she were the woman he wanted to know. His idea of what a sexy woman looked like. Bob felt a pang of jealousy when he looked at the man's body. Although Bob was considered by many people to be a good-looking dude in relatively robust shape, he couldn't compete with the taught and articulated muscles, the pure sexual power of the man in the tattoo. All that energy focused between a woman's legs.

Bob ran his finger over the Polaroid, following the line that detailed her thigh to her belly to her breasts to her lips. He surprised himself when a little moan came out of his mouth.

Bob absently traced a line with his finger slowly down his chest, across his belly, to his crotch. He felt a swelling.

It was a very good tattoo.

2

MAURA LOOKED DOWN on her client. She'd seen his type before. Nervous, scared, hopeful that she would take over and give him release. She never did. That's not why she was here. She was a teacher. She had valuable information to impart and no matter how much they whined or begged, they had to learn to do it themselves. Besides, it's not like she was a whore. If anything, she looked like the head of psychiatry for a large urban hospital. She was somewhat officious, her blond hair cut blunt and to the point, her blue eyes intense. She had an authoritative mouth, not particularly welcoming or warm, with small, slightly angled teeth. Despite what some people called a cold or, charitably, professional appearance, there was something extremely attractive about Maura. It was probably her breasts.

She listened to the familiar whack-a whack-a, the grunts, the short breaths. Using her calmest, most reassuring voice, she offered guidance.

"Relax, Mr. Larga. Take a deep breath."

Larga tried. He sucked air into his saggy, pale body. He exhaled noisily through his thick nostrils and licked his fat lips.

"Relax your abdominal muscles. Relax your thighs."

Larga squirmed in the chair. He was uncomfortable being naked under bright lights. He was embarrassed by what he was doing.

"My arm's getting tired."

Maura had heard this before.

"Orgasm is not the goal."

"I'm getting chapped. I need more lubricant."

She handed him the Astroglide and spoke to him like a reprimanding schoolteacher.

"There are hundreds of different ways to stimulate the tumescent male member. Hammering away with your fist is just one of them."

He blinked up at her, ever hopeful.

"Can you show me?"

Maura picked up a plastic dildo and demonstrated.

"Most men find this one unbelievable."

Larga tried. God bless him. He tried his best. But he couldn't relax and, in the end, went back to whacking away with his fist. Maura sighed. It was so predictable. Some people could relax and benefit from her advice, others just wanted to jerk off in front of a woman. A grunt burst from Larga's mouth. Maura saw that he was nearing orgasm.

"Don't tense. Relax. Start taking deep breaths."

But Larga couldn't relax, and with a loud exhalation ejaculated on his belly. Maura handed him a box of tissues.

"Well, it's a start."

Larga wiped up quickly and started pulling on his clothes.

"You can wash your hands right over there."

He buckled up and went over to the sink. He was in a hurry, like he'd just done something he should be ashamed of. Maura made small talk to ease his guilt.

"So what do you do for a living, Mr. Larga?"

"I write cookbooks."

"That must be fun."

"It's okay."

Larga nodded and ran his fingers through his thinning hair.

"How long have you been a . . . you know . . . a coach?"

"I've been in practice about three years."

Maura watched as Larga looked at her. Or, more accurately, as he looked at her breasts. She was used to this. Ever since she was fourteen she'd watched men look at her face and then slowly drag their eyes down to her chest. Then they would converse with her breasts. It annoyed Maura, but she couldn't really blame them. Her breasts were her most prominent feature. They were large for her thin frame; she looked like a model, a "creepy stick" as her girlfriend said. People always assumed she'd had her tits done, but in truth if she was going to have anything done, she'd have them reduced. They stuck out, called attention to themselves, and caused men to come up to her and say the stupidest things. For example, what Larga was about to say.

"You must be pretty good at it yourself."

"At what?"

"This, you know . . . autoerotica."

Maura smiled and lit some incense.

"Next week. Same time?"

Larga nodded and started out the door.

"Practice what I showed you. Every day."

The door closed and Larga was gone. Maura carefully stripped the sheet off the chair and tossed it in a hamper. She bent down and took a new sheet out of a small cupboard and put it on the chair. She thought about Larga and smiled to herself.

Some people just naturally know how to jerk off.

He wasn't one of them.

3

I T WAS A hectic day at the shop. A Toyota RAV was being eviscerated. Sparks flew everywhere as three men, masked by heavy clothes and protective face shields, butchered the car with arc welders. Gleaming metal entrails fell away as the car quickly became skeletal. The guts were gathered by a teenage boy who picked them up and carted them off. The men worked together calmly and efficiently. They were experts.

The carcass of another car, possibly a Camaro, lay off to the side. Stripped bare, like the leftovers of a piranha attack. Other cars, covered with oil-stained tarps, were parked at the far end of the dilapidated garage waiting to be slaughtered.

The rhythm of the butchery was interrupted when a brand-new Mercedes sedan pulled into the garage and parked right in the middle. The work stopped. The torches clicking off as soon as the workers recognized the man in the Mercedes.

Like a bad hombre in an old western, he climbed out of the car and surveyed the shop like he owned the place. He did. He was Esteban Sola, El Jefe from the tough border town of Juarez, where he oversaw a major drug-smuggling and DEA-agent-murdering operation. Esteban was so successful and so ruthless that he eventually muscled his way into *La Eme*, the Mexican mafia, in Los Angeles. Now he was one of the top lieutenants. A man with his own crew. A man people feared. A man who commanded respect.

The workmen eagerly turned to give Esteban their undivided attention. That or he'd kick the living shit out of them.

"Hola, compañeros."

Esteban spoke with a gravelly voice and an authority that caused most men to feel a vibration in their scrotum.

"Hola, Señor Sola."

Although he was not a handsome man by any stretch—his brown skin was oily and pocked and he wore a bushy black mustache to hide his thin lips—women were strangely attracted to him. They didn't seem to notice that his hair was matted down and slathered with some kind of product from Switzerland that made it appear thick and lustrous when it was actually thin and limp or that his eyes were soft and sensual, betraying a kind of artistic sensibility behind the hard-ass Ray-Bans that he wore day and night. To look at him, without the trappings of power, the fear of violence, and the allure of cash money, you might think he was a busboy. But, getting out of his immaculate Mercedes, accompanied by a slender young gringo named Martin, wearing what can only be described as vaquero Armani, he was an ice-cold blast of cool.

It was calculated. Esteban didn't allow anyone in his crew to shave their heads Pelón style or wear the long socks and short pants so popular with the other Latino gangsters. It was a prison thing. Esteban figured that if you looked like you were from prison, that's where you'd end up. It was much better to look like a movie producer.

"¿Que onda?"

One of the workers stepped forward and extended his hand. Esteban shook it, grabbing the man's hand in a viselike grip. The workman couldn't help but notice the sharp and glittery rings encircling Esteban's fingers. The workman wasn't merely admiring Esteban's fine jewelry. All he could think was, those must really hurt when they hit you.

"We got a couple of new cars we're cuttin' up."

"You steal 'em?"

"No. Some *cholos* from Long Beach."

Esteban laughed.

"I don't trust those *pendejos,* they'd steal my car if they could."

The men laughed. They had to.

Esteban continued, warming to his audience.

"If one of them ever tries to steal *mi coche . . .*" He paused for effect.

"Muerte."

Martin, the dapper gringo, his hair heavy with some kind of gel, wearing an old leather jacket over a bright, big-collared shirt and tight pants that made him look like a wayward rock star, played the sidekick.

"You should give them a demonstration."

The workmen nodded. Esteban, like a magician about to perform his greatest trick, spoke solemnly.

"El Ladrón esta como un culero."

The mention of a *culero,* someone who smuggled drugs by shoving them up his rectum, confused the workmen. This element of mystery helped Esteban's performance.

"Mira."

Esteban led the workman around to the driver's seat to demonstrate.

"If I push this button. It is safe to drive. But if I don't . . . and you trigger these pressure plates . . ."

Esteban looked around and found a heavy plastic box on the floor. He placed the box on the driver's seat of the car and pressed the remote on his key chain.

Bam.

A sharpened stainless steel fleschette burst from under the

seat and tore through the plastic. A would-be car thief would get two feet of stainless steel right up his ass.

"*¿Es la puta madre, no?*"

Esteban laughed out loud and looked over at Martin.

"We should market these . . . much better than The Club."

The workmen were shaken and impressed by this new level of car security. They began to discreetly back away from Esteban. He turned to the workmen and got right to the point.

"*¿Tu viste* Amado?"

The workmen shook their heads.

"He was here yesterday," one of them ventured.

Esteban looked at the workmen, his voice weighed with its full menace. "Tell him to call me."

4

AMADO LAY IN the bathtub. He was a big man, muscular and dark, his face permanently sunburned, worn and cragged by wind, cigarettes, and tequila. Still, he was undeniably handsome with a sensual quality that women found irresistible. There was something about his eyes; even with some serious blood loss, they were intense, focused. Men found it difficult to look Amado in the eye. Even Esteban, a man you wouldn't want to fuck with for any reason, was uncomfortable holding Amado's gaze for too long. It was an animal stare, like he was sizing you up for dinner. For some reason women found this arousing, and would melt into his stare, surrendering to him.

Amado groaned and shifted in the tub. A bag of ice and several towels were strapped to his shoulder where his right arm used to be. His torso was uncovered revealing tattoos of naked women and couples engaged in intercourse. Every possible sexual position explicitly and beautifully rendered. The Kama Sutra inked on his body.

A slick smear of bright red rolled down the porcelain toward the drain, the blood appearing redder than usual in contrast to the brightness of the tub. His jeans were soaked through, the dark trail stretching to his cowboy boots. Amado reached down for the bottle of Herradura tequila that was wedged between his thighs. He pulled it to his lips and took a long gulp. Replacing the bottle he let out a shout.

"¡Pendejo!"

An extremely handsome young man, Norberto, his long hair gleamingly groomed and tied back in a ponytail, entered the room carrying a lime and a knife. The usually cool and stylish Norberto was nervous, sweaty, unsure what to say or do. He had been getting ready to go salsa dancing at Rudolpho's and didn't want to get any blood on his clothes. He had found this crazy purple sharkskin suit at a vintage store and just got it back from having it tailored to fit his slender frame. He could see himself spinning, swaying, and glimmering on the dance floor.

But no, he had answered the door and now had to baby-sit an amputee. It wasn't a choice. Amado was his friend, and more important, his boss. Norberto had to look after him. Still, he felt slightly conflicted. It was understandable given the circumstances.

"You want some lime, man?"

"I want a fuckin' doctor."

"I called. He's coming."

Norberto whipped the butterfly knife open in one deft move and sliced the lime into bite-sized wedges. He held one out. Amado took another long pull on the Herradura, then opened his mouth. Norberto brought the lime up to Amado's lips. He was careful of his fingers as Amado bit down on the lime, sucking the juice out in anger, frustration, and pain.

"Esteban's been calling, man."

"Fuck him."

Norberto reached for the bottle of tequila. Amado swatted him away with his good arm.

"I need this."

Norberto sat down on the toilet next to the bathtub.

"What about me? I need something for my nerves, *cabrón*."

Amado sighed and handed the bottle over. Norberto took a long pull and then popped a piece of lime in his mouth.

"Don't drink it all, *pendejo*."

Norberto handed the bottle back. He looked at Amado.

"Where's your arm, man?"

"I left it in Carlos Vila's garage."

Norberto thought about that for a moment.

"What were you doing in Carlos Vila's garage?"

"Killing him."

"*¿Por qué*, man?"

"Carlos and me, we had a deal. Then that *maricón* decided to sell me out."

"So you killed him, man?"

Amado nodded, took another pull on the bottle. He turned his head and glared at Norberto. Norberto understood immediately and held out another piece of lime for Amado to chomp down on.

"If you killed him, what happened to your arm?"

Amado sighed again.

"I was hanging him in his garage. Make it look like it was *suicidio*, you know? I was up on this ladder fixin' the rope and somehow, man, somehow I hit the fuckin' switch for the automatic door while my arm was stuck in the rails. This fuckin' chain wrapped around my arm and just . . . *mira* . . . look what it did. Just ripped my arm off."

Norberto stifled a laugh.

"*Qué bárbaro*, man."

"It's not funny, *pendejo*."

Norberto straightened up, more out of fear than respect.

"Sorry, man."

"*Pinche puta madre, cabrón*."

Norberto cut another piece of lime as Amado slugged

down more Herradura. Norberto popped the lime into Amado's mouth, avoiding the gnashing teeth.

"*Las placas* is gonna be looking for you, man. You left your fingerprints."

Amado shook his head.

"I wore gloves."

"Yeah, *patrón*, but you left your fuckin' arm there. They'll get your fingerprints right off your fingers."

Amado's expression changed, his face twisting in frustration.

"*¡Carajo!*"

"You're fucked, man."

Amado turned to Norberto.

"Go back and get my fuckin' arm, *pendejo*."

"*¿Ahora?*"

"*Sí, ahora.*"

"What about the doctor?"

"Leave the door open."

"Open? This barrio ain't safe, man."

Amado turned and glared at Norberto, letting his eyes make the threat. Norberto handed Amado the lime and hurried out the door.

5

BOB LAY STRETCHED out on a couch in the classic TV-viewing
pose of the average American male, his oversized T-shirt
pulled up to reveal a fuzzy belly button, his bare feet dangling
over the edge, his head propped up under a couple of ratty-
looking pillows. He was a good-looking young man. He wasn't
beautiful or striking, he was what Maura liked to call normal
handsome. His eyes were strong and symmetrical, his nose dis-
creet. He had a strong chin with a dimple, which he hid with
his goatee, but he felt that loss was compensated by the fact
that his goatee showed off his lips. Even Bob had to admit that
he had very sensual, attractive lips for a straight guy.

Bob took a sip of beer and shifted slightly on the couch. He
was getting comfortable.

The couch was covered in what Bob liked to call hippie
shit, a kind of rough Moroccan fabric that inspired conversa-
tions about hashish and Amsterdam. It was secondhand, like
everything else in the apartment picked up at flea markets and
thrift stores, but Bob liked it. It didn't match any of the other
furniture. The vinyl beauty parlor chairs covered in silver and
pink. The carved wood coffee table with its Mexican tile top.
The black velvet paintings of Chinese landscapes. Bob liked
the eclectic quality of his surroundings. It made him feel like an
artist.

The TV was on, but Bob wasn't watching, he was studying

the Polaroid. There was something about this image. He didn't know exactly, couldn't put his finger on it, couldn't articulate what he found so compelling. It wasn't the usual graphic pornography that he enjoyed, the explicit photographs of wide-eyed and enthusiastic young suckers and fuckers. Maybe it was the simplicity, the lack of four-color glossy detail. Bob didn't know what it was, but there was an assuredness of line, and what Bob could only call aliveness of the woman, that turned Bob on. Like a motherfucking blowtorch.

The sound of keys turning the lock on the front door knocked Bob out of his reverie. Maura came in, threw her keys on the table, and said, "I need to do some yoga."

Bob sat up. "You want a drink?"

"Bob, I'm trying to purify my body, not pollute it."

Bob slammed down the rest of his beer and nodded. He understood. Antioxidizing, toxin flushing, wheat grass juicin'. He knew what she was doing and he was understanding. Understanding was what Bob was good at.

"Hard day, huh?"

"I should've been a doctor. Maybe then they'd listen to me instead of trying to get me to give them a hand job. You wouldn't ask a doctor for a hand job would you?"

"Well . . . if she looked like you I might."

Maura didn't respond. She walked into the kitchen and began sifting through the mail.

Bob got up off the couch and went over to her. He put his arm around her and kissed the back of her neck.

"That was a compliment."

"Not now."

"Why not?"

"Because I'm going to yoga class."

Bob sulked into the kitchen and got another beer out of the fridge. He popped the top off and took a long gulp. He looked over at Maura. Her slim frame. Pretty face. Nice rack. Bob loved her. Or, to be truthful, he loved parts of her. Parts of her body. Parts of her personality. Bob felt that certain sections of Maura, well, you just weren't going to find anything better. Her breasts, for example, or her sense of humor when she was in a good mood. Her tongue. Her chin. Her ears. Her perfectly formed feet. Bob could go on for hours, separating her into desirable and undesirable chunks. Getting smaller and more specific as he went. Deconstructing Maura. Good title for a movie.

"I'm really horny."

"And I'm really not."

"Aw, c'mon."

"Go beat off."

Bob scoffed. He'd heard this before. As if masturbating was the answer to everything.

"You know, some guys actually like to make love to a warm body."

"Yeah, well, this warm body's going to yoga, so if you wanna squirt, you're gonna have to do it yourself."

"Maybe I should make an appointment."

"You can't afford it. Your health insurance doesn't cover it."

Bob was surprised.

"You take insurance?"

"Of course. I'm a health care provider."

Bob nodded dimly.

"What did you think? I was like some kind of massage parlor? Giving hand jobs for thirty bucks?"

"I, uh, I didn't know you took insurance. That's all."

"That's because you never ask about me. You have no interest in me."

Bob rose to his defense, his voice cracking into a high whine.

"That's not true! I just asked you to have sex."

Maura looked at him with an eyebrow raised. Bob stood there, shifting from foot to foot, ready for it. Ready for Maura's volcanic temper to erupt. He'd seen it many times before. The change in her voice, the blood surging to her face, the gulping for air, the shouting, sometimes slamming furniture around. Bob stood as relaxed as possible, like a palm tree waiting for the hurricane to arrive. Maura struggled for self-control.

"I don't have time for this."

With that, Maura walked into the bedroom and pulled off her blouse. Bob watched from the living room, beer gripped tightly, as Maura changed into her yoga clothes.

Maura came back into the room clutching her sticky mat and Mexican blankets.

"See you later, sweetie."

And she was gone.

Norberto didn't waste any time with the back door. He just kicked it in. He clicked on his penlight and swept it around the garage. Crime-scene tape fluttered festively in the wind like streamers from a little kid's birthday party. Otherwise the garage was unexceptional. Old cans of paint stacked on shelves. A shovel. A rake. Plastic containers of transmission fluid. Liquid Plumber. Junk. The penlight beam stopped on a sled. The faded words Radio Flyer painted in red. Norberto, born and raised in Juarez, wasn't immediately sure what it was. He'd heard of sleds, but had never seen one before. He looked at the rails, the wood slats. A sled in LA. What the fuck did Carlos need with a sled? *Raro,* man.

Norberto continued sweeping the room with the tiny beam. He saw a ratchet set from Sears. Norberto knew that those were supposed to be worth some money. He considered boosting it for a second, then changed his mind. The beam of light stopped on the chalk outline where Carlo's body must've been. There was a dark splotch, blood or motor oil, Norberto couldn't tell, next to the outline. A few feet away from that was another chalk outline. This one smaller. About the size and shape of Amado's right arm.

Max Larga stood in his modern, gourmet-equipped kitchen picking his nose. This action was reflected and distorted over and over in the gleaming appliances and cookware that surrounded him. He pulled his pinky out of his nostril and admired the prize. Without thinking he stuck the gleaming mucus ball into his mouth, smacking his thick lips like it was a fresh tiny oyster, and went about preparing dinner.

He took a starched white apron off a hook and strapped it around his corpulent waist. He pulled a roasting pan out of a drawer and plopped a large leg of lamb into it. Larga took fresh marjoram out of the Sub-Zero. Using a large knife he expertly diced the herbs and dumped them in a bowl with a small amount of olive oil. He added salt and pepper and then stuck his hands in the bowl and began mixing. Larga carried the bowl over to the leg of lamb and began rubbing the oil and spices on the meat. His shiny hands caressed the soft, pink meat as he worked the spices into the flesh. Larga found himself getting slightly aroused. He unconsciously pressed his crotch against the butcher-block counter with a gentle rocking motion. He caught himself, his face flushing in embarrassment, when he realized he was using his newly acquired masturbation strokes on the lamb.

He quickly washed his hands, threw the lamb in the oven, and opened a bottle of merlot.

Esteban was frustrated. How many times was he going to sneak guys over the border, give them jobs, give them a chance, give them a fucking life? And what do these fucking *maricóns* do? They fuck it up. They were always fucking things up. They didn't appreciate what crime could do for you. Crime could fucking pay, *cabrón*. Crime could add inches to your cock. Crime could set you up in a life like you never even dreamed. But some people just didn't get it. Esteban knew that Amado didn't get it. Didn't appreciate the opportunity. The Caucasians knew about loyalty. It was the fucking *caballeros* who were trouble. Esteban knew he'd be better off hiring out-of-work linebackers from Texas A & M. At least the dumb white guys appreciated a chance to do something with a little action, a little adrenaline. They'd be loyal. But Esteban felt a certain loyalty himself, a connection with La Raza. Despite all the trouble they caused, he compulsively helped his countrymen.

Esteban put down his beer and looked at Martin. The young man stubbed out his cigarette and stared back at Esteban without blinking. Perhaps because he felt smarter than Esteban or because he was stoned all the time, Martin wasn't afraid to tell Esteban the truth . . . even if it pissed Esteban off. Esteban was wise enough to know not to surround himself with ass kissers. Still, there's something to be said for being surrounded by ass kissers. Esteban sighed.

"I call someone. I tell them to come to me. And what happens? They disappear. What's that?"

"We all need to communicate better."

Esteban scoffed.

"It's beyond that. It's fuckin' disrespectful."

Martin nodded.

"But if we had digital cell phones . . ."

Esteban cut him off.

"I'm thinking we should make an example of him."

"What good would that do?"

Esteban lit a cigarette.

"Part of the job is keeping people afraid of you."

Martin nodded.

"A branding strategy."

Esteban blew smoke out across the room. Christ, this kid was smart. He didn't know what a "branding strategy" was . . . but this kid, with his brains . . . he could go places. If he would only listen to Esteban and learn from his experience.

Esteban understood the difference between book smart and street smart. The high-tech, fast-track, polished-chrome-and-glass world of brokerage firms and high-rise office towers with young secretaries in tight little suits versus the low-tech, testosterone-fueled, down-and-dirty world of cheap motels, panel vans, and arbitration by firing squad.

Martin was white bread. Groomed to be a corporate lawyer. He didn't quite comprehend the subtle nuances of running an organized crime crew for La Eme. He didn't understand that 90 percent of being El Jefe was showing you had *huevos* to spare. Fucking computers and cell phones wouldn't do it. Esteban didn't want his men to call him up, he wanted them to crawl naked through a cactus field if he asked. That's respect. Respect for El Jefe and respect for his *huevos*.

Esteban looked at Martin.

"*Exacto*. We take the *maricón* and we brand his ass."

"We need to find him first."

Esteban stood up.

"Then we find him. *Vamos*."

6

NORBERTO RETURNED TO his house to find the door wide open.

"Fuck, man."

He walked in, closed the door and bolted it shut. He turned and yelled toward the bathroom door.

"I told you to shut the fucking door, man."

There was no answer from the bathroom. Norberto turned and walked towards it.

"You dead?"

He paused. There was no answer.

"I hope you saved me some Herradura, man."

Norberto entered the bathroom. Amado was gone. The tequila was gone. Only a sick-looking streak of drying blood remained. Norberto turned on the water and started cleaning the tub. Blood is hard to clean. Especially if it's dried.

I need some scrubbing fucking bubbles, man. This is a tough stain.

Norberto reached under the sink and pulled out a can of Comet and a scrubby sponge. He shook the Comet out all over the tub. A green dusting of caustic powder fell over the blood. He began to vigorously attack the stain.

Norberto, engrossed in trying to clean the tub, didn't hear Esteban and Martin as they entered the bathroom.

"You having your period, *marción?*"

Norberto wheeled around. Upon seeing Esteban his first instinct was to run for his life. But he knew that was pointless, since Esteban would eventually find him, and there was only one way out of the bathroom anyhow. Thinking quickly, Norberto decided, despite the rapidly spreading stain in his underwear, to play it cool. He affected a casual tone.

"Hey, Esteban. You want me to come clean your tub? No charge, man."

Esteban turned the water off.

"I got a maid."

"Whatever, *cabrón*, you need me, I'm there."

Norberto realized that he was acting a little too easy to please. But by then it was too late. Esteban turned to Martin.

"See this? This *pendejo*'s got no *huevos*. He's wants to lick my asshole."

"No, man. Fuck, no. I don't wanna do that."

Esteban continued, not looking at Norberto.

"I think he's got something to hide."

Norberto knew that pain was on its way.

"What? I'm not hiding nothing, nada."

Martin closed the lid on the toilet and sat down. He opened a small black leather pouch he was carrying in his jacket pocket. It looked like a cigar holder.

"We'll see about that."

Martin took a syringe and a vial of clear liquid out of the pouch. Norberto looked at Esteban.

"What the fuck is that, man?"

Esteban just grinned.

"Don't you wanna ask me something? I got nothing to hide, man. You don't have to do this, man."

Norberto was beginning to freak. Martin held the vial upside down and, just like he'd seen on television, filled the syringe with the clear fluid. He put the vial back in the bag and tapped the air bubble to the top of the syringe.

"What is that shit, man?"

Esteban looked at Norberto. He liked this. This was fun. Watching Norberto shit his pants, beg for his life. This was gonna be good.

"Where's Amado?"

Norberto told the truth.

"He was here, man. I went out to get something and when I came back he was gone."

"What's with the tub?"

Norberto looked at the bloodstain, the Comet, and the scrubby sponge he still clutched tightly in his fist.

"Blood, man. It's just blood."

"Whose blood is it?"

"Amado's."

"Did you kill Amado?"

"No, man."

Esteban laughed.

"He cut himself shaving?"

Norberto looked at Esteban. Then he looked over at Martin. Martin gave the syringe a little squirt. That shit looked evil.

"Look, Esteban, I didn't have nothing to do with this, man."

"Dígame."

"Amado hurt his arm."

"He go to the hospital?"

"No, man, it's more fucked up than that."

Esteban hated to lose his temper. All his heroes, the bad guys in the movies, Marlon Brando as the Godfather or anything with Christopher Walken in it, those guys never lost their temper until they were pushed too far. Esteban admired that.

He wanted to be cool like that. But Brando didn't have to put up with wetback fuckups like he did. Esteban slapped Norberto across the face. Slapped him hard. Norberto reeled, hitting his head against the side of the tub, breaking open a nasty gash. Norberto's blood oozed down into the Comet.

"What happened? What happened to Amado's arm?"

Not wanting to get hit again, Norberto blurted it out.

"It got cut off, man."

The look that crossed Esteban's face was unusual. A mixture of mirth, disgust, and genuine shock.

"Bullshit."

"*Es verdad.*"

Esteban smacked Norberto again.

"Amado killed Carlos Vila, but somehow he got his arm cut off."

Esteban was surprised by this.

"He killed Carlos? *¿Por qué?*"

"I don't know nothing about it, man. But they had some kind of deal and Carlos was cheating Amado. So, you know Amado, he whacked him."

Martin and Esteban exchanged a look. Martin spoke first.

"They can reattach that arm."

Norberto shook his head.

"No, they can't, man."

"With advancements in microsurgery all kinds of things are possible. He may not have full range of motion again, but—"

Norberto interrupted Martin.

"He left his fucking arm there, man. He don't got it."

Esteban leaned in close to Norberto. Norberto squirmed, squinted, and waited for the violence.

"What?"

"He left his arm with Carlos, man."

Esteban stared at Norberto.

"Give him the shot."

Amado woke up. His arm, or more precisely the spot where his arm used to be, was throbbing. His eyes focused on the ceiling. Cottage cheese with specks of glittering gold. A lamp on the bedside table cast a muted yellow glow around the room. Amado twisted his neck and saw that the chest of drawers had been draped with a sheet and was lined with stainless doctor tools. Amado noticed that an IV drip had been attached to his arm. He heard something in the next room and croaked a sound out of his mouth.

The door swung open and a young black man entered.

"You're up? How ya feeling?"

Amado tried to say something. He croaked again.

"Hang on. I know what you need."

The young man brought a cup with a flexi-straw up to Amado's mouth.

"The anesthetic can really dry you out. Go ahead. Drink it."

Amado sucked on the straw. He was disappointed when cool water entered his mouth and trickled down his dried-out throat. The young man looked hopeful.

"Now how are you feeling?"

Amado nodded. He tried to speak.

"Malo."

The young man nodded.

"I'll give you something for the pain. But you're going to have to rest for a few days. You move around too much that arm's gonna open up. Trust me, that won't be good."

Amado nodded as the young man loaded something into some kind of needle and shot it into the IV drip.

"¿Dónde?"

The young man smiled at him.

"My Spanish is really bad. You'll feel better soon."

And before he could respond, Amado was out.

7

D ON DIDN'T LIKE beer. He liked wine. Good wine. He couldn't stand the stuff that passed for chardonnay at The Roost. That's where his partner and the other LAPD detectives liked to go to drink beer and watch sports on TV. Don wanted to go. He enjoyed spending time with his friends and colleagues. He even liked the dim little bar with gnawed booths and sawdust on the floor. But that cheap shit they called wine gave him a headache. One glass and a little pinprick of pain would materialize right behind his left eye. Two glasses and the pinprick would grow to a dull throb and he'd feel slightly nauseous. Three glasses would guarantee a hangover so toxic that Don would consider taking his gun and blowing his brains out. So Don went to the fancy wine bar nestled among the skyscrapers in the financial district downtown.

He liked the bartender, a fresh-faced kid just out of college with a degree in enology. The kid referred to the bar as an enoteca—a wine library. Maybe he was pretentious or just overeducated, but the kid knew his grape juice. Don liked that. It made getting lit seem like an intellectual pursuit. What he didn't like was the clientele. The wine bar was crammed to the rafters after work. Young men and women, lawyers and businesspeople, all smartly dressed in their Brooks Brothers and Ann Taylor suits, schmoozing each other. Talking about cell phones and BMWs, personal trainers and the stock market.

Don didn't fit in with this crowd, but he didn't stand out either. His face had taken a few punches in its youth, but the misshapen nose added a blast of rogue beauty to his handsome, angular, features. He was solidly built with a stocky, muscular body underneath his off-the-rack brown suits and his Fantastic Sam haircut. In fact, without the gun tucked into the back of his pants, Don could easily be mistaken for a salesman or a community college math teacher.

Don watched as the young and well-heeled passed out business cards and tried to make deals. He glanced over at the bartender.

"When I was their age I was trying to get laid. Now all they want is cash."

The bartender nodded.

"Money is the new god."

Don raised his glass.

"I prefer the old ones. Here's to Bacchus."

Don drank.

"You want to try the same wine, another year?"

"Is it a better year?"

The bartender smiled.

"You tell me."

He poured a taste into a fresh glass. Don swirled the wine and gave it an expert sip, lightly sucking air across his tongue as the wine rolled around inside his mouth. Finally he swallowed.

"Currants. Currants and figs."

The bartender smiled.

"I thought you'd like it."

He filled Don's glass, then went off to take more orders, leaving Don to contemplate his drink. Don was a compulsive people watcher, an eavesdropper more out of professional habit than anything else. On a normal night he would listen to the chatter, easily discerning the give-and-take of games commencing and ending, men and women dancing the mating dance, human nature falling into predictable patterns. But tonight he tuned them out. Tonight he was preoccupied. He'd had quite a day.

It started out normal. Shower, shave, shit. Head to Betty's for two eggs, toast, and coffee. Read the sports page. The Dodgers were in spring training, they still needed left-handed hitting. Life as we know it. Then it went straight to the crapper. Detective Lee, the fat Chinese guy from Homicide, called him and told him to get his ass over to a crime scene.

It was a generic enough crime scene. How many times had he seen a body in a garage? Twenty? Thirty? If they weren't in a Dumpster or the bushes they were almost certain to be in the garage. And this was a double homicide, or so it seemed. One identified body and one unidentified arm. Don was sure the rest of the body would turn up somewhere sooner or later. Look in the Dumpsters nearby, was what he told the unies standing around the scene. The Dumpsters and the bushes.

But that was all pretty mundane. The thing that preoccupied Don was that the one identifiable victim was Carlos Vila. Don had spent the better part of the last two years working in the LAPD's Criminal Intelligence Division trying to build a case against the Mexican mafia. His investigations had begun to focus on Esteban Sola, leader of a violent faction of mobsters out of Juarez. Carlos had been Don's informant. Now Carlos was toast and Don had to tie Esteban Sola to Carlos's murder or he was fucked. Two years of work and no conviction, that wouldn't look too good on his record. Don made a mental note to talk to one of the local feds about making a RICO case against Esteban.

The bartender came back.

"Do you want another? Or would you like to try the Saint-Estephe?"

"Take me to France."

Don knew that at eighteen dollars a glass he was running up a bill he couldn't afford, but what the hell. The bartender popped the cork and poured a small taste for Don. He swirled the wine, watching the light glint through the deep red. He inhaled. The wine smelled of earth and flint and melons. Don let the wine hit his tongue. It made him smile.

Bob lay in bed. Maura came in from the shower and looked at him.

"You're still awake?"

"Can't sleep."

Maura threw the towel on a chair and stood in front of him, naked and defiant.

"If you think I'm going to fuck you now—"

Bob tried to interrupt her. He knew where this was going.

"No. No. I—"

She cut him off.

"I don't want to hear it."

"I can't sleep."

"Try harder."

She climbed into bed, her back to him.

"Don't you love me anymore?"

Maura rolled over and looked at him.

"Honestly?"

This was maybe more than Bob had bargained for.

"Sure."

"I love you, Bob. I really do."

"Then what is it? We haven't made love in over a month."

"You really want to know?"

"Sure."

Maura suddenly thought better of what she was about to say, but it was too late to stop it.

"I can't stand the sight of your penis."

"My penis?"

"Any penis."

"Why?"

"They repulse me."

Bob put his head back on his pillow and considered the implications. Maura kissed him on the cheek.

"Maybe you're just tired. Maybe if I—"

She didn't want to hear it.

"I gave at the office. Okay?"

"But—"

"I'm sorry."

Bob was still game.

"You don't have to look at it or touch it or anything. Just let me put it inside you."

Maura looked at him.

"Don't be gross."

Norberto woke up with a splitting headache. Like the worst mescal hangover imaginable. No. Like a hangover from sniffing propellant. Refeo. He tried to move his arms and quickly realized that he was handcuffed to a pole or pipe of some kind. He tugged against it hard, testing. The effort caused blood to rush to his head which, in turn, made him puke on himself. Then he passed out.

Sometimes Martin hated his job. Sure, it had its perks. There was action, travel, a new challenge every day. He got cash,

women, and best of all, a constant supply of high-grade marijuana. But the hours, Christ, the hours sucked. It beat doing a
nine-to-five on your butt in front of a computer trading stocks
or sitting in some stuffy law library reading legal gobbledy-
gook, the kinds of jobs his grad school classmates had fallen
into. That wasn't for him, that kind of life was for losers. People
without imagination. Still, even if he was on call twenty-
four/seven, he'd found time for pleasure. Little things. Scour-
ing vintage clothing stores with Norberto or getting a manicure
from the weird Cambodian ladies. Small pleasures that added
to his quality of life. Small pleasures and plenty of pot.

His parents didn't understand, wouldn't understand at all if
they had any idea what he was really doing. Why couldn't he
take a position at a nice white-shoe law firm or, even better,
score a cushy Wall Street job and become a millionaire like
every other ambitious young American? They believed he was
a "consultant" advising a wealthy Mexican investor. Which he
was, in a sense. He told them that he liked the diversity, real
estate, stocks, venture capital; he was really learning a lot. He
neglected to tell them he was learning the money-laundering
business, the strip-club business, the prostitution business, the
narcotics-trafficking business, and the gun-running business.
Martin didn't know why he was attracted to crime, he just was.

It was cool.

Martin put it all out of his mind as he fired up a big fat joint.
He inhaled deeply, held it, and then exhaled with a long satisfied sigh. He felt his brain climb into a warm water bed and
just . . . float. Martin looked in the mirror behind the polished
granite bar. Why did chrome hurt his eyes? Why did the faucet
and sink have to be so shiny anyway? Why did people with
money want everything to be so fucking shiny? What was up
with that?

Martin reached for his sunglasses even though it was well

past midnight. He took another long drag on the jumbo, put on his shades and watched the smoke drift up to the ceiling.

Esteban's voice snapped him out of it.

"Where's my fucking drink?"

"Comin' right up."

Martin hurriedly chucked ice into four tumblers and filled them halfway up with Don Julio silver. He went around behind the bar and searched for the Cointreau and limes.

"The girls are getting thirsty."

"One minute."

Martin was careful not to let an edge of annoyance creep into his voice. He had seen Esteban lose his temper and stick a man's face in a deep-fat Fry-O-Lator. He'd seen him grind broken glass into someone's rectum. It was best not to piss Esteban off, so Martin always tried to speak in a calm and well-modulated voice. It helped to be stoned.

Esteban sat in the Jacuzzi, letting the warm water bubble around him. He sank in lower, letting his eyes come to just above water level. That way he could get a good look at the two pairs of tits bobbing across the tub from him. He tried to decide. Which were better? One pair was obviously fake. Unnaturally big, unnaturally round, unnaturally perky. With hard plastic nubs on the ends like the doodads that made mannequins look like they had erect nipples. It was the best modern technology could offer, yet Esteban found them unattractive. He could tell they would be hard, not soft. They would not be comforting or sexy. They would be firm and bouncy, like fucking a couple of basketballs. Impressive, but without soul. The other ones, the ones on the Latina, they looked real. Voluptuous and uneven with large terra-cotta aureoles. They were breasts. They had soul.

The girls giggled together and playfully splashed at him. Esteban was careful not to get his hair wet, so he stood up and yelled into the house.

"Where's my fuckin' drink?"

He heard some mumbly bullshit answer come from the house. That and a blast of *mota* smoke. Esteban turned to the girl with the fake tits. He pointed at them.

"Those real?"

"You like them?"

Esteban had heard that question before. He knew that if he said yes, he'd be stuck fucking her later. If he said no, well, that would be rude. Esteban strove for a middle ground.

"I'm curious."

She giggled.

"I had them enhanced."

Esteban nodded. What was there to say? He turned his back on her and yelled into the house.

"The girls are getting thirsty."

Esteban sank back into the water. He let out a sigh, pretending to relax. But how could he fucking relax? He had that punk, Norberto, hog-tied in the downstairs bathroom. He had Amado running around somewhere without his arm. How could someone lose their arm? The arm thing was going to be a problem. Esteban could feel it. Feel it all the way down in the deepest part of his *huevos*. Esteban wondered if he could get Amado a fake arm like the woman's fake tits. They looked real enough.

Martin finally arrived with the drinks. The women giggled and took theirs. One of them said something about a paper umbrella. Esteban slugged half his back in one gulp. It was strong. The sharpness of the lime, the blast of salt, the warmth of the liquor in his guts. He smiled as he felt the tequila spiders crawl up his spine and begin spinning their webs in his brain.

The kid might be some kind of grad school pussy, but he made a good drink.

Martin dropped his robe and eased his body into the Jacuzzi. For a brief stoned moment he felt like shabu-shabu. Sliced meat dunked in boiling water. Esteban had his legs stretched out, he looked like a turkey drumstick. The women with their big round tits could be vegetables, maybe bok choy or mushrooms. The water bubbled.

Broth.

Martin considered his place in the shabu-shabu. He was white, but not tofu. Meat, maybe pork or chicken. Halibut? Or was he that fake crab? He didn't feel out of place like he sometimes felt around Esteban. He felt just fine. Like fake crab.

He smiled at Esteban.

"We're makin' girl soup."

Esteban was too tired for this bullshit.

"Yeah."

The girl with the fake tits piped up.

"Who's got the big spoon to eat me with?"

Esteban looked at Martin.

"Him. He'll eat you."

Martin knew it was an order. He tried some of his Spanish.

"*Seguro*, baby."

Esteban winced.

"First we need to talk. You girls go on upstairs."

The women carried their drinks out of the pool and quickly tiptoed into the house. Esteban turned to Martin.

"I'm worried about something?"

"What?"

"Amado's arm."

Martin knew this was something serious. He had been trying to figure out a way to tell Esteban but was afraid he'd go nuts.

"It's a problem."

Esteban took Martin's drink from him and sucked half of it down.

"How?"

"It's how they got John Gotti."

"What do you mean?"

"For the feds to build a racketeering case against you, they need to tie you to a specific crime. An 'incident,' like a murder, then tie you to the murderer."

"Amado."

"Correct."

"What happened to Gotti?"

"Sammy Gravano killed nineteen people, but Gotti got life in jail for ordering the hits."

"But Gotti didn't shoot anybody."

"Right. But he was the head of a criminal conspiracy. Racketeering."

Esteban finished Martin's drink.

"*Carajo.*"

Martin could only nod. It was fucked up, no doubt about it.

"So we gotta get Amado's arm."

"Unless it's already been processed."

"What if it has?"

"My advice would be we go to Mexico."

Esteban grunted.

"Fuck that, *cabrón.* I didn't work my ass off to go running back to Juarez just because some *culero* got his arm chopped off. No. We're stayin'."

Esteban stood up, the water dripping off him.

"I got some friends. I'll make the calls."

Martin nodded blankly as Esteban climbed out of the Jacuzzi. It was going to be a long night.

Norberto blinked awake again. This time he made sure to take some deep breaths, get some oxygen going to his throbbing head. He smelled old vomit. It made him gag. He felt his hands. The handcuffs were still there. So was the pole. Norberto tested his voice. It worked. Norberto took a chance and yelled for help. It hurt his head, almost made him puke again, but he yelled.

Suddenly the door flew open and Esteban walked in. In the brief blinding flash of light Norberto saw that he was in a bathroom in a nice home. White tile gleamed, clean and inviting. A porcelain sink stood above him, reminding him of a hotel he went to once with a couple of hookers and an ounce of blow. Good memories. Norberto smiled up at Esteban, but only for a second as Esteban began to viciously kick Norberto in the ribs, face, and testicles.

Max Larga sat in front of his big-screen TV. His robe was open and he let a bowl of microwave popcorn warm his nuts. A Japanese cooking show was on. Larga was bored, but it was his job to keep up with current trends in cooking, and Japanese cuisine was hot right now. His editors kept bugging him to write about preparing sushi at home, something Larga knew would cause thousands of cases of food poisoning. He tried to argue against it, but the editors prevailed. So Larga watched. He knew that the quality of the ingredients was the single most important thing. Were there enough fresh fish markets in Peoria? Or would some well-meaning housewife be making maki with week-old catfish? It was all too much to worry about.

Larga shoveled fistfuls of popcorn into his mouth. The fake butter coated his fingers, his fat lips were swollen and shiny from the oil and salt. The warm bowl between his legs gave him a pleasant sensation, and soon he felt himself getting aroused. He thought about all the affairs he'd had in his life. Bored housewives who'd come to watch him give cooking demonstrations. Professional women he'd met on airplanes and in hotel bars. He'd always managed to get laid somehow. But the experience was never fully satisfying. Never as good as a ripe cheese or a well-prepared soup. Larga was concerned that there might be something wrong with him, that there was some aspect of sex that he just didn't understand. That's why he'd gone to the masturbation coach in the first place. Maybe, he figured, if he could pleasure himself, then he could find pleasure with others.

He flicked the TV over to the soft-porn channels and watched a couple of blondes smear chocolate syrup on each others' breasts and slurp it off. Larga's cock grew stiff as he began to stroke it, using the fake butter as a lubricant. He shifted on the sofa and did his homework.

8

OB LOOKED AT his penis. It was early in the morning, and Bob had woken with a blistering hard-on. Stretched out and throbbing, he could admire it in all its glory. Why did Maura find it repulsive? Maybe it wasn't as long as, you know, a porn star's, but he'd never had any complaints. In fact he'd experienced just the opposite. His penis usually earned kudos from the women who encountered it.

And why not? Aesthetically his penis seemed just right. It had a nice organic form, healthy pink color. He kept it clean. He used condoms. Maybe Maura was going lesbo on him. It'd happened before with a girlfriend in college.

Bob looked over at Maura. She didn't look like a lesbian. But then, Bob wasn't sure if you could tell that way. People change.

She was sleeping peacefully on her side, her back to him. He watched her breathing. He remembered the first time he'd watched her sleep. He'd never met anyone so self-assured, so dynamic. In bed she was a pneumatic drill sergeant, barking out commands and inflicting harsh punishments if her orders were not carried out to the letter. Bob was used to women who were awkward, a little shy, mostly sweet, but never like Maura. He used to marvel at her. Maura's drive to orgasm was a planned, sometimes inflicted, sequence of events. Failure was not an option.

She was like that out of bed too. A dynamo. She didn't wait for Bob to hem and haw about what restaurant to go to. She told him when and where. Bob admired her decisiveness. She always picked right. She was an amazing woman, and Bob was infected with enough postfeminist guilt so that he would never admit that she was sometimes overbearing, somewhat obnoxious, and frankly neurotic.

Reflecting on their time together, Bob came to the surprising realization that she had not only swept him off his feet but had put him in a bag and sunk him in the river. Suddenly, his cock deflated. It sagged like a punctured beach ball. Flaccid and done. Bob realized that they would never have sex again.

She found him repulsive. He found her overbearing. Bob sighed. He loved Maura, but he wasn't a retard.

Bob picked the Polaroid of the tattooed arm off the bedside table. He looked at the image and it filled him with longing. *Maybe I can find her*, he thought. *Maybe she'll be sweet and warm and won't think my penis is repulsive.*

Bob got out of bed and started getting ready for work. His ritual, he actually thought of it as a ritual, was the same every morning except Sunday when he liked to stay in bed, read the paper, and have sex as many times as he could before his body screamed for some protein.

But today was Wednesday, so he began the ritual. He unscrewed the Italian espresso maker and filled the bottom half with water, right up to that weird little gasket thing. Then he plopped the metal basket into place and spooned in a heaplette of fine ground coffee. The coffee smelled good. Earthy. Dark. Charged. Bob screwed the top half onto the bottom and turned the flame on. He poured milk into a little pot and put that on the stove to warm.

Then Bob walked into the bathroom. He had just enough time to take a shit before the coffee was ready, this learned from years of experience, the espresso maker designed to give him grace.

As the sound of flushing receded in the background, Bob returned to the kitchen just as the gurgling of the espresso maker became a full-throated roar. Bob cut the gas and poured the coffee and milk into his cup simultaneously, getting the color just right. He did the same into a second cup.

As was his practice, Bob carried the two cups back into the bedroom and put one down on the bedside table next to Maura. She stirred.

"Thanks."

Bob sipped his coffee and cleared his throat. He didn't say, "You're welcome," and he didn't say, "Good morning." He thought about the woman in the Polaroid and a life filled with sweet pleasures. He turned toward her.

"I think you should move out."

That got her attention. She rolled over and gave him a nasty look.

"What?"

"I think you should move out."

"Why?"

"Well, come on, Maura, if you find my penis repulsive and don't want to have sex with me . . ."

"I don't find you repulsive."

"Just my penis?"

Maura turned away from him.

"Yeah."

"Can you tell me why?"

"I don't know why."

"Have you gone gay or something?"

"No."

Maura sat up. Bob watched sadly as her beautiful breasts heaved under her nightgown.

"If it's any consolation, it's not your penis, it's all penises."

"Maybe you're just burned out from your job."

"I don't think that's it."

"Then you should move out."

It was funny, in a way, but Bob didn't feel that bad. He felt slightly numb. But not too bad. No urge to cry or go get drunk. *Maybe,* he thought . . . *maybe I don't love her.*

Bob went into the bathroom to shave. Maura sighed and sipped her coffee. Then she said, "Maybe you should move out."

Bob closed the door. He ran the tap, waiting for the water to get hot, and thought about the apartment where they lived. It wasn't anything special. Just cinder blocks covered in stucco and paint. Really nothing to look at. A giant horseshoe-shaped thing with a gate at the open end and a pool in the middle. Now that he thought about it, Bob realized that the apartment building might seem ugly to some people. But, like most things in Los Angeles, if you looked at it from another angle, say floating on an inflatable raft in the middle of the pool, you wouldn't see the cinder blocks or the trash cans, you'd see several large and graceful palm trees swaying in the breeze against a pure blue sky. If you looked at if from that angle you might think you were in paradise.

Perspective. Bob was trying to put it all in perspective. He opened the door a crack.

"Maybe I will."

On an average day in Los Angeles the weather is clear, the temperature around seventy-five degrees. It rarely rains and it never snows. Modern streets and freeways, with traffic signals designed to provide efficiency of transport, crisscross the great basin, wind up over the hills, and spread out across the valley.

Despite what can only be called ideal driving conditions, there are, on an average day, approximately two hundred traffic accidents. It's unexplainable.

Martin woke up to screeching tires and crumpling metal. The screech was a blinding pain behind his left eye, the crumpling metal was the taste in his mouth. A fender-bender in his brain. A sig-alert in his body. A bong-hit hangover in full bloom. This could be explained.

He looked over at the woman sleeping next to him. Good God, her tits were standing straight up. Virtually antigravity. Martin mused that he must be upside down, in outer space, or in Australia, something that would account for these tits. Then he remembered what those breasts felt like. Hard as fucking stones. He looked at her and shook his head in dismay. Fake tits, dyed blond hair, skin artificially bronzed the color of strained carrots. Maybe she was an illusion. Maybe she was not real at all.

Martin stretched, got out of bed, and slouched toward the shower. He liked to take a shower in the morning. Otherwise he never felt fully awake. He let the hot water caress his body, the scented soap reinvigorating his mind, the steam cutting through last night's reefer fog.

When Martin, fresh from the shower, his soul patch— neatly trimmed, walked into the kitchen, Esteban was already at the table forking mouthfuls of nopalito cactus and scrambled eggs into his mouth. The Latina with the natural breasts who, Martin was to learn, was named Lupe, stood in front of the stove. In the daylight he could see how lovely she was. More Mexican Indian than Mexican Mexican. Black hair to match her black eyes, her skin a luminous terra-cotta. She looked at Martin.

"*Buenos días.*"

Martin nodded.

"Good morning."

Esteban looked up.

"Eat. We gotta lot of shit to do."

Lupe handed Martin a plate and a fork.

"Thanks."

Martin sat down and sipped his coffee. He waited for the acidic brew to hit his tequila-tenderized stomach. It did, and the feeling he got can best be described as queasy. He watched as Esteban dumped vast splotches of hot sauce on his eggs. The same hot sauce that Martin felt hit his tongue like battery acid and gave his lips a raw and unpleasant sensation for most of the day. Esteban spoke with his mouth full.

"I talked to some people down at Parker Center."

"Yeah?"

"The arm's getting delivered later today."

Martin couldn't believe it.

"They don't have it?"

Esteban shook his head.

"They had a lab treat it or preserve it or prepare it or something. Whatever they do with arms. What do I know about it?"

Martin's appetite returned. The coffee settling in and warming his guts like a hot water bottle. He ate his eggs. Maybe they wouldn't have to flee the country after all.

"You know where it is?"

Esteban nodded.

"So . . . we're cool."

Esteban scowled.

Martin realized he'd said the wrong thing when he saw the expression on Esteban's face. He felt his bowels spasm and his testicles retract.

Esteban finally growled.

"It's never that easy."

––––––––

Don stood in the shower. He let the hot water scald his pink body. He'd had a good workout. Free weights. Machines. A half hour on the StairMaster. Derrick, the muscle-freak patrol-man who was like a personal trainer in the police gym, had spotted Don on the bench press and pushed him to lift more weight more times than he ever had before. Heavy iron thrust upward until his arms shook, his back warped, his legs kicked and then . . . then Derrick had him do it again and again until "failure."

He felt his muscles. They were tight, pumped full of blood and more articulated than Don had ever noticed before. The overall effect made him feel powerful, indestructible. Don was ready to kick some ass. In fact, he was champing at the bit. He gave himself an affirmation. Told himself that today would mark the beginning of the end for the Mexican mob from Juarez. They had finally fucked up. He could feel it. He didn't know whose arm it was, or why it was left there, but it just screamed of fuck-up. And that's all Don needed. A chink in the armor. A crack in the wall. Two years of watching and wait-ing, sitting in crappy vans in crappy neighborhoods gathering "intelligence"; spending hours in small smelly rooms inter-viewing punks, losers, and scumbags, as boxes of evidence and information stacked up around his cubicle. For two solid years he'd tracked down one bad lead after another. Every alibi Este-ban had was sphincter-pinching tight. But now the day had come. Something had happened. All Don needed was to figure out what, and it was adios, scumbag, *vaya con Dios.*

Tonight, Don decided, *after I break this case wide open, I'm going to splurge and get a bottle of Opus One. Drink it all by myself. A fat steak and a fat cabernet.* Don smiled at the thought.

Norberto felt a little bit better. His ribs hurt from where he'd been kicked, and the blood from his split lip was caked and dried around his cheek, but all in all he felt better. He assumed that whatever poison they'd injected into him had finally worn off. Norberto shifted a little on the floor, trying to find some tiny degree of comfort. He realized that his pants were soaked with piss. His nice purple sharkskin pants.

The door opened and Esteban came in.

"How're you feeling?"

Norberto was confused. There was a friendly tone in Esteban's voice. What did it mean?

"Esta bien, gracias."

Esteban knelt down and unlocked the handcuffs.

"Take a shower. I'll have clean clothes waiting for you."

"¿Qué pasa, Esteban?"

"Mucho trabajo, cabrón."

When Bob got to the office, Morris was already there, playing Tetris on Bob's computer. Several coolers were lined up on the desk, packed with dry ice and ready for the day's deliveries. Morris shoved a coffee from Starbucks toward Bob.

"Dude, I got you that vanilla thing."

"Thanks."

"I don't know how you can drink that sweet stuff in the morning, man."

"Normally I don't."

Morris looked stricken.

"Did I fuck up?"

Bob shook his head.

"What's on for today?"

Morris turned back to the game with renewed intensity.

"Usual."

His clicking turned frenetic for a moment and then the cloying little jingle sounded.

"Fuck."

"How'd you do?"

"I'll never get past the seventh level. It's like rigged or something."

"It just takes practice."

Morris nodded and started the game again. Bob picked a clipboard off the desk and checked it to see the day's work. He noticed that a large order of organs and tissue was going to the UCLA Medical School.

"Did you get the stuff for UCLA?"

"What?"

"The stuff for UCLA."

"It's upstairs in the lab."

"Dude. Go get it."

Morris concentrated and clicked.

"C'mon, Morris."

Morris shot Bob a disgusted look and turned off the game. He stood up, picking up his Starbucks cup.

"Why you got to give me all the agro, man? All the time, boss, boss, boss."

Morris grabbed a cooler and started to stomp out of the room. Bob felt bad. "I'm sorry. Maura and I broke up this morning."

Morris stopped.

"Wow. Man, sorry to hear that. She's hot."

"Thanks."

"You want to talk or something?"

Bob didn't want to talk.

"Tell you what. I want to get out for a while. You get the

stuff ready and I'll make the run. You can stay here and play
Tetris all afternoon."

Morris broke into a huge grin.

"You rule, man."

Norberto sat in the back of Esteban's car. He'd put on one of
Martin's black gabardine suits, with a vintage fuchsia tuxedo
shirt underneath, and was feeling better. Much better now that
it was apparent that Esteban wasn't going to kill him after all.
In fact, his future was looking good. Esteban had told Norberto that he was a valuable member of the team. With Amado
in trouble, Norberto would need to take more responsibility.
More responsibility meant more money, more respect. Norberto was pleased. He smiled when he thought of last night.
Perhaps enduring the brutality and the strange drug had
proven his strength. He wasn't sure. But, *quizás*, man, *todo es
possible*. All he was sure about was that they were on their way
to help Amado.

He watched as Esteban and that weird gringo dude sat up
front talking about something. Norberto wished that he'd finished his ESL classes. But the teacher at City College was such
a *pendejo* that he just couldn't stand it. He had to quit. Well,
actually, he had to quit after he jumped the hippie gringo
teacher in the parking lot after class and kicked the crap out of
him. The gringo didn't understand that members of *el grupo de
Juarez* were due a certain amount of respect. You couldn't
make fun of them in class. Thinking back on it, Norberto
wasn't sure the gringo had meant to make fun of him, but
either way, it just wasn't cool. You had to stand up for yourself.
Draw the line. Punish those who crossed it. Besides, the gringos always thought they were better than him. It felt good to
send one of them to the emergency room.

It may have been satisfying to go all barbaric on the ESL teacher, but it also made Norberto feel stupid, like he was sub-human or something. Martin had that same effect on him. With all his talk about money and investments and shelters and such, he made Norberto feel stupid. Stupid for sending his money Western Union back to his *padres* in the South. Stupid for keeping cash in a Ziploc bag in the freezer. Like some dumb-shit wetback who didn't know how the world worked. But Norberto knew how the world worked, a little bit, anyway. He knew he should go legit, open a bank account and invest in a real business, a taco stand or something, just to launder the money so he could buy the kinds of things he wanted. Like a Porsche. But he just hated the idea of paying taxes to a country that would turn around and spend the money on law enforce-ment and immigration authorities that wanted to catch him and ship him back to Mexico. *Fuck that,* he thought, *I'm an outlaw.*

Bob took Amado's arm out of the cooler. He carefully pulled back the plastic wrap to reveal the tattoo of the woman. Bob's heart pounded as he looked at her. She was beautiful, even more lusty and erotic on the graying arm than in the Polaroid. Had Bob ever made a woman feel that way? He wasn't sure, but he had tried. Bob was willing to throw himself into any erotic activity. He'd gone down on lots of women but couldn't remember one of them who just threw her head back and let the sensation rock her world. A couple of women had come close, but they'd been drunk.

Was he attracted to uptight women? He wondered. How could a guy like him meet a woman like this? What if a woman like this didn't exist? What if she was like a comic book charac-ter? Could he go down on Wonder Woman? Wasn't she gay?

Bob felt a pang of self-pity shoot through him. Maybe he was too harsh on Maura. What if she was just going through something? Maybe they should go to a therapist, work things out.

Bob looked at the tattoo again. Even if she didn't exist, there must be someone like her. It wouldn't hurt to look. Fuck that, he had to look. If he didn't, he'd regret it for the rest of his life.

Bob wrapped the plastic back around the arm.

Esteban pulled his Mercedes to the curb. He cut the engine. Well aware of his antitheft deterrent under the seat, he was careful not to set the alarm. Martin looked across the street. A drab modern-looking building next to a drab modern-looking building next to a crazy Moroccan stucco strip mall.

"This it?"

Esteban looked over at Martin.

"Yeah. United Pathology."

Norberto squirmed in the backseat, ready for some action.

"¿Vamos?"

Esteban lit a cigarette.

"Patience, cabrón."

Maura stood naked in the bathroom brushing her hair. She thought about what Bob had said. She wasn't angry or hurt. How could she blame him? She was the one who wanted a change. By forcing Bob to be decisive she got what she wanted but was afraid to ask for. Or maybe she got what she thought she wanted but was afraid to ask for. What if she was making a mistake?

Maura watched her voluptuous breasts bounce and heave

in the mirror in rhythm with the movement of the brush through her hair. It suddenly occurred to her that maybe she was just bored. Maybe sex was boring. She thought about all the men she'd had sex with, remembering them. It all blurred for her. In the end it's always the same. In, out, in, out, faster . . . until she came or they came or it was over. What's the fun of that?

9

BOB GENTLY PLACED the arm in the cooler and closed the lid. Just then Morris came back from the lab with several pouches of viscera. Morris looked at the cooler.

"That the arm?"

"Yeah."

"I'm gonna miss that arm, man."

Bob looked at Morris.

"Why?"

Morris shrugged.

"It has personality."

Morris held up the pouches of tissue samples.

"These are ready to go, man."

Bob took the bits in bags and plopped them into the other cooler.

"What do you want for lunch?"

Morris thought about it.

"Burritos."

"We had burritos the other day."

"Burgers."

Bob nodded. It wasn't his idea of a healthy lunch but at least it was different. They almost always had burritos.

"See you later."

Bob took the portable coolers and walked out of the room. Morris smiled. He went immediately to the computer. His thumb stomped down on the space bar, waking the computer from its digital dreams. Morris stretched, cracked his knuckles, and focused. It would take all of his concentration to master the seventh level of Tetris.

Martin continued to talk Esteban's ear off. Something about building a hotel near Mazatlán. Something about a swimming pool that had no edge so you thought you were in the ocean. Esteban didn't know what an edgeless swimming pool was and he didn't really care. His mind kept returning to the blow job administered by Lupe last night. God, could that girl suck. Martin talked about Mazatlán making a comeback. The largest shrimp port in North America was being rediscovered as a tourist mecca by thousands of drunk, topless college kids. Esteban was getting annoyed, he hadn't come this far to go to Mazatlán and open a fucking resort. Try building something in Mexico? The corruption alone would kill you. Yet Martin yammered on about keeping liquidity overseas, numbered off-shore accounts in Barbados, and the relative value of real estate in Costa Rica. It was all about leaving the country. Esteban had killed, literally, to come here, so why the fuck would he want to leave?

He perked up when he saw Bob loading the coolers in the back of the black VW Golf with the United Pathology logo on the side. Esteban noticed another sign, one that said Human Blood in the window of the little car. Also, Driver Carries No Cash on the door. Human blood? What the fuck did they do with that? Martin realized that something was happening.

"That our guy?"

Esteban nodded and started the engine. He watched as Bob climbed into the car and started it up. When Bob turned out of the driveway and drove off down the street, Esteban followed. It was like the old days.

He still knew how to do it. It was easy enough. Esteban remembered when he was first starting out, they'd rear-end a tasty-looking car, usually with a single female inside, then they'd jump out acting all concerned and before anyone knew what hit them, both cars would be gone. A little body work on the stolen car's bumper, a fresh coat of paint, you'd have a new car. Let the cops scour the countryside for that red BMW with a dent. He had a black Beemer without a scratch for sale. Those stolen cars turned out to be seed money for all kinds of things, marijuana, heroin, prostitutes, cheap weapons from Brazil and Italy. Esteban had built an empire off those early carjackings. And, being a smart businessman, he kept on dealing in stolen cars. Only now they chopped them up for parts, the parts being more valuable than the whole car. It was a good business. His "core profit center" or something. That's what Martin called it.

Bob turned up the radio. Normally he listened to an alternative-rock station, but today he was feeling a little out of sorts. He switched over to an R&B oldies station and let the Reverend Al Green speak to him. Smooth, soulful, reassuring. Life has its ups and downs. That's life. Love is sweet and bitter, pain and pleasure in equal parts. That is just the way it is, and at the end of the day, it's all good. Bob understood the truth that Reverend Green was speaking. Intellectually he could grasp it, deal with it. But his guts were churning. Not with anger or hatred or that nauseating feeling you get when you've been betrayed. It was something else. Disappointment.

He was disappointed in Maura. Bob had hoped that she was, for want of a better word, the one. The girl that he would marry and have kids with. He knew it was old-fashioned, but Bob really wanted the domestic life that had eluded him since he was nine years old and his parents bickered, and argued, and fought, and finally divorced. He wanted the picket fence, the two kids, the station wagon, and the dog.

Marvin Gaye came on the radio and did his best to infuse Bob with a little optimism. His spirits lifted. "Sexual healing." There was an idea. A prescription. A course of therapy that Bob could get behind. Because, despite his disappointment, and despite the utter drag of having to split up possessions and move, this was starting to feel like a step in the right direction. An opportunity. A good thing.

A woman in the street caught Bob's eye. She had blond hair stuck up in a ponytail, green capri pants, a white shirt, and black sandals with orangey red toenails. She was slim but not skinny, not a creepy stick; she was nicely proportioned. Would Bob miss those huge heaving tits of Maura's? Yeah. But, hey, man, life goes on. You can't spend your time pining for someone who doesn't want you. The woman in the green capri pants was looking pretty fucking sweet. Sweet enough to distract him momentarily from his quest for a voluptuous Latina.

Bob was still musing about the blonde when his car suddenly lurched violently. He'd been hit.

"Fuck!"

Bob looked in the rearview mirror and saw two big Mexican-looking dudes climb out of a new Mercedes sedan.

Bob turned on his hazard blinker thing and got out. One of the Mexicans, a big one with dark eyes and what looked like a toupee came up to him, concerned.

"*Señor?* Are you okay?"

Martin didn't like driving Esteban's Mercedes. The thought that the touch of a switch, or in the case of an attempted car theft, the nontouch of a switch, could send a sharpened stainless steel shaft right up his ass was just too much. It gave Martin the creeps. It wasn't just unnerving, it was barbaric and unnecessary. Still, when Esteban told him to get behind the wheel and keep the engine running, Martin didn't argue. He did what he was told

Martin watched as Norberto and Esteban approached the poor fucker in the delivery car. The two men feigned concern for about a heatbeat, then . . . Norberto clobbered the guy. Whacked him upside the head with something hard. The guy hit the ground like a big bag of shit. Esteban and Norberto scooped him up and threw him in the trunk of the delivery car. Norberto hopped in the car, Esteban came quickly around to the passenger side of the Benz, and away they went. The whole thing took about fifteen seconds.

Bob regained consciousness in the trunk of a car. A lump about the size of a ping-pong ball was swollen and throbbing just behind his ear. What the fuck had happened? One minute he's talking to these guys and then . . . Bob remembered he'd been rear-ended. He'd obviously been hurt, maybe they were taking him to the hospital. Bob considered that, but it seemed farfetched, weird even. You wouldn't throw a hurt guy in the trunk. You'd call an ambulance or put him in the backseat or something. No, he probably wasn't on his way to the hospital.

Norberto drove the Golf. He let Esteban's Mercedes whip past him and lead the way. A disco beat was softly pumping on the radio. Norberto turned it up. Although *normalmente* he preferred salsa, he thought the old-school disco was *muy curado*. Girls liked it and Norberto was savvy enough to appreciate whatever drove girls to get up off their butts and shake their bodies. Norberto liked the song that was playing. *I will survive. That's me,* he thought. *Not only will I survive, cabrón, but now that I've shown Esteban that I am loyal, I will prosper.*

Esteban felt a dull pain in his lower back. *Carajo.* He used to be able to chuck a *jodido pendejo* like this gringo into the trunk without even breaking a sweat. Now he felt like he'd thrown out his back. And Martin. He wouldn't shut up.

Esteban wondered how this happened. How did everything turn to gazpacho? Then he remembered, Amado. Fucking Amado fucking up. Well, he wouldn't be fucking up for much longer, would he? He would miss him. Amado was a good gangster. A gangster's gangster in some ways. But he'd fucked up. Left his arm at the scene of a crime and endangered the entire family. He had to be dealt with.

Esteban's plan was simple: kill Bob, kill Amado, and burn the evidence. Hell, maybe burn everyone up in a car. Take it out to the desert or up Angeles Crest, light it up and push it off a cliff. Let the forensic pathologists sift through the ashes for some evidence.

Martin was frustrated. Sometimes these fucking mobsters were so thick. There's a problem, you kill everyone. What kind of logic was that? Were those corporate guidelines? Was that any way to run a business? Martin didn't like the idea of murder. It seemed extreme to him. He really didn't like the idea of being prosecuted as an accessory to murder if they were somehow busted.

He tried to calm himself as he rolled a jumbo. His hands were shaking, making the process more difficult. Why did everything have to be so hard? They didn't need to waste the delivery guy just because he was in the wrong place at the wrong time. Martin wanted to convince Esteban that they needed the guy in the trunk. They couldn't just whack him and dump his body, then the cops would know that something was up. They'd know that the evidence had been tampered with and they'd start nosing around until they found something. Esteban's point was that they wouldn't have the evidence so . . . they could go fuck themselves.

Martin got the cigarette paper to stick, and fired up. He held a massive hit in his lungs until they burned and he could feel the air pressure behind his eyes begin to drop. He exhaled a plume of smoke and felt his muscles go lax. Then it came to him.

Martin suddenly realized that what they needed to do was find another arm, switch it with Amado's, and have the guy make the delivery like he normally would. It was crazy. But it was clean. Nothing would be suspect. They would get away with it. How they could convince the guy to do it was another story.

He pitched the idea to Esteban. Esteban told him he was full of shit. He didn't trust the delivery guy, and why should he. They'd send the guy in to Parker Center and next thing they know, they'd be in a lineup. Besides, where would they get another arm? Esteban thought Martin's plan was *tonto*, and he didn't have time for that. Esteban always switched to Spanish when he was annoyed with Martin.

Martin considered it; perhaps Esteban was right. Kill the guy, burn the arm, end of story. But what if they could find an arm easily? Then they could figure something out. Maybe pay the fucking guy. Leverage him somehow. He made, what? Not that much. Slide him ten grand, he delivers the new arm, and call it even. Martin realized he was expending a lot of nervous energy trying to keep the delivery guy from getting whacked. He had his reasons. Bad karma being one.

Don came to work as he always did, walking into the Criminal Intelligence Division with his double cappuccino with nonfat soy milk extra foam, a copy of the *Los Angeles Times* tucked under his arm. Only today there was something different about Don. He always had a spring in his step, but today he had just a little more bounce than usual. He stopped at the little makeshift coffee bar and did something he never did. He took a Krispy Kreme doughnut out of a box. He bit into it and was surprised at how good it tasted. Sweet and yeasty. No wonder they were always lying around the station. Cops love dough-nuts and Don loved being a cop.

Don sat down at his desk, licked the sugar glaze off his fin-gers, and shuffled some papers around. A middle-aged and thick man with dark brown skin and Central American fea-tures sat down at the next desk. A plaque indicated that he was Detective Sergeant Flores. Flores noticed the flakes of sugar on Don's desk.

"I thought you didn't eat that shit."

"I eat all kinds of shit."

"That's what happens when you start kissin' ass. You eat all kinds of shit."

Ah. Wisdom. Don didn't respond. He could've said some-thing about Flores being known as the biggest ass-kisser in the department, or Flores constantly flaunting the fact that he was a Latino, using the race card to get promotions. But Don didn't want to start a ruckus, he wasn't going to let office politics ruin his day. So he changed the subject by getting down to business.

"That arm here yet?"

"The loose limb?"

"Yeah."

Flores looked at some papers as if the answer to Don's question was printed on them.

"Not yet."

"Got an ETA?"

Flores shook his head.

"Sometime today."

Don nodded. That was good. It gave him time to do some paperwork. Don prided himself on his paperwork. He'd seen too many crumbs get off because of some technicality in the way the forms were filled in. Like that fucking mattered. Some guy drives by your house and opens fire with a machine gun. He freely admits that he did it. But then the judge lets him off because some retard fills out the form wrong? It pissed Don off. So he had trained himself to be ferociously anal when doing paperwork. When he took somebody down, they were going down and staying down.

Max Larga stirred the wire whisk around quickly, attempting to get as much air into the egg whites as possible. They needed to be stiff, but not rigid, to add the right amount of fluff. He needed to keep it simple, something that anyone could do. Simplicity was the key to writing a good cookbook. It was one thing to describe, in excruciating minutiae, a rigorous and demanding sequence of complex tasks, but that kind of writing didn't sell cookbooks. In fact, that kind of writing was the problem with his last two cookbooks. It scared people away. His editor had jokingly referred to him as the James Joyce of cookbook authors as he dropped Larga's latest book from the release schedule.

Larga had reacted by decrying his readership as philistines.

But the truth, and it just burned him up, was that people preferred Martha Stewart and her quick-and-easy gourmet
recipes. Martha called it simple elegance. Larga laughed bitterly at that. What did the average housewife in Connecticut or
New Jersey know about elegance? He'd been around the
world. Eaten in the finest restaurants in Europe. Sampled
every edible concoction known to man. He'd even ordered the
weird dish where they press a roast duck through a device
more commonly used to juice apples and serve what comes
gushing out in a little silver cup. Now, that was elegant.

He checked his notes. He'd gotten this recipe from a friend,
a famous chef, because those were the only friends worth having. Friends who would treat you like royalty and suck up to
you with expensive wines and fabulous food. Friends who
would make you feel special, part of an inner circle of people
who were in the know. In return, all Larga had to do was drop
a mention of the chef or the restaurant, to illustrate a point, in
his weekly column.

Larga checked the mascarpone. It was room temperature,
perfect to mix with the egg whites. He worried about whether
this ingredient was too exotic. Would this recipe get cut out
with a simple "You can't get that in Kansas City"? He
shrugged, knowing he'd burn that bridge when he got to it.
Right now he just wanted to see if his simplified version would
be edible. That and he had to get ready to see his masturbation
coach that afternoon.

Norberto hated the safe house. He avoided staying there for
any stretch of time and only came out when he had to. Not that
it was uncomfortable. On the contrary, it was a model suburban home furnished with an entire suite of Ethan Allen furniture, everything bought and delivered at once, a kind of instant

house. But Norberto didn't like sitting on the chairs or sleeping in the beds. He was never relaxed in the house because it all seemed so unreal, like a dream house. Every Mexican's dream of life in El Norte, only fake.

It was in a section of the valley considered to be nice and safe. But Norberto didn't feel safe in Encino. He felt that he stuck out too much around all of the upper-middle-class white people in their SUVs, with their two kids and their big dogs. Like he and Amado were a couple of flies on a big dish of vanilla ice cream. But even if he felt uncomfortable, the neighbors were friendly. They stopped by to say hello, always asking what Norberto had been doing, where they'd gone, etc. Was it nosy or normal? Norberto didn't know. He was always circumspect, sticking to the story Esteban had given him. He and Amado were cousins, they owned a papaya ranch near Guadalajara, they traveled all over the United States trying to convince people that Mexican papayas were superior to Hawaiian.

The last thing Norberto ever wanted to be was some kind of fucking fruit salesman. But that was the cover story and so that's what he was when he was at the house. Mr. Mexican Papaya. *Carajo.* He hated it. But Esteban insisted that it was the best place to stash the large amounts of drugs, and then later, the huge amounts of cash that kept them living the life. Sometimes they'd let someone, an affiliate from out of town, stay there, but they'd never kidnapped someone and brought him here. What would the neighbors say if they heard screaming?

Bob felt the car stop, the engine turn off. He heard the door open and close. He braced himself. What the fuck was going on? Then he heard a garage door being closed. Then . . . nothing. They were just leaving him in the trunk. And man, did he have to pee.

Estcban entered the safe house. He smiled broadly. Clean, ordered, plush. This house was why thousands of hardworking and honest people risked their lives crossing the border to come to America. This was the goal. This was the Alhambra. Esteban had moved on from this slice of suburban heaven, but he still appreciated its power. The American Dream as potent as ever.

He turned to Martin.

"Get me a fucking Tylenol and then tell me again why I shouldn't kill the driver."

Martin walked into the kitchen and grabbed a bottle of Tylenol and a glass of water while Esteban gingerly, a sharp pain racing up and down his spine, stretched himself out on the couch. Martin handed the pills and glass to Esteban.

"Because we need him."

"For what?"

"If the police suspect that the evidence has been tampered with they'll mount a full-scale fuck-fest on us."

"But, *cabrón,* that's what they're trying to do now."

Esteban didn't understand why the kid didn't get it. He wasn't asking the kid to kill the driver, Norberto would be happy to do it, so what was the problem? Why the sudden lack of *cojones?*

Esteban took the Tylenol and lay back on the couch. It occurred to Esteban that perhaps Martin was right. His plan was weird. *Raro.* But maybe that's what they needed. If they could swap arms, make everything seem normal, then the heat would be off. But where would they find another arm? Esteban's back began to throb.

"Go get the arm, let's look at it."

Bob was sweating. It was stuffy and hot in the trunk. Rivulets of perspiration were running off his head, filling his ears, dripping off his neck, soaking his shirt, causing his pants to stick to his legs. Even his fucking toes were wet with perspiration. Bob was sweating the death sweat. Cold fear delivering a weird fever to his body. Adrenal glands pumping overtime, heart pounding, a full-blown pedal-to-the-metal panic attack. Bob was sure that they'd thought he was dead. Killed by the knock to the head. They were going to leave him here to rot until the smell and sheer volume of flies alerted some good Samaritan or the mailman. Then the cops would break into the garage, pop the trunk, and find his withered and rotting carcass.

They might even think it was some bizarre suicide. Distraught over his breakup with Maura he drove to a secluded garage and locked himself in the trunk.

So he was surprised and relieved and scared shitless when he heard the garage door open. Then he heard a voice say, "Dude, we're going to open the trunk. We have guns. Stay perfectly still or we'll fucking toast you."

Bob nodded. Then realized he needed to talk. His voice croaked.

"Okay."

The trunk popped open quickly. Bob blinked. There they were. The two Mexican-looking guys who'd rear-ended him. Behind them a white guy about his age.

"Get out. Slow."

Bob decided to reason with them as he climbed gingerly out of the trunk.

"Listen. Guys. It's not my car. I don't care about the dent."

The young Mexican with the ponytail stuck a gun in Bob's face.

"Don't talk."

The older one looked in the trunk at the two coolers. He turned to Bob. Bob couldn't look in the man's eyes. They were scary.

"Is the arm in the cooler?"

This caught Bob completely off guard.

"Arm? What arm?"

The older, scary Mexican punched Bob hard in the stomach. Bob doubled over, unable to breathe, feeling like his balls had just been shot out of a cannon.

"The arm you're delivering to Parker Center."

Oh.

Bob nodded at one of the coolers. The white guy looked at Bob sympathetically.

"Try to stand up, you'll get your wind back faster."

Bob nodded and tried. He was starting to see spots and floaters in his vision. He thought he might black out. But then short, painful spurts of breathing began. First in the top of his lungs, then slowly working their way down until he was almost breathing normally. Bob noticed that the lump on his head was throbbing again.

"Can I get an aspirin?"

The white guy nodded.

"There's some Tylenol inside."

The Mexican with the ponytail grabbed Bob's arm and began to lead him into what looked like his parents' house.

Maura entered her office and went right to the message machine. She played the messages and was disappointed that Bob hadn't called. Maybe he was just playing a game with her, messing with her head a little. She knew that sometimes he just said stuff to get a reaction. But he'd seemed different this morning. Resolute. If Bob, the most liquid and malleable of personalities, could ever be called resolute. She smiled a little. Maybe her doing this was forcing Bob to grow up. Perhaps there was hope for him after all. She realized that she was ambivalent about leaving him. She didn't really find his cock disgusting. She was just tired of him waving it in her face. She wanted him to be more sensitive. To listen to her. Was that asking too much?

10

THE ARM LAY unwrapped on the kitchen table. The three men stood there staring at it, looking slightly awestruck and puzzled. They obviously weren't used to limbs and organs like Bob was. Bob didn't care about the arm. He held a bag of frozen peas against the lump on his head and gingerly sipped a Coke.

"I feel nauseous. I think you gave me a concussion."

The ponytail guy smiled at him.

"Sorry, *cabrón*. Had to knock you out. You might be a kung fu master or something. Couldn't take no chances, man."

Bob understood. It made him feel a little better. He even felt slightly flattered, a kung fu master? Right on. But now he found himself in a strange position. Was he kidnapped? Were they going to kill him? Should he try to escape? He really didn't know the answer.

The older Mexican guy took a rubber spatula and nudged the arm.

"I never realized he had so many tattoos."

The white guy spoke.

"The police will know that there are tattoos on the arm. We have to find out where he got them done."

The ponytail guy disagreed.

"First we need an arm."

Bob twitched with alarm as the older guy turned toward him.

"He's got two."

Bob shook his head.

"No way, man! No fucking way!"

The older Mexican gave Bob a menacing look. Bob shifted gears.

"C'mon man, my arm does not look anything like that arm."

Bob winced as the Mexican grabbed his arm and roughly jerked him so that his arm was next to Amado's severed arm. Side by side it was easy to see that Bob was right. The severed arm was dark, hairy, and muscular. A man's arm. Bob's arm looked pale, sickly even. An intellectual boy's arm. No amount of tattooing was going to change that. The Mexican looked at Bob.

"You a faggot?"

Bob shook his head.

"No."

"You got a faggot's arm."

Bob didn't respond. He didn't agree, of course. The gay men he knew were extremely buff, muscular, and handsome. His arm didn't look gay at all.

The older Mexican turned to the ponytail guy.

"Find him."

Bob was amazed. The guy with the ponytail just nodded and split. Bob realized that this older, scary Mexican guy was some kind of juiced-up Godfather or something. Why else would a Mexican in a toupee have some clean-cut white guy hanging around with him and be bossing some tough young hombre around like he was a five-year-old? Bob was in some kind of shit. That much was obvious.

Amado sat up in bed watching television. He'd gotten into one of the soap operas, enjoying the backstabbing, lying, and cheating of the characters. It was familiar turf, though he couldn't understand why young Jax didn't take a fucking shotgun to that evil bitch Helena after what she did to Francesca. Maybe Jax just was some kinda fucking *huele-pedos quebrachón.* Amado would've shoved both barrels up Helena's ass and pulled the trigger. Let the *jodida pendeja* have it. *¡Qué te jodas!*

He often found himself shouting at the TV. Attempting to warn someone not to sell their shares in the overseas corporation because it was a trap. A scam. Don't do it! *¡Cuidado!* He'd scream and shout, sometimes waving his arm around frantically, trying to warn them, and then realizing he didn't have an arm anymore. Still it felt like it was there. *Qué raro.*

He was happy to see Norberto when he came into the cheap motel room. Norberto was carrying a greasy brown paper bag. He handed it to Amado.

"How you feeling?"

"How you think?"

Amado opened the bag and was hit by a rich pungent aroma. He broke into a grin.

"*¿Carnitas?*"

"*Carnitas pibil.*"

"*Qué bueno.*"

Norberto sat down on the end of the bed and watched as Amado pulled one of the foil-wrapped tacos out of the bag and struggled with one hand to unwrap it. Norberto made no move to help.

"Do you miss your arm, man?"

"I dream about my fucking arm."

"We got it, you know."

Amado stopped what he was doing.

"What?"

"We got your arm, man. You should see it."

"What're you doing with my fucking arm, *pendejo?*"

"Keeping it from *las placas, maricón.*"

Amado glared at Norberto. Smart-ass little fucker.

"Esteban has my arm?"

"Sí."

"Qué bárbaro."

Amado shook his head and went back to unwrapping the taco. He eventually got the taco out and jammed half of it into his mouth. He chomped down on it, grease and salsa spraying out of his lips. Norberto smiled at him.

"¿Quieres cerveza?"

Amado nodded, a big smile on his face. He was moved by his friend who cared enough to bring tacos and beer. A tiny tear formed in the corner of his left eye. Norberto reached into a grocery bag and pulled out a cold can of Modelo Especial. He popped the can and handed it to Amado.

"Gracias."

"De nada."

Amado took a long pull on the cold beer and then let out a blistering belch. The air was suddenly scented with pork, chilies, and beer. Norberto turned to Amado, serious.

"Esteban needs you, man."

"Needs to kill me."

"No. Stuff's come up. It's important."

Amado looked at Norberto and realized that things had changed. Norberto had moved up in the world, taking direct orders from El Jefe, Esteban himself.

"I thought you were *mi vato.*"

"It's not like that, man. Esteban needs you. He's not gonna kill you."

"That's what he told you."

"That's what I know."

Amado studied Norberto. He figured that the punk was probably packing a nine, or worse, that fucking .38 snubby he liked to carry because he saw it in a movie and thought it looked real cool and vintage.

"Do I have a choice?"

"No."

Amado shrugged.

"Vale."

Esteban was watching Chivas play Morelia on channel 55 when Norberto and Amado walked into the safe house. Martin was talking to the delivery guy, Bob something, in the kitchen, trying to learn more about how to keep the arm preserved. The last thing Esteban wanted in his house was some *fuchi* arm stinking up the place. Esteban stood to greet Amado.

"Cabrón. ¿Qué onda?"

"You tell me."

The two men stared at each other. Esteban suddenly felt unsure of what he was supposed to do. It was a feeling he was unaccustomed to. What had Amado been up to at Carlos Vila's? Was it bad enough that Amado expected him to kill him? Esteban realized that he would have to deal with Amado one way or the other after he was clear of this mess. Sloppy murderers and freelancers were a liability. But he wasn't going to do anything about it right now. Right now his main concern was to keep out of jail. So he just stood there looking at Amado. Finally Norberto broke the tension.

"Amado? You want to see your arm?"
Amado turned to Norberto.
"Yeah."

Bob couldn't believe it when the one-armed dude came into the kitchen. Bob knew it was the arm's owner because this guy was covered in similar tattoos. Women with huge erect tits, men taking them from behind. Voluptuous and busty women with wild tangled hair going down on muscular biker-looking guys, sucking their long hard cocks. And that was just what he could see on the guy's one arm and poking out of his shirt around his neck and chest. It was like the Kama Sutra for Hell's Angels scattered all over the guy's body. Bob was fascinated. He wanted to say something to the guy, but he was mean looking, not scary like the older one, just mean, and Bob really didn't want to be punched in the stomach again, or hit on the head, or worse, so he didn't say anything. He watched as the mean-looking one-armed dude opened the cooler and lifted out his arm.

It was a moment. Sad. Touching. Here was this guy staring at his arm like it was a long-lost child. Bob studied the mean guy's face and saw his eyes well up with tears. Then the older scary guy finally said something.

"*Joder,* that must've hurt."

The mean dude looked at the scary guy, but didn't say anything. He just reached down and touched his arm. He first felt his fingers; then, turning the arm over, he stroked the forearm. Softly, like he could still feel it.

"Get me a drink."

The guy with the ponytail looked at the scary guy, who nodded. Then he went to the cupboard and took out a bottle of tequila. The one-armed dude sat down and knocked back a shot.

Bob pointed to the tattoo of the beautiful woman getting eaten.

"She's beautiful."

The mean dude nodded.

"Felicia."

Bob lit up. It all came out in an excited blurt.

"You mean she's real? This is a real woman? Do you know where she lives? Can I meet her? Do you have her number?"

The white guy, the scary guy, the ponytail guy, and the mean dude all turned and looked at Bob like he'd lost his mind. But Bob didn't care, this might be his only chance, so he kept talking.

"I mean look at her. Just look. Have you ever seen a more beautiful woman in your life? She's . . . she's . . . she's just the bomb, man."

The mean dude burst out laughing. It was a loud, deep, joyous laugh. He laughed until tears sprang from his eyes and he almost choked. Bob watched and, as the laughter continued on and on, he started to get nervous. Maybe he'd put his foot in it this time. Finally the mean dude got control of himself.

"The gringo's in love with Felicia."

The mean dude took his glass and poured some tequila into it. He slid the glass over to Bob.

"Drink."

Bob knocked back the tequila. It burned, in a soothing kind of a way. Bob looked at the mean dude.

"So you know her?"

The mean dude gave Bob a serious once-over, laughed again, then extended his hand.

"Amado."

This was how Bob became introduced to everyone. Amado, Norberto, Esteban, and Martin. Bob felt better knowing their names, but he wasn't sure if they'd given him their real names or some kind of fake names so that if he went to the police he would pass on misinformation. But then, on reflection, Bob felt worse because if those were their real names, that meant they were probably going to kill him so he couldn't give their names to the police.

Morris was desperately spinning shapes into place, clicking the keyboard in a trance. He didn't even look up when a delivery arrived from the Cedar-Sinai Medical Center. The delivery man, a teenage Latino in elaborately baggy jeans and a Che Guevara T-shirt, looked at the screen and snorted derisively.

"Tetris?"

Morris didn't even look up.

"I know, I know, it's old school. But it's a rad game, man."

The teenager wasn't buying it.

"My dad likes it."

"Dude, Tetris challenges your brain. It's like a spatial-relationship road-race disaster movie."

"Yeah, right. Sign this. Then you can go play Pong."

Morris didn't look up from the screen.

"I can't."

"I got places to go."

"One more minute."

"Nope."

"Dude, cut me some."

"Nope."

The delivery man waved his clipboard in front of Morris, almost obscuring the computer screen. Morris grabbed a pen off the desk and tried to sign the clipboard with his left hand without looking.

"This it?"

"Down two inches."

"Here?"

"Close enough."

Morris scribbled his name.

"Thanks, man."

"No sweat."

The delivery man left. Morris continued to play. He didn't notice that what he'd just signed for was a well-developed human fetus in a jar. The fetus floated in solution. Morris concentrated on his game.

Bob was now pretty toasted. He and Amado had killed the bottle of tequila and were sipping beers. Amado had his shirt off and was giving Bob vivid descriptions of each and every tattoo on his body. There must've been a hundred of them. When Bob expressed his admiration, Amado told him that he hadn't even started commemorating women in ink until he'd notched his first hundred on a leather belt. Bob looked at Amado as if he were some kind of rare athlete, someone who had accomplished what few could ever achieve.

Bob thought about his own slight string of conquests. A paltry six or seven. Never torrid one-night stands, always those first tentative meetings, the courtship, and then the relationship. Sure, there had been passion, but nothing worthy of a permanent place on his body, nothing worth the pain of needles and ink, nothing he could call art. Bob longed for something like that. He wanted to abandon himself to animal passions. He wanted to thrust wildly with a voluptuous woman who felt the same way he felt. Bob didn't want to worry about orgasms or foreplay or any of that. He wanted to be inspired to fuck wildly and to inspire someone else to do the same.

Bob watched as Amado drunkenly tried to reattach his arm.

The arm dropped to the kitchen floor with a sickening thud. Juice, Bob didn't know what else to call it, oozed out and smeared Amado's shirt. Amado picked up his arm from the floor and looked at it.

"I miss my arm, Bob."

"I bet you do."

"Never lose your arm, Bob, *nunca*."

Bob nodded.

"I know you didn't lose yours on purpose, and I bet your arm knows it too."

Amado considered that.

"You think so?"

"Absolutely."

Amado's voice caught, it looked like he might cry.

"I never thought about how my arm might feel. I never thought I'd see it again."

Amado was now letting the severed limb sit nonchalantly in his lap. He looked down at it.

"I didn't mean to hurt you."

Amado picked up his arm and cradled it like a newborn. Bob was quiet. He didn't know what to say so he just let Amado make his peace with his arm. Bob could see the Godfather, Esteban, sitting on the couch in the living room talking with Martin, the white guy. Norberto, or Norbert as Bob had called him, had drunk a few shots with them and then retired to a back bedroom to catch up on his sleep.

Bob stood up and patted Amado on the shoulder.

"I'm going to the bathroom. When I come back, let's remember the good things you did with your arm. Let's celebrate that."

Amado looked up at Bob with big wet eyes.

"You're a good man, Bob."

Bob went to pee.

Esteban watched Amado and the gringo drinking and laughing like it was Cinco de Mayo. Let them laugh. They'd both be dead soon enough. Martin was still arguing with him, wanting him to spare the gringo. ¿*Por qué?* Was it because they were both white? Martin never said anything when Esteban had some fucking *cholo* whacked. Now he's got some white guy to deal with and Martin is begging, putting everything at risk.

Esteban realized that Martin had a point. A dead white guy, carjacked while on the job, would be on the news. Once something made the news the police had to pay attention. Having the cops nosing around, asking questions, was never good.

Esteban knew all this, but his guts told him to kill the guy. Loose ends were a bad thing. You let a guy live and you empower him to testify against you in court. That would suck. The last thing Esteban wanted to see was this fucking scrawny slacker gringo standing up in federal court testifying about how Esteban kidnapped him. White people always thought they were better. Esteban didn't know what gave them that idea, it was such bullshit.

Esteban was smart. As smart as any white person, he was sure of that, but he didn't want to let his emotions get in the way of clear thinking. He knew that Martin had a point. So he agreed to let Martin have a talk with the guy, *gringo-a-gringo,* and see if he'd cooperate.

When Bob returned from the bathroom Amado was passed out on the table. He was snoring loudly, a line of drool running from the corner of his mouth to the floor. Bob sat down and watched him sleep. He didn't seem so mean in his sleep. He just seemed like a guy who'd lost his way in a new country.

Lost his way and then lost his arm. Bob felt for him.

Martin came over and sat with Bob. Martin needed to talk to him about something important. He wanted to tell Bob a story so he'd know why they had carjacked him and what they were planning to do with him. While Esteban watched *fútbol* on the television in the living room, Martin recounted the events of the last forty-eight hours that led up to Bob's abduction. Then Martin made Bob an offer.

Bob couldn't believe his ears. Not that he'd ever wanted to be a criminal or involved in a criminal enterprise. Frankly, the idea of jail had always been too frightening for him to even consider breaking the law. But here was a smart guy, a guy with a law degree, a guy who did his undergrad work at Yale, a guy just like him only more handsome, successful, and with better clothes, asking if Bob would work with them on one job. They would pay him ten thousand dollars and all he had to do was deliver the arm—technically a different arm—to Parker Center.

"A ten-thousand-dollar bonus for doing what you'd normally do."

Bob thought about it. He had a moment of indecision. But there was something about Esteban—the same thing that made him scary—that gave Bob confidence. The more he thought about it the more excited he became. Martin waited for an answer. Finally . . .

"I'll do it. But . . ."

Martin was taken aback.

"Bob, you're not really in a position to negotiate."

"You don't know what I want."

Martin nodded.

"Okay. What do you want?"

"I want to meet Felicia."

"Who's Felicia?"

Bob lifted Amado's arm off the table and pointed to the tattoo.

"That's Felicia."

Esteban was surprised that Bob came around so easily. He could see that Bob, like Martin, was attracted to the glamorous aspect of the criminal life. Caucasians can be so naive. They think being a gangster is all fast cars, beautiful women, and cash. They watch too many movies. Esteban knew firsthand how much work was involved in maintaining a successful life of crime. The long hours, the late nights, the constant anxiety. Most of the older members of *la familia* had developed angina from the stress. An unlucky few were rotting away in jail somewhere. Others had just dropped dead from massive coronaries while pumping some whore. Viagra deaths, he called them. The drug turns your *explorador* into Superman and leaves the rest of you a saggy old *abuelo* trying desperately to keep up. Wheezing and huffing, hardly enjoying it at all. It was tragic, grown men acting like teenagers, but still Esteban figured that it was better to go out having fun with a woman than being shot in the head while sitting in your car.

The scrawny gringo came into the room holding a can of beer. Esteban gave him the glare and was satisfied to see the gringo look away. Esteban cleared his throat.

"You understand what this means?"

Bob looked first at Martin, then back to Esteban.

"I think so."

"You'll become an accessory to murder, and that is some heavy shit, my friend."

Bob hesitated.

"I'm not going to kill anyone."

Esteban could barely conceal his irritation. The nerve some people have. Thinking it's easy to just go kill someone. Like anyone could do it. Even Amado, who had years of experience, bungled a simple hit.

"No. You're not going to kill anyone."

Martin interrupted.

"But you will be an accessory. I want you to understand that."

Bob nodded.

"I understand."

"You could go to jail."

Esteban gave him the look.

"If you go to the police, we will kill you."

Bob was almost annoyed.

"I get it."

Esteban watched as Bob stood and pondered the possibilities. You could almost see the wheels turning in his brain. It wouldn't have surprised Esteban if Bob had asked for a piece of paper and pencil so he could draw a line down the middle and write the pros on one side and the cons on the other. *Americanos* have no *huevos*.

But Bob surprised him.

"If I get to meet Felicia, it'll be worth it."

Esteban laughed out loud.

"You believe a woman is worth the risk?"

Bob nodded. He had never been so sure of anything in his life.

"She's not just any woman."

Esteban shook his head in amazement.

"Just so you understand."

Bob sat down on the couch next to Martin. Martin slipped into business mode, closing the deal.

"The deal is we're going to give Bob here ten thousand dollars and a night with Felicia."

"And what does Bob give us?"

"He will deliver the arm, the new arm, and tell everyone that he's been distraught over breaking up with his girlfriend and that's why he's late."

"Did you break up with your girlfriend?"

"Kind of."

"What do you mean?"

"We had a fight."

Esteban sat back and sighed.

"I hope it was a good fight."

Bob nodded.

"Pretty good."

Martin chimed in.

"We could drive by and you could finish it off. I mean, really break up with her. That way the story would stick."

Bob was enthusiastic.

"I'd like to do that before I see Felicia. You know, make it official and all. That way it wouldn't be like I was cheating on her."

Esteban just looked at the two gringos. *Carajo*. What a fucking mess.

"We still need an arm."

11

I T WAS ONE of those great days in Los Angeles. The kind you see when you watch the Rose Parade on TV. The golden sun slicing across the city bringing health, wealth, and warmth to the world. The blue sky spreading cheerfully overhead. The kind of day that makes you think that people in LA live in some fantastic world of promise, like vitamin C land or something.

Only city buses drove by instead of floral floats as Don sat on the steps of Parker Center and ate a big greasy hamburger with Detective Flores and a couple of uniformed officers.

Other LAPD personnel stood in line at the roach coach waiting for their food. Don felt great. It was great to be a police officer. Great to be out there making the world a better place. Great to be eating this big gloppy burger in the sun with his comrades. Don knew that tonight he'd have to have a green salad and maybe a little sashimi to counteract the effects of this gutbomb, but that was a small price to pay for the absolutely glorious way he felt right here, right now.

Don dipped his fries into a little paper cup of ketchup and mused. He imagined Esteban Sola stripped of his toupee and wearing a bright orange LA County Jail jumpsuit. Don relished the image of Esteban standing, bent and cuffed, ready to be deported to a Mexican jail. For too long Don had watched as Esteban had strutted and preened and lorded over people. It was raw arrogance and nothing pissed Don off more than that. That's why he'd targeted Esteban, made it his personal mission to bring that motherfucking Juarez wetback down.

Don slurped his diet root beer. He turned to Flores.

"That evidence delivered yet?"

Flores looked up, his mouth packed with *carne asada* burrito, and shook his head. No.

"Well, I can't wait all day. I'm gonna make some calls and find out where this thing is."

Don crumpled his gutbomb wrapper and arced it into the trash. He wiped his hands on his pants like a man and headed back into the building.

Don drove the dirty brown Caprice out of Parker Center. He didn't understand why the UC cars always had to be dirty brown Chevrolets. Parked in a line in the LAPD parking lot they looked like giant piles of dog crap. What kind of message did that send? Why not have the detectives zipping around LA in BMWs or a Lincoln Town Car or something? The shit brown was just as recognizable to the crumbs as a black-and-white, it didn't fool anyone, so why not mix it up? Driving one of these cars gave Don an understanding of why some detectives were on the take. It was not esteem building. Sitting behind the wheel of a big stinking turd, who wouldn't consider collecting a little extra cash now and then?

Don didn't understand where this delivery guy could've gone. He'd called United Pathology and gotten a list of all of the scheduled stops. The guy hadn't gone to a single one. So, like the good detective he was, Don was going to hit the streets and investigate. Anything was better than sitting around the office writing for Flores' gas to begin.

Larga never knew what to wear to these sessions. He felt uncomfortable wearing jeans because she made him take them all the way off. Something about constricting the blood flow to the prostate. The prostate needing oxygen to make more of that slimy stuff it made. Shorts? Shorts just seemed so gay. Larga stood naked in front of the mirror. He turned sideways and saw his big gut sagging outward in profile. Perhaps sweatpants. Larga dug through his closet and pulled out a matching nylon jogging suit, the kind that fat guys in New Jersey wear when they're driving their Camaros around in the afternoon. He'd bought it when he'd decided to take up jogging. He'd worn it once.

Don pulled up in front of United Pathology. A big building full of dead stuff. Even though he'd seen hundreds of dead bodies, something about this building gave him the creeps. Maybe it was because when Don found the bodies they were still people. Even a corpse has personality. Personal effects. A life lived and lost. Here, in the pathology lab, it was reduced to tissue, fluids, samples. No life. No character. The last thing Don wanted was some Poindexter poking around his body when he was dead. Hopefully you really are dead when you're dead. Don entered the building.

Morris sat in front of the computer waiting for a Web site to open. It took a fucking ice age to load, and when it was done it was the same old thing. Morris had been to several sites offering "free" photos, and all of them had demanded a credit card number as "proof" that the viewer was over twenty-one. As if a teenager couldn't get a credit card. As if someone under twenty-one shouldn't be allowed to look at pornography. *Shit,* Morris thought, *I've been banging the beaver since I was fifteen.* It was a very annoying way to spend the afternoon.

Morris looked up as some dude in a sports coat came in. The guy smiled and flashed a badge. He didn't do it fast like they do in the movies. He held it out a really long time, as if Morris was too stupid to read.

"Hey."

The police dude cleared his throat.

"Hi. I'm looking for a piece of evidence. It was supposed to be delivered to Parker Center today."

"You mean the arm?"

"Yes."

"It should be there already."

"It's not."

Morris looked at the guy, then he looked at his screen. Spunk.com had loaded and, shit, it was gay porn. Morris tried to click the page off, but it was still loading and just hung there, literally. Morris started to sweat. He impulsively punched the button and just turned the monitor off.

"Well, it should be any minute."

"It's not there."

"It should be."

"I know it should be, but it isn't. That's why I'm here."

"It'll get there."

"Where is it?"

"Is it important?"

"Yes."

"Then it'll get there."

Don cleared his throat.

"It's not there."

Morris wondered why this guy was so dense.

"What do you want me to do about it?"

"I want you to tell me where it is."

Morris shrugged.

"Dude, I don't know."

The police guy leaned in acting all heavy and pissed off. He reached around and turned the monitor back on.

"What're you doin', man?"

"Where's the arm?"

"En route."

"En route to where?"

"Parker Center."

"But it's not at Parker Center."

"Right. It's en route."

The monitor came back on with several graphic and revealing images of male on male intercourse. Morris began to squirm.

"Oh, man, that's not what I wanted."

The cop guy smiled like he had something on Morris.

"Who has the arm?"

"Bob."

Morris clicked the image away. This time it disappeared.

"Where's Bob?"

"Fuck if I know, man. He should be at Parker Center."

Bob sat in the front seat as Norberto drove. Esteban and Martin were in back. Amado had decided to remain at the safe house, his favorite *telenovela* was about to come on and he didn't want to miss it.

"Turn right here."

Bob was directing them to Maura's office. It was in a nondescript box of a building.

Bob was sweating. He was starting to have some doubts

about the whole deal. Second thoughts. Third thoughts.
Fourth and fifth thoughts. On the one hand he was excited to
be on this adventure. *You don't really know how boring your
life is*, he thought, *until adventure comes conking you in the
head and stuffing you in a trunk.*

But on the other hand Bob knew that he was not a bad guy.
He wasn't a thief or a murderer and he didn't really want to
become one.

By the sixth thought, he had rationalized it. He was going
to be all right. He wasn't going to kill anyone. He was only
playing his part in an unfolding drama. How could he judge it?
It was just beginning.

The seventh thought, however, was just like the second. *If I
don't do what they say, they'll kill me. They might kill me anyway.* That was eight.

"You can park in the lot behind the building. She vali-
dates."

"Not if you really break up with her."

Bob considered that.

"Right."

Bob got out of the car and entered the building. Bob
thought about what he'd say to Maura. He wished he was
angry. Really fucking pissed off. Wished that he could scream
and call her a bitch, throw something, break a plate or knock
over a table . . . you know, make a good show of it. But Bob
wasn't in the mood. In fact, the more he thought about breaking up with her, the happier he became. He'd been stuck in
this boring bohemian lifestyle for so long that he'd forgotten
what it was like to be excited by other possibilities. It was a
great big world, and here he'd been sitting on the couch watching TV, drinking beer, and sending e-mails to his friends. What
had he been thinking? Now he was a new man with a new
career, a dangerous and exciting one, and perhaps, a new

woman in his life. A fiery, voluptuous Latina who could teach him Spanish and make him her sex slave all at the same time. He was practically giddy.

Bob bounded up the stairs to Maura's office.

Esteban was worried. How much time did they have to pull this off? Would it even work? He knew that as long as the cops didn't have Amado's arm or Amado—figuring that a man missing an arm would be as much circumstantial evidence as an arm missing a man—they couldn't build a case. Without either there was no way they could tie Carlo's murder to him, it would be over. *Terminara.* But when he thought about it, that seemed so *flojo.* Better to take it one step further. Give them some kind of clue that would have them chasing their tails for months if not years. A real *"¡Qué te jodas!"* right in the fucking face of the *federales.* Let the *jalapeños* know who's boss. That, he thought, would be *mejor.* Better than *mejor,* it would be *la puta madre.*

Suddenly Norberto turned from the front and nudged Esteban.

"Mira."

Esteban followed Norberto's gaze and watched as a plump gringo in a track suit climbed out of a Saab.

"El es un poco gordo como Amado."

"Cierto."

Norberto reached into his pocket and pulled out a heavy sap. Martin started squirming.

"I don't know guys, maybe this is a bad idea."

Esteban glared at Martin. He watched as the *jodiendo gringo* withered right in front of him.

"Creo que el niño se ha meado en los pantalones."

Norberto laughed.

"Qué lástima."

Martin sat up and pointed at Norberto.

"Don't think I can't understand what you guys are saying, because I do. Mostly."

Esteban growled.

"Understand this. We need an arm. El Gordo has an arm. *¿Entiendes?*"

Martin nodded.

Norberto and Esteban climbed out of the car.

Max Larga woke up to the gentle rocking of a car in traffic. It was dark and his head was throbbing. He didn't remember much. He was on his way to his appointment and then he woke up in the trunk of a car. What the hell was going on? Why was he in a trunk? You don't just dump someone in a trunk. This was not how civilized people behaved, he was sure of that. Not that he was uncomfortable, it was a spacious trunk.

Larga decided he needed to get to the bottom of whatever was going on. He began to kick the trunk lid as hard as he could. It didn't take long before he got tired of that, it didn't seem to be making much difference. So he felt around in the trunk for something hard. He came up with a tire iron and began to pound that against the frame, the hood, whatever made the loudest noise.

Larga felt a sense of triumph when the car finally slowed to a stop. He heard the driver's side door open. He couldn't wait, he was going to give them hell. You can't just put Max Larga in the trunk of your car and not answer for it.

The trunk lid was thrown open. Larga was temporarily blinded by the light, but he could distinctly see a Mexican man with a ponytail swinging a baseball bat right at his head.

Don was annoyed. He wasn't getting anywhere. He'd called Flores at Parker Center. There was no sign of Bob, the delivery guy, or the arm. He'd called UCLA where Bob was scheduled to drop some tissue samples for the medical students. Nothing. Don knew something was wrong . . . but what?

"Tell me, does Bob take drugs?"

Morris squirmed.

"I don't know."

"Of course you know."

"You can't expect me to be a narc, man."

"So he does do drugs. Is that what you're saying?"

Morris clammed up.

"You're not going to tell me?"

"I got nothing to say until my lawyer gets here."

"But you're not under arrest."

That made Morris think.

"Did you do something that might lead to your arrest?"

"No."

"Then just answer the question."

Don watched as the kid worked it out in his brain, replaying in his mind some lawyer show that he'd seen on television, trying to remember how it ended. Don had seen this countless times in interview rooms and crime scenes. Once a crumb even asked him if he remembered a *Columbo* episode. As if Don was patterning his line of questions after a TV show. Don still hadn't decided whether all these cop shows and lawyer shows had made his job easier or more difficult. People seemed to think that what he did was more glamorous, which definitely helped when he went out on a date.

"Does Bob have a drug problem?"

"Dude, I don't think it's a problem."

"But he does puff the occasional joint."

"Maybe. He likes beer. I know that."

"So do you think he's at a bar?"

Morris scratched his head.

"Maybe. He was pretty crabby when he came in this morning."

"Why was that?"

"His girlfriend dumped him. Harsh."

Don smiled. Now things were starting to make sense. They always did. Once you had enough information, everything made sense.

"That *is* harsh."

"Yeah."

"So . . . where do you think he might be?"

Martin sat in the back and felt a feeling of dread wash over his body. He watched as Bob, the idiot delivery guy, sat in front and pounded out a drumbeat on the dashboard.

"Hey, guys, can I ask you something?"

Esteban turned to Bob.

"Sure."

"Can I change my name?"

"Legally?"

"No, what I mean is, would you guys call me Roberto instead of Bob?"

Esteban laughed.

"Cierto, Roberto, cierto."

Norberto playfully whacked Bob on the head.

"Roberto!"

Bob nodded.

"Me llamo Roberto."

Esteban laughed again.

"Already you're speaking Spanish, Roberto. *Muy bien.*"

Bob broke into a huge grin, smiling like he'd just dropped a double hit of ecstasy. Martin remembered the feeling of excitement, of belonging, that he got when he first joined up with Esteban. Now he just felt sleazy, his conscience working against him, stealing his appetite, taking away his erection when he was supposed to be banging some hot chick with fake tits. Martin felt a migraine coming on. Maybe it was the fucking kidnap victim in the trunk who was battering the shit out of the lid. Like he could dig his way through reinforced German steel.

The fat guy's clanging and thumping was a reminder to Martin. What, exactly, were they going to do with him? Tattoo him and then chop his arm off? Obviously. That was the point of the whole harebrained scheme. But then what? Dump his body in the desert? And who was going to do the chopping? Martin tried to remember if he'd been high when this stupid idea came to him. Probably.

Martin wished he could fire up a jumbo right now and just forget the whole thing was happening.

The fucking guy in the trunk just wouldn't stop. Martin looked around. Esteban didn't even seem to notice. Norberto was talking to Bob about *rock en español.* But it was really getting under Martin's skin.

"Can we make him stop?"

Esteban turned to Martin, that fucking superior smile on his face.

"Is it bothering you?"

"I'm worried that someone might hear it."

"And?"

"And know that we've got a guy locked in the trunk."

Esteban nodded to Norberto and then turned back to Martin.

"Don't worry so much."

"That's my job. I have to worry. Someone has to watch your back, Esteban."

Esteban smirked again with that fucking superior smile, like he had to constantly prove that Latinos were better than whites.

"I have many people watching my back."

The car pulled over and Norberto took a baseball bat from under the front seat and got out.

Then it was quiet.

12

MAURA LOOKED AT her watch. Her client was half an hour late. He'd have to pay full price for the session. Maura didn't appreciate no-shows, her policy was that you had to give at least twenty-four hours' notice to cancel. There was a knock at the door.

"You're late."

The words were out of her mouth before she realized that it wasn't Larga but someone else. The man identified himself as a detective from the LAPD. Maura saw him quickly scan the room with his eyes.

"I'm not a whore. This is a legitimate business."

"I'm not with Vice, so even if you are a whore, I don't care. I want to ask you a few questions about your boyfriend."

"Bob?"

The detective nodded.

"Can I sit?"

"Sure."

Maura took the clean sheet off the chair and the detective settled in.

"Have you seen Bob today?"

"What has he done?"

"Nothing. We're just looking for him."

"If he hasn't done anything, why are you looking for him?"

Maura watched the detective heave a sigh.

"Why is everybody so suspicious nowadays?"

Maura thought about that. She didn't think Bob would do anything crazy, but then again he was acting really weird.

"We broke up."

"Was it his idea?"

"It was mine."

"Was he upset?"

"Yes."

"Do you have any idea where he might go? Who he might see when he's upset?"

"Did you try the apartment?"

The detective sighed again.

"Of course."

Maura thought. If Bob was in trouble, where would he go? It was funny, she realized, you could think you know someone really well, on a really intimate level, but when it came down to it, you didn't know them at all. She turned to the detective and shrugged.

"I don't know."

"Does he have any hobbies? Anything he likes to do?"

"He likes his computer."

"Does he frequent an Internet café, something like that?"

"Not that I know of."

"When did you break up with him?"

"I told him last night that I couldn't stand the sight of his penis."

The detective gave her a funny look. Maura defended herself.

"I'm just sick of it. That's not a crime."

"Do you think he'll come back?"

"He told me he never wanted to see me again."

Maura suddenly broke down and started sobbing. The detective reached over and handed her a box of tissues.

"I'll never see him again."

"Isn't that what you wanted?"

Maura blew her nose. She didn't know what she wanted. What she wanted changed every day. Who the fuck actually knows what they want? Does anybody? A show of hands?

"I guess."

The detective was growing impatient, and shifted in the chair.

"What do you do here?"

"I'm a masturbation coach."

She looked at the detective, expecting the reaction she always got, the disbelieving and dismayed bug-eyed jaw drop. Instead, he seemed genuinely intrigued.

"Yeah? Is that like some kind of therapy?"

Maura nodded.

"There are many ways to enhance the orgasmic experience. There are breathing and relaxation techniques, different kinds of grips and strokes. A couple of sessions can really improve the quality of your masturbation."

The detective stood and extended his hand.

"Do you have a card?"

Esteban stood in the kitchen of the safe house. Greasy wrappers from a take-out meal were strewn on the counter. Esteban belched. Greasy food never went down easily for him. He preferred good Mexican food. Not the kind you found in crappy Mexican restaurants up here but the kind you found in Mexico. Fresh, with flavor. There were a few spots around Los Angeles that he liked. La Serenata de Garibaldi in East LA. Another place way the hell out in the Valley. But even the gringos knew about those places. Esteban belched again and popped a Tums. Maybe he should open his own restaurant, get that molé recipe from his *madre*. Restaurants were excellent businesses for laundering money.

The sudden stench of marijuana got his attention. He walked into the living room to find Bob, Martin, Norberto, and Amado all stoned and watching a tape-delayed soccer game from Guadalajara. Esteban was suddenly hit with a strong desire to go back to his own house and crawl into his Jacuzzi with Lupe and her natural breasts. There are times, he realized, when being an organized crime boss was a real fucking drag.

Esteban walked in and faced the men. Norberto held up a burning joint.

"*¿Quieres tostar el churro, Esteban?*"

"No."

Esteban picked up the remote, and flicked off the TV. Amado groaned.

"*Qué bárbaro.*"

Esteban turned to Norberto.

"Did you call the tattoo man?"

Norberto carefully stubbed the joint out with his fingers.

"*Sí.*"

"*¿Y? ¿Dónde?*"

"I don't know, man. *No se.*"

Amado looked up.

"He likes the *caballo*. We should go to his shop."

Esteban sighed. Great. A fucking junkie tattoo artist. Esteban didn't approve of drugs. Even if he made millions of dollars off their importation. People who took drugs couldn't be trusted. They were weak. Easily turned by the *federales.*

The four men continued to stare at the TV even though it was off. That must be some *hierba buena.* Esteban growled.

"*Vamos.*"

Norberto was getting tired of being bossed around. Tired of driving Esteban around like he was some kind of fucking chauffeur. Here he was enjoying himself, minding his own business, watching TV with Amado and the gringos and . . . and El Patrón comes and kills the buzz.

Norberto lifted the lid of the trunk and checked on *El Gordo.* Dried blood was crusted in the guy's hair where he had blasted him with the bat. *This dude is fucking out,* thought Norberto. But he was still breathing, that was a good thing. Norberto was relieved. He'd thought he killed the guy. All the excitement of the day, the tension of the situation, and then the fucking guy goes and starts banging the inside of the trunk. It really irritated Norberto. He didn't mean to hit the guy so hard.

The delivery guy, Roberto, sat up front between Norberto and Amado. Norberto had grown to like the guy. He thought Roberto was cool, and smart too, smart like Martin. Maybe when Norberto was head of his own crew, he'd have a smart gringo giving him advice like Esteban did. Maybe he and Roberto could start a crew together after this was all over. That'd be sweet. It's cool to have a gringo sidekick to boss around.

Don was annoyed. In the old days people had real vices. You're looking for a guy who likes to gamble, you find him at the track or one of those card rooms in Commerce. A guy likes to drink, you find him at his local bar. A guy's a sex addict, you find him in bed. This guy Bob, what was his vice? Surfing the Internet? What was that? Don pondered the possibilities. He could canvass all the cyber cafés in Los Angeles, or look for some scraggly guy in a park typing into a laptop. Or he could do what he did. He went to UCLA to see if Bob had made his delivery there.

The first thing Don noticed when he entered the lab was a funky smell. It was a mix of chemical preservatives, stomach acids, and rotting flesh that assaulted his nostrils and made him gag. He walked past a group of four med students who were busy performing an autopsy on what looked to be a sixty-year-old Caucasian female. Don had seen his fair share of guts and corpses, but they were always in context. There was something about the detached way the students were working that made him feel slightly queasy.

One of the students scooped the intestines up and over.

"Are you going Friday night?"

"Where?"

"Party at Jill's apartment."

"I wasn't invited."

"You are now."

"What's the purple thing?"

"That's the liver, right there."

"Why does it look all splotchy?"

"Hard to say, let's cut a sample."

Don walked to the back of the lab and found a teaching assistant filing some papers. Don identified himself.

The car was parked in front of a tattoo parlor in Hollywood. Bob watched as Esteban and Amado went in. Bob turned to Norberto.

"Maybe I'll get a tattoo."

Norberto smiled at Bob.

"Yeah, *ese,* get the fuckin' Virgin of Guadalupe inked on your chest."

"I was thinking maybe something, I don't know, something tough."

"Nothing's tougher than a virgin, man."

Norberto broke up laughing. Bob smiled, but he was deep in thought. Maybe like a tiger or a dragon or something on his arm. Then again, maybe this wasn't such a good idea.

"We're not going to kill him, are we?"

"No, man. Nobody fucks up, nobody dies."

Suddenly the car lurched as the weight in the trunk began to shift and stir.

"Looks like sleepy head is waking up."

Norberto took a bottle of water out of a paper bag and unscrewed the lid, then reached into his pocket and pulled out a tiny vial. He quickly dumped the contents of the vial into the bottle of water and screwed the cap back on.

"What's that?"

"Rophinol."

"What's that do?"

"It knocks them out, man. Knocks them out and they don't remember shit when they wake up."

Esteban stuck his head out of the tattoo parlor door and signaled for them to come in.

Bob was more than a little nervous when they went around to open the trunk.

"What if he tries to get away?"

"Relax, man, he won't even know his name."

Norberto popped the trunk. Inside, the stocky guy in the track suit lay curled up and disoriented. He blinked up at Norberto and flinched, expecting to get hit again. Norberto spoke to him in a soothing voice.

"It's cool, man. You're all right. You must be thirsty. Here, have some water."

The guy just nodded blankly and took the water from Norberto. He drained it in a few gluttonous gulps.

"Can you get up? Do you need some help?"

The guy tried, but his legs must've been asleep or something. Bob and Norberto each grabbed an arm and hoisted the guy out of the trunk. The guy looked at Bob.

"Thanks."

"No problem man. Feel like getting a tattoo?"

The guy looked up at the garish designs painted on the tattoo shop's facade.

"A tattoo?"

Norberto patted the guy on the shoulder.

"Yeah, man, everybody's got a fuckin' tattoo now. It's all the rage."

Don was getting frustrated. Sure, the pieces of the puzzle were starting to fall into place. It was only a matter of time before he tracked Bob down. But right now, when he could be processing that arm, running the prints, beginning to piece together an indictment that could bring the Mexican mafia in southern California to its knees and make Don a law enforcement hero all in one fell swoop, right now Don was in the second act of a wild-goose chase, and it was starting to piss him off.

Don went over the checklist in his mind. He'd been to Bob's place of employment, apartment, and girlfriend's place of employment. Don smiled thinking about that. Who ever heard of a masturbation coach? Don had never given masturbation much thought. Sometimes he felt slightly, er, engorged, and just did it. It helped him fall asleep when he was stressed out. But he had to admit that the idea of a coach was exciting. Or maybe it was the idea of that particular coach. She was really attractive. He pulled her card out of his pocket and looked at it. Then he thought better of it. Maybe he just needed a girlfriend. Don put the card away.

Don hadn't had a girlfriend in about a year. He didn't know why. It wasn't as if his friends weren't always trying to set him up with some Amanda, Karen, or Dana. He'd just gotten into his work. With the exception of his enological pursuits, Don had done nothing but work. He had pored over every wiretap word by word, he had begun to learn Spanish, had gone through the income tax returns like an auditor, studied phone bills; thousands of tiny details about Esteban had been scrutinized. To clear his head, to keep his sanity, Don had spent nearly every night drinking a bottle of good wine. Drinking alone in that fancy wine bar. Letting the wine wash the minutiae away in broad burgundy strokes.

Don sat in his car, stuck in traffic. This was annoying. Why did Bob have to break up with his girlfriend today? Why couldn't he just do his job? Don was doing his. He wasn't mooning over some lost love somewhere. He considered arresting Bob for obstruction, not that the DA could ever make it stick, but just to fuck with him. Let him stew in jail for a few days. Run him around a little, just like he was running Don around now.

Don had to laugh at himself. He was not normally a vindictive person. He didn't usually get emotional about the small glitches that occur in any investigation. But Don had to admit that he was growing tired of his obsession. It had gotten to him. Ground him down. That's why he was so anxious to find Bob and get that arm over to Processing.

Bob and Norberto led the stocky guy into the tattoo parlor. The drugs were kicking in fast, the guy's legs functioning sporadically and then not at all. Bob shifted his grip.

"Heavy fucker."

Norberto agreed.

"Gringos eat too much, man. They eat the fuckin' world."

After they went through the front door a bearded man in a

tattered leather motorcycle jacket and ripped jeans flipped the sign around so it read "Closed" and locked the door behind them. When the biker guy walked he produced a distinct rhythm, his biker boots clomp-clomping as a long wallet chain ka-chinged against his leg. Bob was impressed, not so much with the place but with himself. *Here I am in a real tattoo parlor with a real Hell's Angel–looking tattoo artist. Cool.*

The tattoo artist looked at Larga.

"This the guy?"

Esteban nodded.

"He looks fucked-up, man."

Norberto answered this one.

"He is, man, trust me."

The biker shrugged.

"Put him in the chair and hold him down."

Bob and Norberto dragged Larga to a chair in back and plopped him down. Larga flopped over like a dead geranium.

Amado had met them there and nodded to Bob like, *Job well done.* A little sheepish, Bob nodded back, then turned and took in his surroundings. He couldn't believe all the different designs displayed on the wall. There were hundreds of them. Cool-looking Celtic bands, panthers, Mayan suns, Maori tribal face tattoos. There were pictures of Japanese dudes whose entire bodies were covered with the most incredible and colorful tattoos. Bob was excited, he desperately wanted a tattoo. He thought it would perfectly symbolize his newfound freedom. But what image? Then Bob was struck by another thought. He turned to the bearded tattoo artist.

"Does it hurt?"

The tattoo artist smiled at him.

"What do you think?"

Martin stood near the back and watched as the tattoo artist, who looked like the poster boy for a Harley Davidson ad, held Amado's severed arm under a light. The old biker looked at Amado.

"What was her name?"

Amado grunted.

"Felicia."

The tattoo artist looked back at the arm.

"I can't make it look exactly the same. It's gonna look new. No way I can fix that."

Esteban had an expression on his face that Martin had seen before. It was the look of a man who had reached his limit, who was ready to explode into a rage and kill everyone in the room. But Martin knew that Esteban had a masochistic streak. He would hold the rage in as long as he could. He would push it down into his belly and hold it there. He would be needing some Maalox soon.

"The police haven't seen it yet, they just have some photos. It'll be fine."

Norberto chimed in.

"It doesn't have to be exact, *cabrón*. Just make it close enough."

Martin watched as Bob went over to Esteban.

"Can I get one?"

Martin held his breath. He was certain Esteban was just going to punch Bob in the stomach. Martin had seen it countless times. He knew that getting hit in the stomach hurt, it knocked the wind out of you, but no matter how excruciating the pain, you had to stay on your feet. If you fell to the floor, Esteban would kick you until you were unconscious.

But, to Martin's surprise, Esteban laughed.

"Sure."

A stream of drool suddenly spilled out of the fat guy's mouth. The tattoo artist looked concerned.

"Is he dead?"

"He's just sleepy."

"He looks dead."

Norberto patted the fat guy on the head.

"No man, I just slipped him some Rophinal."

"What's that?"

"You know, man, it's the date-rape drug."

"What is it?"

"Guys slip it to *las mujeres* and it knocks them out. *Entonces tú puedes meterla hasta los puños.* When they wake up they can't remember anything."

Esteban leaned in for a better view.

"No te acuerdas de nada?"

Norberto nodded and pointed to Larga's unconscious body.

"Yeah, man, you can fuck him if you want. He'll never know."

The men looked at each other for an excruciating minute. Esteban broke the silence.

"Jesús Cristo, pendejo. No somos bujarrones."

Norberto shrugged.

"He wouldn't know, that's all I'm saying."

Martin looked at his hands. They were wrapped around the back of a chair, white-knuckled, digging into the wood until they hurt. Martin released his grip, clenched and unclenched his fists. He couldn't believe how tense he was. *At this rate I'll be dead of a heart attack before I'm thirty,* he thought. He needed to talk to Esteban about letting him get an office. He needed some kind of sanctuary from this madness. Running around, riding in cars, kidnapping people, it was all getting to be a little much. Martin realized he really needed a smoke. He nodded to Esteban.

"I need some air."

Esteban didn't seem to care, and for that matter nobody else seemed to care either, so Martin walked through the tattoo shop, past the ratty back room with its old TV set and battered refrigerator. He opened the back door and stepped out into the sunlight. The alley behind the tattoo parlor was nice. Sunny and clean and quiet. The light hitting the warm red bricks and spilling down to the pocked asphalt. Martin looked around, and didn't see anyone. He pulled a nice smooth jumbo out of his pocket and fired it up. As he exhaled a deep plume of gray into the air he realized that if he had an office, he could smoke all day. Plop his butt on a couch, put his feet up, pop open a cold can of soda and zone out. He'd still get his work done. He was responsible. But he wouldn't have to ride around in the car endlessly. He'd demand that Esteban make appointments. He took a heavy pull on the joint and held it in his lungs. He liked this idea.

Norberto came out and silently took the joint from Martin's fingers. He took a hit.

"Nice day."

Amado watched as the tattoo artist worked diligently to counterfeit his severed arm. His arm was lying right next to Larga's as the artist went back and forth, measuring, calculating the scale and line, trying to make it as close to perfection as he could.

It was like some kind of strange dream. A *sueño con locotes* calling the shots. The big boss, El Pez Gordo, Esteban stood over the tattoo artist like a nervous schoolteacher, making sure he didn't fuck it up. Amado remembered when Esteban was tough, really tough. In the old days he dealt with problems quickly, showing no mercy. He never lost his cool, he had ice in his veins.

Nowadays he just acted tough. Amado could tell by the look in his eyes. He knew Esteban was afraid. He had gone gringo, *agringarse.* In the old days, Esteban would've just shrugged, and said, "*Chingado.*" And that would have been that. If *las placas* bust us, they bust us. That's *la vida.* Now all Esteban seemed to care about was staying in El Norte and making big money, trying to be legit, respectable. As if being a fucking gangster wasn't respectable enough. Of course Amado realized that there was an upside to Esteban's change of heart, because in the old days he would be dead by now.

Bob made up his mind. He turned to the tattoo artist.

"Could I get, like, a coffee cup right here on my arm, you know, and spell Felicia's name in the steam?"

"How big?"

"Not too big. A little one."

Bob held his finger and thumb about two inches apart.

"Sit down."

Esteban stepped forward.

"Do we have time for this?"

The tattoo artist looked at him.

"The outline ink needs to set before I do the shading. It won't take long."

Bob winced as the machine, kind of like an engraver—a skin engraver—started buzzing. It hurt, but not as bad as he thought it would.

Bob looked up at Amado.

"When do I get to meet her?"

"Felicia?"

"That's the deal."

Amado and Esteban exchanged glances.

"You want to meet her tonight?"

"That'd be awesome."

Esteban nodded.

"We need to get you an alibi. Someplace where you spent the night."

Bob turned to the tattoo artist.

"I'm really upset because I broke up with my girlfriend."

The tattoo artist nodded and stroked his beard philosophically.

"Fuckin' chicks, man."

Then he went back to tattooing.

Bob looked over at the guy in the matching track suit. Kidnapped, knocked out, tattooed. Wow. Talk about being in the wrong place at the wrong time. Bob felt sorry for him. Of course, Bob realized, none of this was his fault. They had originally planned to kill him and destroy the arm, then the smart white guy had come up with this other plan. That saved his life. His life for a stranger's arm. It wasn't great, but it was better than the alternative.

Bob was curious about the fat guy. He reached over and pulled a wallet out of the tracksuit. Esteban growled.

"What are you doing?"

"I just want to see who this guy is."

With one hand Bob flipped the wallet open and saw the driver's license.

"Max Larga."

Bob flipped through the wallet.

"He's an organ donor."

Esteban ripped the wallet out of Bob's hand.

"Look, *pendejo,* you don't want to know too much about people. *¿Entiendes?*"

"Why not?"

"Just trust me on this. It's better not to know."

Bob looked at Amado. Amado nodded.

"Es mejor, Roberto, *es mejor."*

Bob nodded.

"Okay."

Bob looked at his arm and watched as the tattoo artist inked and dabbed, inked and dabbed. A beautiful coffee cup and saucer were appearing.

"Can you put some color in?"

"No problem."

Amado stood up and looked at the clock. He turned to the tattoo artist.

"You got a TV?"

"In the back."

"My *telenovela*'s starting."

"Make yourself at home."

Amado walked into the back, past Esteban who was rolling his eyes. He found the TV and a ratty old couch. Amado clicked on the tube, walked over to the wheezing refrigerator and opened it. He pulled out a long-neck Budwieser and settled in on the couch to watch his show. The thick sweet smell of *mota* came drifting in from the alley where Norberto and Martin were getting stoned.

As the theme music for the telenovela began, Norberto came scurrying in.

"¡Ay, qué padre!"

Amado made a shushing sound as Norberto flopped on the couch next to him.

The lead actress—Amado had a huge crush on her—
walked into a doctor's office on the small screen. Amado
turned to Norberto.

"Ella es cojonuda."

"Como tú."

Amado smiled at the compliment. He was proud of his reputation, he had *cojones*, and everyone knew it. No matter what
anyone said, *cojones* counted.

13

DON RETURNED TO Parker Center. He was beat. He had a headache. The drive back from Hollywood hadn't helped. He felt frayed, like everything he'd been working for was starting to unravel because some loser broke up with his girlfriend. He realized he should've stopped at a Starbucks and gotten a latte or something.

Flores was at his desk reading the paper when Don sat down next to him.

"Didn't you already read that?"

Flores looked up.

"Yeah."

"So why're you reading it again."

"I'm bored."

Don rifled through his messages.

"The evidence ever show up anywhere?"

"The arm?"

"Yeah, the arm."

"Nope."

Don slammed some paper into his trash can in frustration.

"Where the fuck is it?"

"Wait a day, you'll be able to smell it."

Don wrinkled his nose. He did not like the smell of dead things. That was one of the reasons he'd moved from Homicide to Criminal Intelligence. Much better to sit in a van pulling surveillance for twenty-four mind-numbing hours than to pop the trunk on a Ford Taurus at LAX that's got a month-old corpse. Even though the delay was driving him crazy, Don was glad that they'd sent the arm to the lab for treatment.

"They treated it. It won't smell."

Flores put down his paper.

"Yeah, right."

"Well, it's not supposed to smell as bad."

"Dead things smell."

Flores went back to reading his paper. Don headed for the coffeemaker. He needed some caffeine. It might help him focus. He knew that when he got frustrated his brain had a tendency to become fragmented, to drift off down meaningless tributaries, winding around until it finally came to a complete and utter dead end. Don needed to get back to basics. Back to the who, what, why, when, where, and how of criminal investigation.

He poured a cup of the thick institutional brew, stirred in a packet of chemical sweetener and a blop of Irish crème-flavored nondairy additive, and headed back to his desk. Don had always considered himself a good judge of character. His instincts were sharp. First things first. Find Bob. Don sipped his coffee and thought about it. If he were Bob and he'd just broken up with his girlfriend, what would he do? Don knew instantly what he'd do. He'd go crawling back to Maura. He turned to Flores.

"I'm going to be putting in some overtime tonight."

Flores didn't even bother to look up from the paper. He was asleep.

Esteban was amazed. Despite the fact that one of the arms was gray and getting a little shriveled, they were almost identical.

"You, my friend, are a true artist."

The biker smiled.

"Give it some time to set and it'll look even better."

Esteban grunted.

"It's good enough right now."

The biker stood up and wiped the ink off his fingers.

"I know I shouldn't ask, but I have to admit I'm curious what you're going to do with these two arms."

Esteban smiled. This was the part he liked, the gossip that would circulate around the criminal underworld of Los Angeles for the next few weeks. No one would know exactly what he was up to, they would just know that he was carrying around a severed arm. This would enhance his reputation. Make people wonder. Instill a little fear. It was good for business.

"It's a practical joke."

"A joke?"

"On the police."

The biker grinned.

"Those are the best kind."

Norberto was shaken. He'd been so stoned that he'd forgotten to turn off Esteban's psycho antitheft device. He was just lowering himself into the driver's seat when Esteban shouted at him. Another second and he'd have gotten fifteen inches of cold metal fleshette rammed up his ass. But Esteban shouted, causing him to launch himself out of the car in the nick of time. He sprawled on the street, his heart pounding so fast he thought it might come popping right out of his chest.

It had been a *milagro*. Some saint was looking down on him and decided to spare him. Maybe this was a lesson. Maybe an omen. Norberto didn't know for sure, but he knew it was something. Someone was trying to send him a message.

Even as his mind filled with the Holy Spirit and his adrenal glands pulsated furiously, Norberto felt so relaxed, and so high, that all he could do was lie on the street laughing uncontrollably. He was sure he'd shit himself. And that only made him laugh harder.

Amado extended his hand.

"Come on, *pendejo,* get up."

Norberto couldn't. He was paralyzed with laughter. Tears rolled down his cheeks.

"I shit myself, *cabrón.*"

"You still have to get up, *vato.*"

Norberto saw Esteban out of the corner of his eye. Esteban's face was screwed up and cold. Killer cold. It scared Norberto straight enough to take Amado's hand and stand up.

"Sorry. Sorry, Esteban."

Esteban took the keys from Norberto.

"Vamos."

Norberto wiped the tears from his eyes and went around to the passenger side. His face flushed with embarrassment, just like when he went to school and the teachers made fun of him for doing something stupid. Norberto hated that feeling. He got in the car and buckled his seat belt.

Bob was sitting in back with Martin. The fat guy was crushed between the two gringos, his head flopped over onto Bob's shoulder, a thin line of spittle running the length of his torso. Bob pushed the fat guy over toward Martin. Martin pushed him back.

"What the fuck're you doin' man?"

"My tattoo's getting jammed against the door."

"Well, you should've thought of that."

"I thought we were going to put him back in the trunk."

Norberto loved to hear the gringos bicker. That whiny nasal edge coming into their voices. There was never any threat of violence. No one would throw a punch or pull a knife. Gringos were too polite. They'll just argue like old women for the rest of the ride home.

Norberto wiggled his butt against the seat trying to feel if he had actually shit himself. He didn't detect anything sticky or slimy so . . . *no problema,* man. He could sit back, relax, let Esteban drive, and see if he could locate the buzz he'd had before.

Then Esteban turned to him, and said, "We need a chain saw."

And that killed what was left of his buzz.

Maura watched as her last client of the day, a thin wisp of a man with a giant penis, slowly reached orgasm. What a strange day she'd had.

Even though her thoughts were elsewhere she spoke soothingly to the man in the chair as he stroked his cock furiously.

"Relax. Breathe into the sensation. Let it ascend slowly up your spine until it reaches your cerebral cortex."

A surprisingly small drop of spunk leaped out of him and landed on his arm. Maura handed him a box of tissues.

"Let the energy of the orgasm flow through your entire body, refreshing, replenishing, and reenergizing you."

It suddenly flashed in her mind that maybe that's what Bob's problem was. He'd repressed his wild side for so long that now he was on some kind of rampage. Bob was in trouble. He would probably lose his job. The police were looking for him. He was moving out. He'd probably end up homeless. Maura hoped that didn't happen. Bob on a rampage was still Bob.

Bob sat in the back of the car pinned under the unconscious fat guy. His tattoo was being rubbed raw against the door. Bob pushed the fat guy over toward Martin, but Martin must've had some kind of leverage because Bob pushed as hard as he could and the only thing that changed was the fat guy's breathing.

When the car made a turn to the left, Bob's arm stung under the weight of the fat guy combined with the centrifugal force of the car. Bob was worried that his tattoo might smear or become damaged. He put his foot on the door, deciding to wait until the car made a hard right and then use his leg to muscle the fat guy over on Martin.

While this reverse tug-of-war was going on, Martin sat there reading him the riot act. Telling him that he didn't know the first fucking thing about La Eme. As if Martin were Don Corleone and Bob some chump who'd just fallen off the turnip truck. The more Martin talked, the more annoyed Bob became. He realized that there is nothing worse than a know-it-all stoner telling you what your problem is.

In the front seat Bob saw that Amado and Norberto were chuckling. Laughing at the two white boys in the back. Talking about them softly in Spanish. Bob felt a pressure beginning to build in his chest. He tried to control it, but Martin was still going on and on.

Bob snapped. He shifted in his seat for a better angle and then drove his right fist into the side of Martin's head.

"Shut up."

Sucker punched, Martin's head snapped hard to one side and banged against the window frame. Then he slumped against the door. Lights out.

Bob shoved the fat guy over on top of Martin.

Then he had a thought. Dread washed over Bob. He wondered if he'd crossed the line and now they were going to kill him. But that didn't happen. Esteban turned to Bob and looked him right in the eye.

"*Gracias, Roberto.*"

Bob nodded that knowing head bob that means "It's cool" or "No problem."

Amado and Norberto giggled in the front seat like schoolgirls.

"*Qué bárbaro.*"

Amado turned to Esteban, and said, "Maybe we should change his name from Roberto to Lucho because he likes to fight."

Bob smiled. Maybe smacking Martin upside the head was a good thing. It improved his standing with the guys and, surprisingly, relaxed him. He flexed his hand, the knuckles red from impact. Bob felt good. He rolled down his window and took a breath of fresh air. He checked his tattoo to see if it was all right. It was still as beautiful as ever.

Don sat in his car across the street from Maura's apartment building just off Sunset Boulevard in the Silverlake neighborhood of LA. Don had told the captain that he needed to put in some overtime to try to track down some missing evidence, but that was only part of it. Don couldn't help himself. There was something about Maura that he found so interesting and so compelling that here he was, sitting in his car, waiting for her to come home.

He saw her drive past in an old Galaxy 500. The car looked to be in pretty good shape; she must've had it restored. A cool car for a cool woman. The more he learned about her, the more he liked her. Don watched her get out of her car and enter the building. He admired the way she walked. She had a

purpose, a sense of herself. And those tits. The way they
heaved slightly as she moved. Don tried not to think about
women in the overtly sexual way he heard in the precinct
locker room. In his mind, he was looking for someone with
more than a nice rack. Still, when a man's confronted with a
pair of breasts, well, he can't help but think in those terms. He
watched her ass as she walked into her building. Nice rack,
tight ass. She was a great-looking package.

Don knew from experience to give her a few minutes to use
the bathroom, check her messages, and relax a little. Otherwise
she'd be unsettled and try to get rid of him. Give her some time
and she might even welcome him in, pour him a glass of wine.
Don smiled at the thought of that. He looked at his watch.
Twenty minutes.

The more Maura thought about it, the angrier she got. Who
the fuck did Bob think he was? She had been the one who was
changing her life, putting the wheels in motion, building up a
head of steam. She was the one who was going to venture forth
into the big and exciting world. But no. Bob had beaten her to
the punch. He'd stolen her thunder. Cut her off from her
momentum. Let the air out of her tires. Now she was stuck
looking at all their crappy furniture in this funky old apartment. Her life with Bob hung from her neck like a giant inflatable mascot in a used-car lot. A forty-foot plastic albatross.
God, it pissed her off.

She saw his laptop sitting on the desk and impulsively slid it
into the trash can with a satisfying thunk. She looked at if for a
moment, realized the immaturity of her act, and then reached
in and put it back on the desk. It pissed her off that she was so
pissed off. Who was Bob that he could push her buttons like
that? He was just a fucking guy. A young dude. Oh, he had

some special qualities, she had to admit, but nothing earth-shattering. No, Bob was not one in a million, he was one of a million. Maura realized she was grinding her teeth.

The knock on the door came as a relief.

"I hope I'm not bothering you."

Maura recognized the detective.

"No. Please."

"Thanks."

"Have a seat."

She closed the door behind him and pointed to the couch. She saw the detective take in the room with a couple of quick sweeping glances.

"Can I get you something to drink?"

"Sure."

"I could make coffee. Or I've got some wine."

"Wine sounds great."

The detective sat on the couch as Maura hurried into the kitchen. She returned with two glasses and a bottle of pinot noir from somewhere in Oregon.

"Sorry, this is all I've got."

The detective smiled at her.

"That's a good bottle."

She was surprised.

"You like wine?"

"It's sort of a passion of mine."

Maura shrugged.

"I thought cops drank beer."

"We usually do."

She expertly uncorked the bottle and poured him a glass.

"Thanks."

She watched as he spun the wine around to aerate it and then took a small slurpy sip, allowing the wine to dance on his tongue.

"Nice."

"It's one of my favorites."

The detective inhaled deeply.

"It's a little young still. If you like this you should really try the wines from the Loire Valley."

"I love French wines."

"Then I know just the place. Care to have dinner to-night?"

This took Maura by surprise. She'd planned to go to her yoga class and try and get centered, work her anger out. But the wine was warming her up, making her feel soft and happy. Why not go out with the detective? Fall off the horse and get right back in the saddle. Besides, he hadn't cringed or mocked her or laughed nervously when she told him what she did. He was different.

"I'd love to, but . . ."

"But what?"

"I forgot your name."

"Don."

Maura sipped her wine and smiled at him.

"Don."

Martin's jaw hurt. His face burned with embarrassment. He wanted to scream. He wanted to throw something. But he couldn't. He knew enough from being around Esteban that a man just sucks it up. You get punched, it's not supposed to bother you. You just shrug, say *"No chingues,"* and move on. These stupid fucking cowboys. They were never going to move into the legit business world if they hung on to those macho attitudes. Martin wondered why Esteban didn't stick up for him. He could've killed Bob right then and there.

And Bob? What was he thinking? Martin had been instrumental in saving his life and as his reward he got sucker punched. That's not right.

The more Martin thought about it, the angrier he got. Here he was working to keep his boss out of jail and some fucking delivery boy alive, and what do they do? They laugh at him. They abuse him.

The car pulled into the driveway of the safe house. Norberto turned and saw that Martin was conscious.

"You okay?"

"Yeah."

Bob looked over at Martin.

"Sorry, man. I just lost it for a second."

Martin shot Bob his toughest glare.

"Don't let it happen again."

Bob nodded.

"Cool."

Martin saw Esteban and Amado chuckling as they climbed out of the car. Bob and Norberto dragged the fat tattooed guy in the tracksuit out of the back and carried him into the house. Martin noticed one of the neighbors, a churchgoing middle school principal who was always friendly, walking his golden retriever. Esteban saw the neighbor too.

"How are you?"

"Good."

"Beautiful day, isn't it?"

"It's a fine day."

The neighbor watched as Norberto and Bob dragged the fat guy through the front door.

"Is your friend all right?"

Esteban looked at Martin before turning back to the neighbor with a shrug.

"Tequila."

The neighbor nodded. He had heard about the powerful effects of distilled agave.

"You've got to be careful with that stuff."

Esteban couldn't have agreed more.

"To be sure."

Martin stepped forward.

"Did you like the papayas we sent?"

"Oh, yes, thank you very much. They were very good. In fact I was telling my wife that I wish we could grow papayas in our backyard."

Esteban laughed.

"Then you would put me out of business, amigo."

The neighbor chuckled.

"Oh, I doubt that."

Suddenly, the golden retriever got a scent of something and started growling and tugging at his leash. The neighbor bent down and scratched the dog's ears.

"What is it boy? What have you got?"

The dog was pulling for all he was worth. The neighbor yanked back on the leash.

"Whoa, there, Frankie."

The dog began dragging the neighbor toward the car. Esteban looked over and noticed that the top had come off the cooler in the trunk, exposing Amado's arm.

The dog barked.

"Martin. Keep the lid on the meat."

Martin slammed the lid on the cooler and quickly hustled it inside the house. The neighbor tried to calm his dog. He looked up at Esteban apologetically.

"I just fed him, but I guess he's still hungry."

"Steaks. We're barbecuing later."

Maura sat across the table and listened while Don told her how he became a detective. It was a simple, straightforward story, but she was captivated. He looked rugged and handsome in the flickering candlelight. Not a movie star, but a well-respected character actor. That's why she found him attractive, he had character. A cop who knew more about wine and food than anyone she'd ever met. A cop who seemed to understand her, who didn't judge her. She couldn't help it, she found herself attracted to him.

The waiter filled her glass with wine that seemed to glow like a big fat ruby.

"What do you think?"

"This is yummy."

"The French. I don't know how they do it."

"Have you ever been to France?"

Don shook his head.

"No. But someday I want to live there."

"Me, too."

Don leaned forward conspiratorially.

"To be honest, I'm afraid to go. I don't speak a word of French."

Maura smiled at him.

"I do."

Esteban sat on the couch with his feet on the coffee table. He was tired. Beat. He needed a nap. *Chingao.* These fucking people.

Martin came in and deposited a fresh margarita in front of him.

"*Gracias,* Martin."

Martin sat down on the chair across from him.

"I'm having second thoughts about this Bob guy."

"Roberto?"

"Yes. Roberto, Bob, whatever the fuck you want to call him."

Esteban sipped his drink. It was good. Sharp, sweet, and warm as it flowed through his body.

"What do you mean?"

"I don't know if we can trust him."

This sudden change of heart sent off alarm bells inside of Esteban. He knew that Martin was mad because he'd gotten coldcocked, but to stab Roberto in the back so soon made Esteban think that Martin was some kind of *rata. If he turns on Roberto, how long before he turns on me?*

"Why do you say that?"

Martin shrugged.

"Just a feeling I get."

"Are you afraid of him?"

Martin reacted.

"Why would you say that? I'm not afraid of him. Why would I be afraid of him?"

Esteban sipped his drink.

"Just asking."

Esteban liked putting Martin on the spot. He liked watching the smart-ass gringo squirm.

"What do you suggest?"

"Kill him."

Esteban looked flatly at Martin.

"You want me to kill him?"

"Yes."

"Why don't you kill him."

"Can I?"

"I don't know, hombre, can you?"

"Do I have your permission?"

"After he delivers the arm to the police."

Martin stood up.

"Thanks."

Esteban held up a hand to stop him.

"You have to do it. I don't want to find out you sent Norberto or anybody else. You got the *cojones*, it's okay with me. But you got to be the one to do it. *¿Entiendes?*"

Martin nodded.

"I understand."

Martin walked out of the room. Esteban smiled to himself. That fucking kid was no matador, he had trouble squashing a bug. There was no way he could bring himself to kill Roberto. Although Esteban had a feeling Roberto might be capable of killing Martin.

The hardware store was unusually busy. Or maybe that's the way it is in the Valley. Suburban people like to fix up their homes. So there they were, out in force, buying faucets and hammers, electrical doodads and lengths of plastic tubing, brushes and rollers. A couple gallons of paint were hooked up to a machine that was shaking them violently. Norberto stopped and watched. *I'd like to see what would happen if you stuck a cat in there,* he thought.

"Can I help you, sir?"

Norberto looked up and saw an eager young man wearing a bright red vest. The name Franco was embroidered on the vest. There was no way this guy was really named Franco.

"Is that your name?"

The eager young man pushed his woodshop-style glasses up on his nose and looked down at his vest.

"Oh, sorry, man. I, like, grabbed it off the hook when I came in. My name's Teddy."

"Well, Teddy, I'm looking for some kind of tool to cut up some branches."

"Tree branches? Like you're going to trim a tree?"

"Exactly."

"How thick are the branches?"

Norberto thought for a second.

"Like my arm."

Teddy reached for Norberto's arm. Norberto took an instinctive step back. Teddy stopped and pulled out a tape measure.

"I need to measure."

Norberto held out his arm. He couldn't help but flex his muscle, trying to make the arm thick like the fat guy's.

Teddy took the measurement and calculated.

"You're going to need a chain saw, man. There's, like, no other way."

Teddy pointed Norberto over to where several chain saws were displayed. Norberto studied them, trying to figure out which one would be powerful enough to do the job quickly. From the descriptions on the boxes these things could sever the leg off an elephant in a matter of seconds.

Norberto looked around for Teddy. He saw Bob bouncing on his toes, as nervous as a little kid on the first day of school. Bob kept picking up stuff, a weed whacker, a lawn sprinkler, a leaf blower, and putting them back on the shelf.

"Roberto. *Tranquilo.*"

Bob came over.

"Sorry. I'm just excited about tonight."

Norberto nodded sagely.

"Felicia."

"Yeah. I can't wait."

"Well, first we got some work to do, *vato*."

Bob looked at the chain saws. His face fell.

"Us? You and me?"

Norberto nodded.

"Nosotros."

Norberto studied Bob's face. Now was the time when most people turned and ran. But Bob didn't.

"Yeah, but we're not going to kill him, right? We're going to take him to the hospital after we get his arm, right?"

Norberto looked at Bob.

"We won't kill him, okay?"

"Promise?"

Norberto held up his hand like a Boy Scout.

"I'm not going to kill him, I promise."

Bob smiled, relieved. Then he had a thought.

"It's going to get messy. We should get some plastic ponchos and a couple of tarps."

Norberto smiled.

"Seguro, Roberto, *seguro."*

Larga was still dreaming, but his dream began to take on an unpleasant and painful buzz. It was his arm. His arm was being stung by bees, hundreds of them. Poking away with their little stingers, pumping bee venom until his arm began to swell up to Elephant Man proportions. It was horrible. Swelling until it seemed like it would explode.

Larga bolted awake. He looked at his arm and was shocked to see raw and slightly scabby tattoos. He looked around the room. He realized that he had no idea where he was or how he'd gotten there.

He looked at his arm again. He made a fist and saw the word *Hola* appear as his fingers came together. Larga was confused. Why would he write a Spanish greeting on his knuckles? He twisted his arm in the light. Aside from some minor crosses and dots, stuff that looked like gang markings, the main feature on his arm was a stunning naked woman with a man performing cunnilingus on her. How did that get there? He didn't remember going to a tattoo parlor. In fact, he didn't remember much at all.

Larga had never wanted a tattoo. He'd never even been remotely interested in tattoos. But he had to admit, aesthetically speaking, whoever had done this was a fine artist. The expressiveness of line, the play of ink in skin, it was beautiful. It changed him. *Hola.*

He stood up, wobbly at first, and walked over to a mirror hanging on the wall. He pulled up his sleeve and flexed his muscle. It hurt, the skin still tender, but it gave him an aura of toughness. A raw animal quality. He knew it was ridiculous, a tattooed cookbook author, but maybe this was a side of him that no one would know about. A hidden wild side. A leather jacket, big boots, mirrored sunglasses version of him. He could get a Harley and go out on Sundays, smoke cigars in roadhouses, show everyone his nasty tattoo.

But before he could do that, he had to figure out where he was and what was going on.

Martin sat in front of the television and lit a joint. Events, he realized, had gotten out of hand. Normally the criminal enterprise ran like a well-oiled machine. Goods and services were provided. The cash flowed. Simple. Easy. Nothing more complex than the business models he'd created as a project in his first year of graduate school.

As he held in a toke, Martin mused about how he had come up with all these labyrinthine money-laundering schemes, with layer upon layer of legitimate businesses funneling excess cash to dummy corporations in the Bahamas. He had spent weeks figuring it out, building it up until it was solid. Rock fucking solid. Of course, Esteban didn't get it. Esteban understood business at the most basic level. The Paleolithic model. The sophisticated structures that Martin concocted, with their rococo flourishes of multiple retirement accounts in four countries, were simply over Esteban's head.

Old-school criminal enterprise only worked as long as it was under the radar. Once the feds caught on to what you were doing, they'd dedicate themselves to raining shit on you. But Esteban didn't care. He would rather keep the money in a vault in the basement. Never mind that the IRS could drag him into court for tax evasion. Take away the vault of cash, the safe house, the other house, the car, the satellite phone, everything. Clean him out like a fucking rainbow trout. Leave him on the street with twelve dollars and an old pair of shoes.

Then Esteban would wish he'd listened. Then he'd want those legit businesses for the tax shelters they provided. Keep his ass out of jail. Even if he went to jail he'd still have beaucoup bucks waiting for him when he got out. He wouldn't end up some haggard old busboy clearing tables at El Chavo.

Martin stubbed the roach out on the side of the coffee table and kicked back. He thought about his parents. They never listened to him. They had a plan for him. They pulled the strings. He'd never realized before just how fucking controlling they'd been. They told him what schools to go to, what friends to have. If they didn't like his girlfriend, he'd get a new one. They wanted him to get an MBA, he got one. But did they ever once listen to what *he* wanted? Did Esteban? Did anyone listen to him?

Martin chuckled to himself. He had done all right so far. He lived his life so that he didn't have to do what he didn't want to do. He didn't want to wear a suit. He didn't want to work in some corporate tower. He didn't want to help anyone get rich except himself. It was pretty cushy, he had to admit.

Martin's brain traipsed through the wonderland of his life, until it returned to the current mess. Events had gotten out of hand. Things were out of control. Amado had freelanced and created a problem. The arm was a problem. The police were a problem. Bob was a problem. The fat guy they'd kidnapped and tattooed was a problem. There were lots of fucking problems. Problems that threatened to take down Martin's cushy life. Things had to be taken care of. Decisions had to be made.

Maybe Esteban was right. The quickest way from point A to point B is a straight line. Martin liked the logic of that. The simplest way to deal with all these problems would be to line everyone up against a wall and shoot them. Then burn the house to the ground.

Sometimes messy problems require messy solutions.

Larga tiptoed to the door of his room and slowly turned the knob. He expected it to be locked and was a little frightened when it turned all the way and opened. His heart began to beat quicker. He stood frozen, the door cracked, listening. He heard the murmur of a television and the distinct sound of a man snoring. He opened the door just enough for him to fit though, about halfway. Even with wall-to-wall carpeting, the floorboards of the house creaked and squealed as he tried to sneak down the hall. It was excruciating. As if he were accompanied by the UCLA marching band.

In the living room he saw a young white man watching television. Larga couldn't be sure if the man was awake or asleep, but the stench of marijuana was so strong Larga was certain that he was stoned. Larga decided to try the back door. He crept around toward the kitchen. The sound of snoring resonated from one of the other bedrooms in the house. Larga peeked into the bedroom and saw a large dark figure laid out on the bed.

Holding his breath, his heart ready to seize up, his bowels urging him to shit, his bladder throbbing, Larga crept into the kitchen. He blew a silent sigh of relief when he found the kitchen empty. He looked around for a phone. His plan was to make a quick call to 911 and then run out the back door and down the street as fast as he could.

Then he heard the car pull into the driveway. Cold sweat erupted from his forehead. He wanted to grab the phone, but there wasn't time. He saw a small broom closet against the far wall and quickly climbed inside.

He'd barely gotten the door closed when two men carrying a chain saw entered the kitchen. He heard the Mexican man speak to the Anglo.

"I'm going to need a beer before we do this."

"I'm going to need a couple."

He heard the fridge open and the distinct *phisst* of two twist-offs being popped.

When the two men left the kitchen, Larga made his move. He opened the broom-closet door and stepped out. He looked around and, suddenly, felt very lucky. In the middle of the kitchen table, on top of a brand-new chain-saw box, was a set of car keys.

Larga grabbed the keys and slipped out the back door.

Night had fallen and the darkness wrapped around him and

comforted him as he fumbled with the keys. He saw a
Mercedes-Benz parked in the driveway. The distinctive key
was easy to find on the chain.

He opened the door and slid in, making sure to lock it
behind him. No more surprises. Now he was in control. He figured he'd go straight to the nearest police precinct and tell
them what had happened. He realized he needed the address,
but that would be easy enough once he got going.

He knew that once he started the car, he'd have to move
quickly. They, whoever they were, were not going to be happy.
They might chase him. They might shoot at him. But they
wouldn't catch him. He was determined. He was escaping.
They didn't know who they were dealing with. You can't kidnap Max Larga.

Larga realized that he was experiencing a feeling he'd never
felt before. He felt exhilarated. Alive. Like Steve McQueen in
The Great Escape. Only Larga would be pulling away in style.
He'd always wanted a Mercedes. He wondered if they'd let
him keep the car as a trophy. A fuck-you to the bad guys who'd
kidnapped him. He looked down at his tattoo and smiled.
Today was turning out all right.

He slid the key into the ignition and realized that he'd never
even driven a Mercedes. This was going to be a treat.

You just don't fuck with Max Larga. He'd always thought
that, proving it in little ways, winning the picayune disputes
with his editors. He'd always managed to get even somehow.
They didn't think the American public was ready for porta-
bello mushrooms. What the fuck did they know? He'd write
an article detailing the texture, the taste, the sensual delights of
portabellos, and the next thing you know every supermarket in
the country had to have them. It was the same with crème
fraîche. You think it's just sour cream from France? No. It's

crème fucking fraîche, buddy. It's different. It's a whole other thing.

He'd fought these battles and won. He'd proved them wrong. He'd proved them wrong again and again. Now he was proving these guys wrong.

You just don't fuck with Max Larga.

His heart pounded in his chest, his palms were clammy, and yet he couldn't suppress a genuine smirk as he put his foot to the gas and turned the key. For a brief moment he thought the car had a dead battery. Why wasn't it turning over?

Then he felt the pain.

He tried to speak, but only heard a small gurgle. Something cold had entered his body and he could feel his warmth draining out of him.

Then he was dead.

14

MAURA DIDN'T KNOW why she was kissing the detective. Was it revenge? Proving to herself that Bob didn't matter? Maybe he never did. Or was it the two bottles of expensive wine they'd consumed with dinner? Maybe it was the dinner itself, perfect and soul-satisfying, with thick garlic-laden sauces that warmed her body like she was wrapped in a warm blanket. Maybe it was the detective. He was handsome enough. And she'd never been with a man who was, well, so straight. A man's man. A cop. Maybe it was all of the above.

They were sitting in his car in front of her apartment complex. It wasn't comfortable or uncomfortable. She liked feeling his hot wine-spiked tongue in her mouth. She felt his hand caress her lower back, slide up her rib cage, and gently brush her breasts. She reached around to pull him closer and felt a large, hard lump under his jacket.

"What's that?"

"That's my gun."

"You have a gun?"

Don nodded.

"I'm required to carry it at all times. It's part of the job."

Maura felt a strange vibration in her stomach.

"Can I see it?"

"Sure."

Don reached behind him and pulled out a snub-nosed .38

in a clip-on holster. Maura blinked. Even in the darkness of the car, the metal gleamed at her, cold and blue.

"Can I hold it?"

"Just be careful."

Don handed her the gun. She was surprised at how heavy it was. It had gravity.

"Have you ever used it?"

"You mean shot it?"

"Have you ever shot someone?"

Don nodded.

"Yeah."

"Did you kill him?"

Don nodded again.

"Reluctantly."

She felt a spasm in her thighs.

"Did he die?"

"Yeah."

"You must be a good shot."

"They train us not to miss."

She handed the gun back to him. She felt a sensation between her legs that she hadn't felt in a long time. She was wet. Soaking.

"Let's go inside."

Esteban was annoyed. His margarita buzz was gone, and all that was left was a dull pain in his head and a metallic taste in his mouth. He stood in the driveway looking at his car. It was ruined. Blood all over the driver's seat and floor. Maybe such a violent antitheft device was not such a good idea after all. Still, it was better than the fucking guy running to the cops. That was for sure.

Amado pulled up in his car and saw what had happened.

"He tried to get away?"

"*Sí.*"

"*Chingao.*"

Esteban could only nod. Of course it was fucked.

"Everything's set with Felicia. She's in a motel in Glendale."

Esteban growled.

"One mess at a time."

Esteban turned when he heard the sound of the chain saw. He looked up the driveway and saw Bob and Norberto in plastic ponchos get to work on the fat guy. Bob held the arm out, Norberto gunned the chain saw, and seconds later the arm was swinging in Bob's hands.

Amado nodded at Esteban.

"That's a good saw."

Norberto was impressed. He fired up the chain saw and it went through the fat guy's shoulder like a knife through butter. *Muy rapido.* Even the bone, the shoulder joint, didn't slow the saw down. Only the sound changed a little. It went up an octave.

A pink hamburger spray of meat and bone rose up and drifted in the air. Specks and blops of God-knows-what cartwheeled off the blade. Good thing Roberto had thought to get these ponchos, this shit would ruin his clothes.

Roberto was there to catch the arm. Since it was logical that his fingerprints would be on it.

The neighbor came out, not surprising, what with the sound of the chain saw running at night. Esteban was there to head him off.

"Sorry about the noise. We had a problem with a tree and our cable reception."

"Oh, that's all right. I was wondering if I could borrow it for a minute."

"Now?"

"It'd just take a sec."

Esteban looked up the driveway at Norberto.

"He wants to borrow the saw."

Norberto looked down at the saw. Illuminated by the garage light, the chain saw's blade looked like a fucking horror show.

"Un momento."

Norberto went over to the garden hose and washed off the chains as best he could. This, he realized, is why he hated the suburbs. You could hack some fucker to bits in the middle of Hollywood and no one would notice. They might turn their music up a little louder, but they wouldn't come over to say howdy.

Bob stood in the middle of the backyard letting the arm drain into the grass. Blood came out in a syrupy drip. Bob had dealt with dead body parts before. It had been his job at United Pathology. But most of those were cold and disinfected, processed and wrapped in plastic like American cheese. They weren't alive. This arm was different. It was still warm. It even pulsed and twitched a little when the saw went through it.

Bob was trembling. He was surprised that he hadn't freaked out. He'd wanted to. A part of his brain had urged him to run off screaming down the street. But then, that wouldn't be very smart. They'd come after him and kill him. Bob didn't want that. So here he was, trembling in the backyard, wearing a plastic poncho under a clear night sky, helping chop some dead guy's arm off.

He felt sorry for the guy. No one really wanted to kill him.

But the guy had tried to escape and, well, he shouldn't have. It was really too bad.

Bob had developed an affection for him. He didn't know why. They hadn't even spoken a word to each other, Larga being beaten, drugged, or just unconscious the whole time, but Bob had been his caretaker, his guardian, and he felt some disappointment.

Bob watched as Norberto took the chain saw over to the neighbor's house. His arm was getting tired of holding the arm out. You wouldn't think that someone's arm would weigh so much.

As the chain saw roared from next door, Esteban came over and looked at the arm.

"You okay?"

Bob nodded. Esteban patted him on the shoulder and gave him a smile.

"The first time I did something like this it made me puke."

"I'm okay."

Esteban mussed Bob's hair. It was an affectionate, paternal gesture.

"Bueno, Roberto. Qué bueno."

Martin was making a pot of coffee. He knew that they'd have a long night ahead of them. What with having to dispose of a body and a car. Of course, the car was easy. The chop shop was already sending a tow truck to pick it up. It'd be in pieces and on the way to Costa Rica by sunrise. But the body was now a big messy blob dripping forensic evidence everywhere they dragged it.

Martin considered making it a two-fer. Killing Bob and dumping his scrawny ass in with the blob. Just dig one big hole in the desert and call it a day. But he realized they needed Bob. Bob had to deliver the arm. Then he could die.

Martin carefully poured the coffee into a thermos. He turned and saw Bob and Esteban looking at the two arms side by side on the table. The arms were laid out on newspaper like two freshly caught walleyed pike. The whole scene reminded Martin of fishing trips he'd taken with his father and grandfather. Men standing around admiring their catch, the smell of fresh blood and fresh coffee hanging in the air, maybe they'd play a couple hands of pinochle before bed.

Amado entered and looked at the arms on the table. He couldn't tell which one was his. He guessed that it was the slightly grayer one. The other looked fairly fresh and still pinkish. It made him sad. He missed his arm and felt phantom pangs and sensations. As if his fingers were touching something soft, like fur, sometimes something rough, like his beard. But there weren't any fingers to touch anything. It just felt like it.

Amado looked at Esteban. Esteban gave him a nod.

"Roberto, *vamos.*"

Bob turned around.

"Felicia?"

"*Sí.* She's waiting."

Amado watched as Bob looked at Esteban for approval. Esteban nodded and Bob smiled.

"Thanks, man. I owe you."

Amado watched as Esteban mussed Bob's hair again.

"Enjoy yourself, Roberto. You have earned it."

Out of the corner of his eye, Amado caught Martin glaring at Bob. It was a look that Amado had seen before. The evil eye. *El ojo diabólico.* A look ripe with jealousy and murder. Amado had gotten that look from men who hated him because of the women he had. Men who were jealous of his power, his connections. Carlos Vila had that look and had tried to rip off Amado. That's why Carlos Vila was dead. Amado realized that he'd have to watch out for Martin. If he made a move to kill Bob, it could only cause more trouble.

Any qualms, scruples, or doubts Don may have had about getting involved with someone he was investigating were flushed from his mind the instant her hot, probing tongue had entered his mouth. He knew it wasn't smart, but it'd been a long time since he'd last gotten laid and he wasn't going to let a little thing like ethics get in his way. Besides, it's not like it's against the law.

Don reached around behind Maura's back and unfastened her bra with a deft snap of the fingers. He'd always had this talent, not that he'd had much opportunity to practice it in the last few years. His former girlfriend, a rough-and-tumble assistant district attorney, had small, squishy little breasts and never wore a bra. But somehow his fingers remembered.

As soon as Maura's tits became unmoored, she pulled her shirt off over her head and pushed Don onto his back. Don couldn't believe how hot she was. Her skin against his skin. Her body and his body creating humidity. She unbuckled his pants and tugged them off. He reached for her crotch but she caught his hand and pushed it up to her breasts. Don was happy to stroke her nipples and watch her back arch in pleasure.

For the briefest possible nanosecond Don thought he should put a condom on. He thought he should say something about the importance of safe sex. This thought crossed his mind. But Maura had taken a firm grip on his cock and was now guiding it inside her.

As Maura began to ride him in urgent animal spasms, Don felt that his entire soul, his inner being, was slowly being pulled into her by the rhythm. He saw her face contorting in pleasure, her breasts swinging to the motion yet reaching for him. His body responded. Automatic and enthusiastic. Thoughts only got in the way.

What happened next was new for both of them. It was like being in a hot, sweaty sauna when someone suddenly pours a bucket of water on the white-hot lava rocks. There was an explosion of heat, sensation, fluids. Maura spoke in half-syllables, the contractions in her body and the endorphin surge in her brain short-circuiting her speech. Don felt a sharp quiver deep in his spine. And then it snowballed, building until his entire body was ringing like a tuning fork, the energy becoming unbearably intense until it rocketed out of him in a series of eye-popping seizures. For a brief moment they were transported to a world that was unbearably delicious, sensual and tranquil, comforting and releasing.

It was moist.

Amado drove the car with one hand. Bob sat next to him. He was impressed with Amado. Amazed at how quickly he'd adapted to living life with one less arm. Could Bob have done that? Or would Bob be in some outpatient physical-therapy clinic whining about how he couldn't wipe his ass anymore? Amado didn't do that. He just got on with it.

Bob smiled to himself. He was beginning to learn the difference between boys and men. He was a boy. Amado was a man.

It didn't take long before the thought, a dark and withering fear, entered his consciousness. Bob suddenly feared that Felicia wouldn't want a boy, that she'd want a man like Amado, a man she'd been with before. Bob was suddenly filled with crippling performance anxiety.

"What's she like?"

"Felicia?"

"Yeah."

Bob watched a smile sprout across Amado's face.

"You'll see."

"What if she doesn't like me?"

Amado turned and looked at him.

"Don't be nervous."

"I can't help it."

"These things are natural, *cabrón*. Don't worry."

The more Bob tried not to worry, the more worried he became. He began to have doubts. Maybe joining up with hardened criminals, kidnapping and dismembering innocent bystanders, maybe this wasn't such a good idea. Maybe these people weren't his friends after all. He tried to push those thoughts from his mind. He was here. He was in a car. He was on his way to make love to a beautiful, sensual woman. He just needed to relax. Relax and get a hard-on. One big erection and everything would be okay.

Bob exhaled.

"Amado, what's the secret to being a great lover?"

Amado looked at Bob.

"Roberto? You don't know?"

"I don't think I'm a great lover."

Amado steered the car with his knees while he lit a cigarette.

"There is no secret, Roberto. There is only one thing that makes a great lover."

"What?"

Amado turned to Bob, a twinkle in his eye.

"Enthusiasm."

"Enthusiasm?"

"*Sí*, Roberto, enthusiasm."

Larga's bloody one-armed corpse lay rolled up in a tarp in the middle of the backyard. Martin and Norberto watched as a tow truck dragged the Mercedes down the driveway and off into the night. Martin clutched the thermos in one hand, then turned to Norberto.

"Where do you want to dump him?"

Norberto lifted a can of beer to his lips and drained it before expelling a thunderous belch.

"I like the Joshua Tree Park."

"Joshua Tree's too far. Let's just go up Angeles Crest."

"Maybe, but it's easier to dig a hole in the desert than in the mountains, man. And besides, everybody dumps their bodies in the park. The fuckin' place is getting crowded, man."

Martin groaned.

"Are you telling me you'd rather drive an extra hour because the park is too trendy?"

"*Exacto.*"

Esteban watched from the kitchen window as Norberto and Martin loaded the body into the back of a Ford Explorer. They climbed in the car and drove off. Esteban was tired. He took some ice from the freezer and began to mix himself a drink. He put the ice, five cubes, in a tumbler and then poured Don Julio Silver in about halfway. Cointreau, which was much better than Grand Marnier or triple sec because it wasn't too sweet and tasted more like oranges, filled the glass up to the three-quarter mark. One whole lime, quartered and squeezed, filled up the rest.

Esteban stuck his finger in the drink and stirred. As he stirred, his mind sifted through a sequence of possible scenarios. Martin had asked permission to kill Bob. Esteban didn't know why. The fact that Martin had suddenly become homicidal, something very out of character, made Esteban suspicious. If he could flip so quickly one way, he could flop back the other. A couple of flip-flops and Martin would be testifying against him in court.

Esteban tasted his margarita. It was good, but not as good as the ones Martin made. *Qué lástima.* Esteban would miss those drinks.

Felicia sat on the bed in the Travelodge Motel watching TV. She was dressed trashy-sexy in a diaphanous red fuck gown she'd picked up at Victoria's Secret in the Galleria. She'd gotten some lipstick to match at Nordstrom's and had carefully painted her lips a labial red. She thought about getting some stiletto-heeled slippers, but decided that was just going too far. Besides, she looked hot in the gown, her breasts clearly visible through the fabric, the cut making her ass look larger than it really was. These were both good things.

A lukewarm bottle of Modelo Especial sat on the nightstand. She didn't want to drink too much, but she'd gotten bored waiting and cracked open a beer. Her mind drifted from the sitcom on TV to her situation in the motel. She didn't like where she was. Didn't like being put in this position. She wasn't a whore. But she owed Esteban a favor and he'd called on her to repay it. It wasn't something she'd normally do, but she knew she had to do it.

It was complicated.

When Amado told her about the gringo and how he'd fallen in love with a tattoo, well, she was intrigued. Besides, she hardly ever went out with gringos and, after being reassured that he wasn't a dwarf or a freak, just a guy who liked computers, she'd agreed. She was curious. It was hard to meet people in LA.

Besides, Felicia enjoyed sex. She enjoyed it a lot. It was her favorite pastime. Better than going to the movies, more relaxing than going to the beach, more fun than dancing. In fact, she'd rather be fucking than doing almost anything.

It's not like she was some kind of sex addict like the kind she'd seen on the TV talk shows. She didn't need to have sex constantly. She just liked to. She was promiscuous. Deal with it.

Felicia heard a soft knocking. She stood up, twisted her nipples so they'd jump out a little, and answered the door.

Amado came in first and gave her a quick peck on the cheek. Then he stepped back and looked her up and down.

"Caramelo mio."

"You like?"

"Muy caliente."

"Gracias."

Felicia noticed that there was something different about Amado.

"Amado, you look great."

Amado grinned.

"I do?"

"Did you get a haircut?"

"No."

"Lose some weight?"

Amado turned sideways so she could see that he was missing an arm.

"Chingao! What happened?"

Amado shrugged.

"Accidente."

"You okay?"

"Sí, todo bien."

Felicia didn't know what else to say. Amado seemed himself, even if part of him was now missing.

"You want to meet Roberto?"

"Claro que si."

Amado went out the door and came back with a nervous young gringo.

"Felicia, meet Roberto."

Felicia smiled.

"Hola, Roberto."

"Ili."

Felicia couldn't help herself, when she saw the trembling anglo in front of her, she giggled.

"Relax, Roberto. We're going to have fun."

Bob nodded.

"Okay."

Amado patted Bob on the shoulder.

"See you in the morning."

Amado winked at Felicia and then was gone. Felicia locked the door behind him and then turned toward Bob.

"You like?"

She watched as Bob looked at her, his eyes locking on her with the same kind of fervor she'd seen in Salvadoreños when they saw the Virgin of Guadalupe. She moved for him, walking back and forth, letting him have a good look. Packing every step with an animal sensuality, she twirled in front of him. Teasing him. Allowing her body's movements to arouse them both. Her breasts swinging freely behind the red veil. Her hips, her ass, her pussy open for him to see. She felt her body, supple and strong, yet heavy like ripe fruit. Her skin starting to heat up, her juices beginning to flow. She was ready to be picked.

She watched him watching her. His lips trembling, his knuckles white as he clutched his hands together.

And then something happened. She saw a look in the young gringo's eyes that she had never seen before.

Bob fell to his knees and began weeping. Felicia stopped. She was concerned, but kept her distance.

"Roberto, is something wrong?"

"No. Everything's perfect. Just perfect."

Tears streamed down his cheeks as he just knelt there, looking at her with that look on his face. He was grateful. He was in rapture.

She sensed a surrender in him. To what, she didn't know, but she could tell that he wasn't dangerous. He wouldn't hurt her or get weird. She went over to him and stroked his hair. She spoke to him tenderly.

"Why are you crying?"

Bob choked back his tears and raised his head to look at her.

"Because you are real."

A surge of emotion rolled through her body, taking her by surprise. She knelt down next to Bob and wrapped her arms around him. Bob responded, holding her tightly. Felicia could feel his hot, sweet breath against her neck. They stayed that way for a long time.

Norberto drove. They hadn't even gotten off the freeway when Martin started in on his plan. He laid it out in casual, almost joking terms. Norberto listened intently, following Martin's logic, step by step.

The plan was simple. Kill Roberto because he was a liability, an amateur who'd easily crack under interrogation. Give Amado's arm to the police. Let them arrest Amado for murder and then indict Esteban for racketeering. With those two in jail, Martin and Norberto could move in on Esteban's business, take them over like they were doing him a favor, and make millions.

Norberto recognized that the plan was a good one. Martin was a smart guy. He'd figured it all out. Letting the cops come in and do the dirty work was a nice touch. It kept Norberto's hands clean. Made him a victim of Esteban and Amado's stupidity. For once he would be the smart one. Norberto liked that. He liked that a lot.

He didn't, however, like the idea of killing Roberto. He enjoyed having him around. But he wasn't the kind of man who'd let a thing like affection stand in the way of millions of dollars. He'd gutted people for a lot less.

The only thing that gave him pause was the simple fact that he'd never trusted Martin. Never liked him. Martin had that superior anglo attitude. The same attitude that the ESL teacher had when Norberto beat the living shit out of him. But maybe all anglos had this problem. Maybe they all needed to be taught a lesson. Would the other factions of La Eme let a gringo run the crew? *No way, José.* What would they think of Norberto taking orders from a gringo? Norberto realized the only way to make this work was to follow Martin's plan to the letter and then kill him. Besides, if Martin made him kill Roberto, it would make him feel better to return the favor.

Maura woke up. Her body was relaxed. Loose and filled with heat like she'd just spent the last two hours going through an intense set of asanas in her yoga class. The detective's body was tangled up with hers. She could feel his warmth, the moisture trapped between them where they touched. She could smell the wine on his breath. She stretched and slipped her body out of the knot they'd made.

She thought about what they'd done. She'd never had sex like that. But she realized that it wasn't like Don had done anything to her. It wasn't his skill or expertise. It was her mood, her energy. She had fully committed to the act. She climbed out of bed and walked toward the bathroom. She saw his pants puddled on the floor where she'd thrown them. She reached down and felt around for the heavy metal.

Maura shot a furtive glance over at the detective. He was sound asleep. A big man-lump on the bed. She gently pulled the gun out of its holster and held it in her hands. She'd always been afraid of guns. She believed that they should be banned. They were dangerous. They killed people. From a politically correct point of view she shouldn't even be with a man who had a gun. And she definitely shouldn't be standing naked in the middle of her bedroom holding his gun.

But she couldn't help herself. She felt something inside her. A compulsion. An urgency. She held the gun in one hand and touched herself with the other. Breathless, excited, and honestly a little worried about herself, she came in less than a minute.

No matter how deep you dug, the fucking holes were never big enough. That's the way it seemed to Norberto. He'd buried all shapes and sizes of people out here in the desert and it was never easy. Norberto couldn't help but chuckle to himself. It always seemed to him that he was digging in the exact same spot where he buried the last guy, yet he never unearthed an old grave while digging a new one. Freaky.

Norberto wiped the sweat out of his eyes and looked around for Martin. Their work was lit by one pathetic beam from a flashlight wedged between a couple of rocks. Luckily the stars were out, so they could see what they were doing

without attracting attention. Like there was anyone around to
see them.

Norberto heard the crunch of shoes on dirt and turned to
see Martin coming back from the car with a couple bottles of
water.

"You gonna help me, man, or what?"

"I was thirsty."

Martin handed Norberto a bottle. Norberto drained it in a
few greedy gulps while Martin picked up the flashlight and
examined the hole.

"It looks big enough."

"No way, man."

"Let's dump him in and see."

Norberto looked at Martin. Martin shone the light in his
face.

"Get that outta my face, *maricón*."

"Sorry."

Norberto couldn't hide his annoyance.

"Once we dump him in, it's, like, impossible to get him out,
man. So we got to make sure it's big."

"It looks big."

"What if it isn't?"

"I told you we should've dumped him in the forest."

"I told you, they find 'em in the forest."

"They can't find all of them."

"I don't care about all of them. I care about this one and we
don't want them finding this one."

Norberto was getting pissed. There's a right way to do
things and a wrong way to do things. Why be half-assed about
hiding evidence? This was a time to do things the right way.

He watched as Martin fired up a joint.

"What are you doing, man?"

"You want some?"

"I want some help diggin' this fucking hole."

"I'm just taking a break."

Norberto glared at Martin. Then he realized that Martin couldn't see his glare in the dark. Couldn't see shit. Norberto watched as Martin's silhouette blew a thick plume of smoke into the air. He knew Martin would be worthless now.

"Fuck it."

Norberto went back to digging.

Felicia woke up and crawled out of bed. She went into the bathroom and flicked on the light. She sat on the toilet and thought about Roberto. Never in her life had she felt such devotion. Where did it come from? Roberto had fallen in love with a tattoo that looked like her. Actually it looked like lots of women she knew, but for some reason Roberto thought it was her. Was he crazy? No. She didn't think he was crazy. Not in a clinical way. If he was crazy what did that say about her? She had felt a connection with him from the moment he entered the motel room.

Something was happening. She looked in the mirror and was surprised to see that she was smiling. She couldn't help herself.

15

AMADO DROVE. BOB sat next to him with a moony grin on his face. Amado recognized the look as his own after he'd spent a night with a woman. Feeling hollowed out and reborn, spent and revitalized, all at the same time. You get kind of sex-goofy.

"You had a good night, Roberto?"

Bob grinned and nodded.

"Thanks, man. Thanks a lot."

Amado laughed.

"You want to get a tattoo?"

"No, man. I want to get a ring. I want to marry her."

Amado shook his head. Gringos were locos. Why were they always getting married?

"*Carajo,* Roberto. What did she do to you?"

Bob started to answer, but then just grinned and shook his head. Amado laughed again.

"You're not going to tell me? It's some big secret?"

"No, Amado. No secret. I want to keep it to myself."

Amado nodded. He respected that. He himself didn't like to recount his exploits to his friends. He would show them a tattoo. But he liked to savor the memories of his sexual encounters in privacy. Just like Bob. Amado couldn't quite wrap his mind around the realization that he and Bob were similar in some way. Not that they looked alike—they could not be more different—or that they came from the same back-

ground. There, too, they couldn't be further apart. But there
was something about Bob, a surprising soulfulness, that
Amado connected to and admired.

Amado decided to change the subject.

"Are you ready for today, Roberto?"

Bob looked over at him.

"You did your part. I'll do mine."

"All you gotta do is tell the truth."

Bob nodded and ran through the alibi.

"I broke up with my girlfriend. I was very upset. I drove
around for hours. I went to a bar. I met someone. We spent the
night at the Travelodge in Glendale."

"Exacto."

"And do you know what the good thing is about that?"

"What?"

"It's all true."

"Exacto, Roberto. You should never lie."

"I could pass a polygraph test."

"Exactamente."

Bob looked out the window at the passing strip malls and
car dealerships, the landscape of the Valley.

"Can we stop at a Starbucks? I could really use a latte."

Felicia sat on the bed in the motel room drinking coffee and
watching TV. She was wrapped in several clean white towels,
her body slathered with free moisturizer. Her hair perfumed
and soft from the free shampoo and conditioner. She stretched
and lounged and felt very, very good. She didn't have to check
out until noon so she lay back and enjoyed the comfort and
tranquility of the king-size bed, the cool hum of the air conditioner, the safety of a sanitized toilet. Now, this was living.

She thought about Roberto. She hadn't noticed his tattoo,

the one with her name on it, until they'd been in the shower that morning. Felicia felt so honored that she'd given him a blow job right then and there. Her knees on the wet tile with the nonslip strips, hot water streaming over them. His face obscured by clouds of steam. His moans echoing off the walls. She liked that. She was doing something dirty, but she felt really clean.

As she watched the *noticias* on Channel 34, she began to feel different. Her instinct was to resist this feeling. It was a wonderful feeling, but at the same time it was threatening. She valued her independence. It was her *vida,* and if she gave this feeling a chance it would take over. So she tried to push this feeling as far away as possible. She filed her nails, then applied a new layer of color.

This worked for a little while, and then an image of Roberto, kissing her tenderly on the ankle, would pop into her mind. She found herself thinking about him. Remembering what his skin felt like, how his mouth tasted. He was a good kisser and had a nice big cock. But what stuck with her was the way he had looked at her. His eyes shone with a passion, a force, like one of those pictures of Jesus. His eyes filled with devotion. But his love and devotion wasn't for all the sinners of the world, Roberto's love was for her.

She had never felt love like that before. Not once. Sure, many men had said that they loved her, but once they'd fucked her they didn't seem to love her as much as they claimed. She was used to it. She had steeled her heart against it. When they said they loved her, she didn't believe them, and, even better, she didn't care. But he hadn't said anything. He didn't have to.

The more she thought about Roberto, the stronger the feeling became. It finally became so powerful and insistent that she couldn't push it away any longer. She succumbed. She let the feeling wash over her in a delicious rush. It made her nervous.

It scared her. Because this feeling had a life, an energy, and a power. It could hurt her. It could cut deep into her heart. It could change her for the better or it could fuck her over. But she couldn't resist. It felt too good. She was *enamorada*.

.

Don sat at the kitchen table, his fingers tracing the funky yellow Formica boomerangs as he sipped a cup of coffee. Maura was wearing a fuzzy bathrobe and spreading butter on some toast. She waved a piece of toast at him.

"Sure you're not hungry?"

Don shook his head.

"I've got to get going."

Maura took her toast and sat at the table. There was an awkward pause, a beat of indecision and dread.

"Am I going to see you again?"

Don sighed. He had been afraid to ask this question in case he got the answer he didn't want to hear. But she just flat-out asked. She wasn't afraid. This, Don realized, was one of the things that made her so attractive. She didn't play games. If she wanted something, she asked for it. It was refreshing.

"I hope so."

Maura smiled. Now it was Don's turn.

"I'd like to see you tonight. If you're not too busy."

"Can I cook for you?"

Don reached out across the table and gently took her hand.

"Whatever you want to do."

Maura smiled.

"Then I'll cook."

Don finished his coffee and stood up to go.

"I hate to bring up work, but if you hear from your exboyfriend would you call me?"

"Can I call you just to talk?"

Don smiled.

"Absolutely."

Don patted himself, feeling for his gun, his badge, the tools of his trade. Reassured that they were all in place, he walked over and gave her a kiss. Maura held on to him, stroking his back, giving his ass a playful squeeze, her hand stopping and holding on his gun for a moment, and then she broke from the embrace.

"I'll see you tonight."

Norberto and Martin sat in a booth at Denny's. Norberto was famished, exhausted, *agotado,* having just spent the night working like a fucking *campesino.* He wasn't in the mood to talk, especially not in English. When he was tired, or really drunk, or sick, his ability to *habla Inglés* left him. It just vanished. He knew Martin was one of those gringos who thought they spoke Spanish. They would speak loudly and confidently with all the vocabulary and syntax of a first-grader. Norberto hadn't gone to college, he couldn't claim to be an expert or anything, but listening to gringos fracture grammar and mix tenses was just annoying.

So Norberto didn't say anything. He dipped his paper napkin in his water glass and tried to wipe some of the grit off his face. He looked across the table at Martin, who was staring out the window with a stony grin plastered on his face. All Norberto could think of was what a *maricón* Martin was. At one point he had wanted to shoot Martin and dump him in the hole with the dead guy. But, typical, the hole was barely big enough for the dead guy by himself, and there was no fucking way he was going to dig it bigger.

Norberto realized that Martin might be smart but he was also lazy. *Flojo.* Lazy was dangerous. Lazy made mistakes. He would have to keep his eye on Martin. Make sure he didn't get sloppy and leave loose ends. Loose ends were always followed if not by *las placas* then by Esteban. He didn't know how they did it, but somehow loose ends always unraveled whatever scam you were pulling. That's why Carlos Vila was dead.

Norberto drank his coffee, then his water. He was dehydrated, grumpy, and really hungry.

Martin was hungry too. His appetite fueled more by the effects of copious quantities of marijuana than by physical effort. Still, he'd helped chuck the corpse into the hole. He'd helped cover it up. He wasn't a laborer. He wasn't a—Martin had to catch himself when he thought of this one—Mexican. He had a graduate degree. He worked with his mind, not with his back. Sorry, but that's just the way it was.

Despite what Norberto thought, and Martin could tell he was annoyed, Martin was thinking. Planning. Being strategic. Maybe he didn't help dig the hole, but he put his mind to work, doing his best to keep it from looking like a fresh grave in the middle of the desert. He'd had the great idea of building a campfire on top of the grave to make it look like it was some kind of campsite.

Norberto hadn't appreciated the genius of that. He'd had to argue with Norberto about that for an hour while the sun slowly crept over the horizon. Martin hadn't realized how stupid Norberto was until now. Maybe it'd been a mistake to bring him in on the plan. There were advantages, of course, to having Norberto be so dumb. It would keep him from plotting against him. Norberto would need Martin, not just to pull this off but to help run the business after Esteban and Amado were put away. Norberto's stupidity gave Martin a kind of job security.

Martin sipped his chocolate malt, washing the dirt out of

his throat with its cold icy granules, and watched as Norberto demolished a Grand Slam breakfast. A grand slam. Clear the bases. Bring it all home. That's what Martin was going to do, and when he was done, then Norberto would appreciate his genius. It was like a game of chess. Anyone could move the pieces, that was just logistics, lifting, grunt work. It was strategy that won the game.

Don drove home to quickly shave and change his clothes. Today was going to be a good one. Whatever forces that propelled the universe—be they energies of coincidence or karma—had conspired to bless him. Not only did he have a break in his case but his search for Bob had led him to this incredible woman. Don had gotten lucky.

Esteban carried his copy of *La Opinion* into the kitchen. He opened a cupboard and took out a small glass. He took a jug of freshly squeezed orange juice out of the refrigerator, pausing for just a beat when he saw the two severed arms together on a cookie sheet on the bottom shelf. Esteban would be glad to get rid of those things. He never liked to have anything remotely resembling evidence around for long. He'd never store a shipment of drugs at his own home, always using warehouses, storage units, or, in an emergency, this safe house.

He sat at the kitchen table, sipped his orange juice, and read the paper. This new *presidente* in Mexico could be trouble. He was not part of the old guard that had kept Mexico in a kind of feudal society for centuries, with rich landowners, industrialists, and gangsters as kings and shoguns. He wasn't a socialist, thank God, but he was a reformer. A reformer who made a lot of speeches about improving the lives of the Mexi-

can working class. Part of that would be eliminating the drug
trade and cracking down on corruption. Esteban chuckled. As
if that would improve their lives.

Esteban relied on a time-honored tradition of bribes and
corruption, giving officials their "little bites," to move product
through the country and over the border. How else could
your average civil servant afford a satellite dish, a DVD player,
or a Jeep Cherokee? But if this new guy was going to start
cracking down, it could cause problems. Not that it would ever
stop the flow of product into the States, there was just too
much money to be made, but it could cause headaches, disrup-
tions. *Carajo,* this new *presidente* was going to be a fucking
pain in the ass.

Esteban looked up as he heard Bob and Amado pull into
the driveway. He watched as the two men climbed out of the
car, laughing and joking like they were old friends. As much as
he liked Bob, Esteban was still a little unsure. It was a risk he
wouldn't normally take, but then this was not a normal situation. Still, there was something about him that seemed trust-
worthy. He was sincere. Not jaded like Martin and other
Anglos that Esteban knew. Anglos always seemed to think that
they were entitled to everything. As if working was somehow
beneath them. It was a kind of culturally inbred arrogance. It
was not an attractive quality to someone who'd worked his way
up from the strawberry fields.

Bob and Amado strolled into the kitchen. Bob was carrying
a couple of cups from Starbucks. He handed one to Esteban.

"I didn't know what you liked so I got you a cappuccino."

Esteban took the coffee from Bob, touched by the gesture.

"*Gracias,* Roberto. I like cappuccino."

Esteban and Bob locked eyes for a moment. Esteban was
surprised and, he had to admit, pleased when Bob didn't look
away. Bob wasn't threatened by him.

"Roberto, did Felicia help you find your *huevos?*"

"What?"

"Your balls."

Bob blushed, a sly grin on his face. Amado smacked him on the back.

"He's ready."

Esteban sipped his cappuccino.

"You ready, Roberto?"

"Yeah. I guess."

Esteban got serious.

"I'll tell you something about the police. *Las placas* can tell when you're lying. They got some kind of sense about it. So the secret is simple. Do not lie. Tell them the truth. Maybe not the whole truth. But you tell them enough of the truth and they'll believe you."

"Because I'm telling the truth."

"*Exacto.* And remember, you're not excited. You're upset. This thing with your girlfriend was very upsetting."

"I should be depressed?"

Amado joined in.

"Yes, a little sad, I think."

"But I'd be lying. I'm not sad."

Amado and Esteban exchanged looks.

"So you were celebrating after your breakup?"

Bob smiled at the men.

"I was celebrating."

"*Bueno.* Whatever is the most honest."

Bob finished his coffee and put it down on the table.

"Where's the arm?"

Esteban pointed.

"In the fridge."

It felt strange to be back behind the wheel of the delivery car. Bob clicked on the radio, which was still tuned to the same station he'd been listening to before his life had changed so radically. Bob knew that he'd have to work at the lab for a week or two, then give notice. He had to be smart about it, he couldn't just walk in and quit. That might give away the fact that he'd been up to something. Unless he got fired. That would work.

As he drove toward Parker Center he thought about Felicia. He compared her to Maura. He couldn't help himself. He started to chastise himself for all the time he'd wasted being with her when he could've been with Felicia. But then he realized that he'd been happy with Maura. They'd had fun together. They'd loved each other. Maybe it wasn't the intense love he felt for Felicia, but it wasn't a waste. Maybe if he hadn't been with Maura he wouldn't have been ready for a woman like Felicia. Bob began to wonder if the world really was random like he'd always thought. Maybe there was a kind of plan to everything after all. It sure seemed like it.

Bob was beginning to believe in something. The higher power that the drunks and dope fiends talk about. The force, like in *Star Wars.* The laws of karma. The will of Allah. Jah love. It was real. He could feel it.

Don was pissed. He had left specific instructions with the evidence room clerk that the minute, no, the second that the arm was delivered they were to call him and detain the delivery guy. But they hadn't. In fact, they hadn't even called him and told him the arm had been delivered. He'd had to call down to ask.

Don didn't wait for the elevator. He took the stairs, running down two at a time. He'd had a hunch that Bob was a normal, honest guy. That he'd been distraught over being dumped. And who wouldn't with a woman like Maura? Still, after he got the arm sent over for fingerprints and DNA testing, he'd track Bob down and have a little chat with him. Help him get his priorities straight.

Don went into the evidence room. He tried to hide his annoyance, not that the clerk would've noticed. The clerk, a pudgy guy with extremely thick blond eyebrows, showed him the cooler. Don popped the lid and looked in. There it was. The arm last seen on the floor of Carlos Vila's garage. Now Don would find out who it belonged to. Because he still couldn't figure out why they'd leave Carlos's body but take the body of the second victim. It just didn't make sense.

This was the part of his job that he enjoyed. Taking a collection of seemingly unrelated evidence and information and slowly piecing together a picture of what had happened. It was like archeology.

The clerk looked over his shoulder.

"That's what you were waiting for?"

"Yeah."

"Do I need to keep it cold?"

"Just keep it in the cooler."

"You want me to send it to the lab?"

Don looked at the clerk.

"Yes."

The clerk was oblivious to Don's sarcastic tone.

"Okay."

"Can you put a rush on it?"

"You have to call the lab for that."

"All right. You get it over there right away and I'll call the lab."

The clerk nodded.

"I can do that."

Maura was beginning to lose her patience. It wasn't like her, but this new client just wasn't getting it. Not that he was nervous or inhibited. In fact, he couldn't wait to take off his clothes and wave his hard-on at her. But his motion, his stroke, it was spastic. Herky-jerky. She spoke to him softly, trying to get him to slow down, smooth out, enjoy the sensations. But he couldn't do it. Like he had Tourette's syndrome in his right arm.

It was the opposite of her night with Don. A night filled with smooth, gliding sensations. Their bodies linking up in the same rhythm.

Watching this guy was like chewing aluminum foil or hearing someone run their fingernails across a blackboard. It was horrible.

Maura couldn't take it anymore. She impulsively did something she'd sworn she'd never do. She stopped him and took his cock in her hand.

"Here, let me show you."

She jacked him off in a jiffy.

Amado sat on the couch watching his *telenovela*. It was a slow day on the hacienda. Fernando was up to something and Gloria was busy seducing the local padre. Amado was hoping that the priest wouldn't fall for her cheap come-on. You decide to dedicate your life to the Church, then that's what you do. It's your calling.

Amado had a calling. He had devoted his life to thieving, fucking, and drinking. He embraced the sins of the flesh. He celebrated them by turning his body into an icon of carnal acts. He'd have to be loco to go into a church and declare himself a man worthy of God's everlasting love. Just like the padre would have to be loco to suddenly fall into Gloria's arms.

He could see that the padre was tempted; who wouldn't be,

looking down into Gloria's cleavage, which was as deep and mysterious as the Marianas Trench, but Amado hoped that the padre would come to his senses, have a little integrity. The padre needed to remember why he'd chosen the path of God and resist the fleeting joys that Gloria offered. Otherwise he could never hold mass again.

Norberto and Martin entered the house. Norberto was filthy. He took his shoes off at the front door so as not to track dirt through the house.

"Hola."

Amado looked up from the TV.

"Hola, pendejo. ¿Cómo fue?"

"Bien. Todo bien."

Martin chimed in.

"Everything's cool."

"Curado, vato."

Amado could tell from their body language that everything was not cool. But he played it off. Martin shifted his weight from foot to foot.

"Is Esteban here?"

"He went home."

Martin nodded.

"Maybe I'll give him a call. Just to, you know, check in."

"You do that."

"Is your arm still here?"

"It's in the fridge."

Martin nodded.

"We should get rid of it."

"Why?"

Norberto piped up.

"It's evidence, man."

"It's my arm."

"If the cops find it . . ."

"Las placas won't find it. *¿Entiendes?"*

Amado shot them a withering glance. But Martin wouldn't let it go.

"Esteban said that we should get rid of it."

"It's not El Jefe's arm."

"What are you going to do with it?"

Amado didn't know the answer to that one.

"Keep it around."

"Until the police find it."

"It's my arm, *pendejo.*"

He watched as Martin and Norberto exchanged glances.

"I need a shower, man."

Amado didn't say anything. Gloria was stroking the padre's thigh.

"Yo necesito descansar, también."

Amado looked up at Norberto.

"Vale, cabrón."

Norberto and Martin stood there for a beat and then shuffled off. Amado rolled his eyes. They were hiding something. Either they'd botched the burial or they were planning something. Or they were stoned. With Martin you could never tell, he always seemed a little squirrelly. A *baboso* who thought he knew everything but really had a lot to learn about the way things work. Amado knew that, whatever they were trying to pull, the learning curve was going to be steep and hairy for Martin and Norberto.

He turned back to the TV just in time to see the padre fall into Gloria's arms, burying his head between her huge soft breasts and praying for God's forgiveness for what he was about to do.

Amado hated hypocrites.

Morris was still playing Tetris when Bob walked in.

"How high are you?"

Morris stopped playing.

"How high are you, man? Where the fuck have you been?"

"Out."

"Duh."

"Anybody notice I was gone?"

"Just the boss, the police, everyone at UCLA."

"The boss mad?"

Morris shook his head.

"He's worried, dude. We were all worried."

"About me?"

"Yeah."

Bob smiled.

"I didn't know you cared."

"I'm not gay. I didn't care, like, that much."

Bob laughed.

"I better go tell the boss."

"You better call the cops, too."

"Yeah. Yeah."

Bob turned to go.

"You must've really loved her, man."

Bob stopped.

"Who?"

"Your girlfriend."

Bob reminded himself to tell the truth.

"Yeah, I did."

Esteban lowered himself into his bubbling Jacuzzi. He felt the tension of the last twenty-four hours begin to melt away. Amado had made a gazpacho out of everything, but at the end of the day he was still one of the few men that Esteban could

count on. Count on and trust. He'd have a word with Amado
about whatever freelancing he was doing with Carlos Vila, but
he didn't want Amado dead. He was too valuable.

Lupe came out with a bowl of guacamole and some chips.
She was wearing a dark blue one-piece swimsuit, and Esteban
couldn't help but admire her body as she climbed into the
Jacuzzi and put the dip down in front of him.

"Gracias."

"De nada."

She smiled at him. She had a beautiful smile.

Esteban wondered if it wasn't time for him to settle down.
Maybe get married. He'd always figured he'd end up married
to an American, that'd make it easy to get a green card. But
American women were so thin, skinny and preoccupied with
shopping and their appearance. Esteban found them repulsive.
They chatted endlessly about how they looked, how other
women looked, and how they or their friends would look after
surgical enhancements were completed. They lacked soul.

Esteban took a chip and dipped it into the guacamole. The
cool thick avocado coated his tongue. It was somehow spicy,
biting, and soothing all at the same time. It tasted of earth and
sun, cilantro and jalapeño, onion and lime. It reminded him of
Mexico. The good parts he'd left behind. Guacamole, he realized, was very soulful.

Lupe smiled at him as he ate another mouthful.

"Te gusta?"

"Sí. Muy rico."

He watched as she slowly submerged herself in the water.
He admired her. She didn't need a bikini or fake tits. She was
who she was and she was beautiful that way. She was honest
and earthy and soulful. Like guacamole.

———

Maura walked around to the front of the building. A sign told her that the entrance was in the rear. It seemed strange to her, there was a perfectly functional front door, but it had a metal gate across it. It was probably a security precaution, although if someone were going to rob the store they could just as easily use the back door.

She walked up and around, down the alley, to the back of the building. She pulled open the glass doors, passed a serious-looking metal detector, and took a look around. It was a little overwhelming. She'd never been in a gun store before, and the variety and sheer number of guns took her by surprise. The air was a heady mix of oil and gunpowder, metal and wood. Intoxicating.

Maura strolled slowly through the room, entranced. What was it about these things? What caused her insides to quiver when she held one? Maura didn't understand what was happening to her. All she knew was that when she held a gun in her hand it triggered something deep inside. It was a connection to a primal, sexual power. Life and death, creation and destruction. Explosion and silence. It was nothing she'd ever felt before.

She laughed at herself

A friendly employee came up to her and spoke directly to her breasts.

"Lookin' for home protection? Or somethin' to carry in your purse?"

"I don't know."

In fact, she had no idea what she was doing there.

"Lookin' for somethin' versatile?"

"Let's start with that."

The employee, a round and red-faced American with an LA Dodgers cap, sized her up.

"This your first time?"

Maura nodded.

"Don't be scared. You use these right, they'll never hurt you."

"Okay."

He walked around behind a glass display case filled with all makes and models of handguns. There were scary black Glocks, lethal-looking Walthers, efficient Smith & Wessons, a truckload of semiautomatic handguns, revolvers, and all manner of death-delivering devices. He pulled out a Beretta nine-millimeter semiautomatic. It was big, black, menacing. It meant business. The kind of gun that bad guys used in the movies.

He pulled back the top part to reveal the chamber.

"A Beretta nine-millimeter semiautomatic. Italian made. Excellent quality. Double action. Fifteen-shot magazine. Guaranteed to drop an intruder before he can get his pants down."

Maura picked up the gun. It was surprisingly heavy.

"I got it in a slightly smaller version called a Centurion. That's what some of the female police officers are using."

Maura pushed down on a lever and the pistol sprang together with a vicious snap.

"Yikes."

"Just keep your fingers clear. That sucker can pinch like the devil."

Maura didn't like the gun, it had no personality.

"I want a more old-fashioned-looking gun."

"Like a cowboy gun?"

"Like the detectives carry in the movies."

"I gotcha."

He pulled out a Colt Detective Special. A snubby little pocket revolver with a two-inch barrel. It was not inspiring. Maura held it like it was a dead fish.

"Do you have something a little . . . bigger?"

"Surely."

He pulled out a Colt Anaconda and plopped it on a felt pad. Now, this was a gun. Shiny and silver with a long nine-inch barrel and a big wooden grip.

"It's heavy. You might have trouble getting a good shot off with this one."

"It's really pretty."

He nodded.

"Yeah, it's a good-looking pistol. Effective, too. Six shot. Combat-style finger grooves. Full-length ejector-rod housing, ventilated barrel rib, because you got yourself a real long barrel there, wide-spur hammer, stainless steel."

The more he described the gun, the sexier it sounded. Maura could feel her pulse quicken, her palms getting sweaty, as she held the pistol in her hands.

"How much?"

"Six hundred bucks."

Maura was surprised. That wasn't expensive for such an incredible machine.

"I'll take it."

The helpful employee looked at her.

"Can I be honest?"

"Sure."

"You're not going to be able to shoot this too good. It's just too damn big for your pretty little hands."

Maura didn't care about shooting the gun.

"I just like the way it looks."

"There's lots of guns that'd be good for you to shoot. They're pretty too."

"I want this one."

"I just want you to be happy."

Maura smiled at him.

"I'm happy."

Bob couldn't believe it. It was just like on TV. Two detectives had picked him up at the office and driven him down to Parker Center. They hadn't said anything at all in the car. The ride was taken in complete silence. Then he was whisked up an elevator and brought here, to this small interrogation room.

Bob sat at a cruddy institutional table on a metal folding chair. Fluorescent lights hummed down from the ceiling. There wasn't a window, only some kind of see-through two-way mirror on one wall. Stale air drifted in through a vent.

The detective sat on the other side of the table drinking a cup of coffee. Bob watched the detective as he wrote down information on a notepad. He was trying to put some kind of chronology together.

"And after you confronted her at her office?"

"It wasn't a confrontation. We were just talking."

"Okay. What did you do after you talked?"

"Drove around."

"Where?"

"Hollywood. Up Laurel Canyon and down into Studio City."

"Did you stop anywhere?"

"I think I stopped at Starbucks."

"Which Starbucks would that be?"

"I don't know. There's, like, a million of them."

Although the questioning was thorough, even intense at times, Bob never felt too nervous. He didn't sweat or tremble. He did sometimes hesitate, but he wasn't cocky or cool. He had just the right level of nervousness. He wanted to appear a little nervous. After all, even a completely innocent individual gets anxious around the police.

"Was this in the Valley?"

Bob nodded.

"Yeah. I think so."

The detective made a note.

"During this time were you under the influence of alcohol or drugs?"

"I'm not a drunk driver, okay?"

The detective looked at him.

"I don't care if you were, I just want to know."

Bob sighed.

"I'd had a couple of drinks."

"What kind of drinks?"

"Tequila."

"Where did you drink the tequila?"

"In my car."

"You were driving around drinking tequila in your car."

"I was parked."

"Do you recall where you were parked?"

"Some street somewhere."

"In Studio City?"

"Burbank, I think."

"Then what did you do?"

"I fell asleep."

"In your car?"

"Yeah."

"Didn't it occur to you that you had things to deliver?"

"Well, yeah."

"So why didn't you?"

"I was upset."

"You were upset."

"Yeah, and I didn't want to work."

"You could've driven back to the lab and asked for the day off."

Bob nodded.

"I wish I'd thought of that."

The detective made more notes in his notepad. Bob gave him a very sincere look.

"I'm sorry if I messed up something. I didn't mean to."

The detective kept his expression serious.

"You've hampered a very important murder investigation."

"I'm really sorry. I didn't know."

"You knew it was something to be delivered to the police, correct?"

"Yeah."

"Why wouldn't that be important?"

Bob hung his head.

"I see your point. I'm really sorry."

"It's a little late for 'sorry,' Bob."

"Am I under arrest?"

"Not yet."

Bob wondered why the detective was working alone. Two guys had picked him up. If this was the bad cop, Bob wanted to see the good cop in action. The one who'd be sympathetic to Bob's emotional distress. Of course, if this was the good cop and the other one was going to come in and break his arm . . . it was fine just having the one detective.

"So you didn't return to the office after five or go home. You kept the car. Did you spend the night in the car?"

"No."

"Where did you go?"

"I stayed in a motel."

"Where? Do you remember?"

How could he forget.

"The Travelodge in Glendale."

The detective wrote that down and then gave Bob a very hard look.

"I'm going to check this out. Anything you want to change about your story?"

Bob looked him right in the eyes.

"No."

"You're sure?"

The detective was pressing, trying to get in Bob's face, rattle his cage. He succeeded, Bob lost his temper and began to rant.

"Hey, man, I'm sorry I didn't make the delivery on time. Okay? I'm really sorry. But I have a life too. I had problems and I had to deal with them. Okay? So before you go judging me, think about what you'd do if your girlfriend dumped you. All right?"

Don watched as a uniformed officer escorted Bob out of the interrogation room. There was something about Bob that bothered Don. He couldn't be sure if it was because Bob was Maura's ex-boyfriend. It was possible that Don's feelings for Maura were contaminating his impression of Bob. But it seemed to him that Bob's response was just a little too contrived. Don had seen it before. People who think they know how the police think they should respond. Not overly dramatic, not overly detached. It was a kind of response that people had when they were guilty and had watched too many cop shows.

Don told Bob that he was going to have to sit tight while he checked out his story. Bob had protested about being held without being under arrest; that is, until Don had started to oblige him with obstruction of justice charges.

Don didn't know why people got all pissed off about being held. If they were innocent, you'd think they'd want to be cooperative. But he knew from experience that the innocent ones always put up the biggest stink about hanging out in the precinct. And Bob had put up a big stink.

Still, it wouldn't be long, all it would take was a visit to the Travelodge in Glendale and he'd know the truth. If Bob was lying, this gave Don the license and leverage to turn up the heat, tighten the screws, and really fuck with the guy.

Martin sat in the backyard smoking a jumbo. Like a mantra, the words *No guts, no glory* kept rolling through his head. You had to break some eggs to make an omelette. You had to roll a joint before you could smoke it. No guts, no glory. One small step for man, one giant leap for mankind.

Norberto came out into the backyard. He was drinking a beer. Martin offered him the joint, but he shook his head and said, "I'm having second thoughts about the plan."

Martin blinked. This was just so fucking typical. A few wispy clouds drifted along, violently white against the intense blue sky. He turned to Norberto.

"No guts, no glory."

"What?"

"No guts, no glory."

Norberto nodded like he understood.

"Yeah, but what if it backfires? *Nos chingamos,* man."

"It won't backfire. It's airtight."

"I don't know, man. You're counting on something that could easily fuck up."

"What?"

"Las placas."

"The police?"

"Yeah, man. You're counting on the fucking jalapeños to come and arrest everybody. What if they don't?"

"They will."

Norberto shook his head.

"If they were so good, they'd have busted us by now."

Martin turned on Norberto, he couldn't hide his anger.

"They don't have anything to bust us for. And you know why? Because of me. Because I make the plans. I launder the money. I take care of the legal shit. That's why."

"Or we're just lucky."

The roach burned Martin's finger. The pain short-circuited his anger. He stood there for a beat as his synapses bounced around like Ping-Pong balls in that bouncy air-blower machine they use to pick the Lotto numbers. Finally, everything settled back into place. He stubbed the roach out on the ground and fixed his gaze on Norberto. Norberto's sudden reluctance was killing his buzz.

"You're just scared."

"Maybe, man. Maybe."

"I'll watch your back."

Norberto drained his beer.

"The people we're up against, they don't bother sneakin' up behind you, man."

Bob sat in the holding cell with a couple of other men. It was drab and smelly. His cellmates, one a ferocious-looking Vietnamese teenager, the other a burly Latino in his thirties, were stretched out on the hard benches. The Vietnamese boy looked slightly green, with a slick sheen of cold sweat covering his body, like he was going through some kind of jones for a sack of glue. The Latino just lay there like a boned chicken. They seemed resigned to whatever the Fates had in store.

Bob figured that the detective had him put in the cell to intimidate him, get him to crack, but the only threatening thing he could see was an exposed toilet that sat in the corner.

It was threatening because Bob had to piss. His bladder had swollen beyond the normal limits it might reach when stuck in traffic. It had grown from a dull reminder to a sharp, aching throb. His kidneys were even getting into the act, sending scaring bolts of pain through his lower back. But Bob couldn't bring himself to urinate. He was intimidated.

There was no sound in the cell. No talking, no radio. Bob's pee would be the only source of news and entertainment in the room. Bob knew that if he got up and just trickled, he would be sodomized by noon. But if he got up and let loose a powerful and impressive stream, they'd back off. They wouldn't fuck with him. It was performance anxiety of a whole new kind.

A single tear welled up in Bob's eye and ran down his cheek. His bladder was screaming for release. He had no idea how much longer he might be held, it could be hours, but he did know that if he didn't stand and deliver, he was going to wet himself. That wouldn't be good.

Bob stood and quietly padded over to the steel toilet. He lifted the lid and slowly unzipped. He was glad he had his back to his cell mates as his penis turtled into his pants. It just wouldn't stick its head out. Bob was reluctant to tug on his dick too much. He didn't want them to think he was jacking off. He carefully pulled his penis out and held it with his right hand.

Nothing happened. He tried to relax. He thought about Felicia, walking though a park, a trip to the beach, anything to take him away from this stinky cell, these two guys, this shiny toilet, and this unbearable pain.

He took a deep breath and let out a sigh.

And then it began. It started softly. As if his fears were now about to become reality. But the sheer volume of urine in his body kept that from happening. It slowly gained power and momentum. Bob's entire posture shifted. Another tear ran down his cheek. It was as if he had been holding his breath for a year and now he could take in some fresh air. His penis hung out bravely, looking and sounding much larger than it ever had before. Bob smiled.

He was pissing like a racehorse.

Don came back from the Travelodge in Glendale and found the envelope on his desk. Flores sat at the next desk reading the sports page.

"When did this get here?"

"While you were out."

"Why didn't you call me?"

"And spoil the surprise?"

Don ripped open the envelope and looked at the report.

"Who the hell is Max Larga?"

Flores shrugged.

"You're the detective."

Bob was showing his tattoo to the Latino man in the holding cell when Don came down for him. Bob knew his story would hold up. He had made small talk with the clerk at the Travelodge when he checked out. Now he listened as Don told him that he was being released but that the LAPD would reserve the right to press obstruction-of-justice charges at a later time if they found him uncooperative or lying or complicit. It was just so much blah, blah, blah. Bob nodded. Getting out of there was his primary concern. They were starting to serve a lunch of creamed corn and some kind of meat patty. The smell was nauseating, overpowering, like boiled dog food. Even though it brought up a slight gag reflex it was also, strangely, making his stomach growl.

As they were leaving the holding area, Don turned to him.
"Does the name Max Larga ring any bells?"

"Who?"

"Max Larga."

Bob appeared thoughtful.

"No. Sorry."

Don handed him his business card.

"If you do remember who he is, or think of anything, let me know. Okay?"

Bob took the card.

"Sure."

Martin walked into the house. Amado lay snoring on the sofa, the TV still rattling away in Spanish. Norberto had gone back to his apartment. Martin walked into the kitchen and opened the refrigerator door. Inside, wrapped in Saran Wrap, was Amado's arm. In the harsh light of the fridge it looked like a leftover sandwich or something. Martin blinked at it through his sensimilla-tinted eyeballs. He saw a jar of pickles and had to have one. He stood, with the door open, and fished an icy pickle out of the jar. The cold crunch and briny taste snapped him back to his mission. No guts, no glory.

As he chewed on the pickle and looked at the severed arm, Martin heard voices in his head: his parents urging him to finish business school and get that MBA; his friends bragging about mergers and acquisitions; even his old swim team coach in high school. They all said the same thing. Make something of yourself. Be a winner.

Martin put the pickles back, grabbed the arm, secured the plastic around it, and scurried out of the house.

16

DON WATCHED AS Bob punched the button for the elevator. He watched as Bob looked around nonchalantly, like he visited a police station every day. He watched as Bob picked at his fingernails, looked at his feet, and practically jumped out of his skin when the elevator finally arrived.

The sensation, an unpleasant gnawing feeling, started in the pit of his stomach. Don felt it build and rise up into his chest. It was his instinct telling him that something was not kosher. He smelled a rat.

Bob had been too uninterested in Larga. Studiously casual. Just like when he was waiting for the elevator. Don saw how Bob was bouncing in his shoes. Did he think he'd gotten away with something?

Don checked himself. Could it be that he was jealous of Bob? After all, Bob had been Maura's boyfriend. She had chosen to move in with him. They lived together. Something Don had not yet managed to accomplish. She must've loved Bob at some point. Don realized that he didn't know her that well. She had shared her life with Bob, a man who couldn't be more different than Don. If she'd done that, what did she see in Don? Maybe she had matured. Learned a lesson living with a slacker gadfly like Bob. Maybe now she wanted a grown-up man. Stable, honest, and hardworking. Yeah, that was it. He decided to give her the benefit of the doubt.

But Don was annoyed. His feelings for Maura had put the whammy on his instincts. He reminded himself that he'd worked too hard to let this investigation get away from him. He needed to be fully focused. He needed to scrutinize every detail. Look for inconsistencies. Make connections between disparate incidents. Piece the puzzle together.

Don's fully focused, steel-trap policeman's mind drifted for a moment. A flash of Maura's breasts, golden in candlelight and heaving in unison, shook him. He needed another doughnut.

Bob walked out of Parker Center and into the deep orange glare of a Los Angeles sunset. He felt great. Energized. On top of the world. He'd survived a police interrogation and actually pulled it off. God, was it making him horny.

He couldn't wait to tell Esteban how he'd handled the cops. Expertly, in his opinion. They didn't have a fucking clue. His story was believable, he told the truth, it hung together. In frustration, they'd tried to sweat him in a holding tank filled with hardened and dangerous criminals, but they didn't crack him. In fact, he'd earned the respect of his cellmates with his prodigious pissing ability. He was tougher than they thought, smarter than they knew. His cock stiffened slightly in his pants. A call to celebrate.

Esteban had made him memorize a special number to call when he got out. He was supposed to find a pay phone and dial the number, say his name, and then hang up and wait. Esteban said he'd return the call in less than five minutes. It was some kind of satellite deal. Untraceable. Or if it was traceable it would only lead back to some pay phone on the street somewhere and not to Bob. Bob knew he should call Esteban, but something else was on his mind. He found a pay phone and called Felicia.

The can of Comet and scrubby sponge were still in the bath-tub. So was the bloodstain. *There's no fucking way it's coming out now,* Norberto thought. But he realized he wouldn't want to take a bath in the tub if he could still see the stain, so he got to work. He ran cold water and scrubbed as hard as he could. It was like sanding porcelain, but it was working. The stain was lifting.

Norberto thought about what Martin had said. The more he thought about it, the more ridiculous it sounded. Did he really believe that the other crews in *La Eme* would just sit around with their thumbs up their asses while he and Martin took over Esteban's powerful and lucrative enterprise? Why wouldn't someone from another crew move in? Someone like Jared Samuel or Tomás Hernández would pounce on their operation so fast they wouldn't have time to grab their cocks and pray.

If he were really going to try and take power from Esteban he'd need someone like Amado, someone whom everyone respected. He'd need that or he'd be fucked. That, and a whole lot of guns.

Norberto shook his head in disbelief. He was glad he'd come to his senses and told Martin to forget about it. But how did he let Martin talk him into it in the first place? How could he be so stupid? He must've been high to even think it could work. Then he remembered.

He *was* high.

Martin turned off Ventura onto Laurel and began the drive up the canyon. He was heading over the hill into Hollywood. He figured he'd drop the arm off at the police station in West Hollywood. Let the LAPD and the West Hollywood police fight over jurisdiction. Create a bureaucratic clusterfuck.

The arm was resting on the passenger seat. It jiggled and bounced and, at least to Martin, seemed to become uncomfortably animated. It was starting to creep him out a little. Even in the plastic he could see the fingers moving, reminding him of a horror movie he'd once seen in which the hand of a murderer acted on its own, killing anyone who got near it. Amado had murdered people. This was definitely the arm of a murderer.

Martin stopped at a light and put the arm under the seat.

The light changed and he continued up, leaving the Valley behind him. When he reached the ridgeline of the mountains and saw the view, Martin made a quick right turn and pulled over. He got out of the car, away from the arm which was still making his skin crawl, and stood looking at the vista as twilight descended.

All of Los Angeles, the great grid, stretched out in front of him. It carpeted a vast basin, going off in every direction as far as he could see. The city twinkled in its own atmosphere, the lights looking like strangely vivacious galaxy. Overhead, jet streams caught the last rays of the sun and glowed pink in the darkening sky.

Martin liked Los Angeles. It offered such a plastic facade. The sunshine and palm trees, convertibles and blondes. *We love it*. But if you really looked at the city, if you dug beneath the ever-tightening facelift it showed the world, you'd find that it was a much more complex, much more sinister, place.

On the surface you had one layer. The layer of people doing their daily things. Working. Shopping. Going to school. Dating. Mating. The obvious layer. Under that you had another layer. An invisible subculture that trades with the obvious layer. Money for drugs. Money for sex. Money for bootleg DVDs. Money for the things that make living in the obvious layer bearable. Money paid by hardworking people, struggling to get by or struggling to pay for their new BMW, desperate for any small pleasure that would take them away from their pain and make them feel special. Billions of dollars sucked into a dark labyrinth in the name of fleeting pleasures. More money than the fucking IRS will ever collect, circulating in an invisible world.

And beneath that world, another invisible world. And another. Like those Russian dolls that nestle inside each other, getting smaller and smaller.

Martin was skilled at taking the money from the invisible layers and, like a Las Vegas magician, making it real. Making it part of the obvious layer. It was a good trick. But he'd been doing it for others, and now it was time to become entrepreneurial.

Martin began to roll another jumbo. He was surprised to discover that he was almost out of weed.

Don had finished typing the request for a search warrant. He'd been informed that the courts were backed up today and that if it was an emergency they could push it through; otherwise, wait until tomorrow. Normally Don would've tried to push it through, making some kind of claim that Larga might still be alive inside his house and they needed to rescue him immediately. But Don was pretty sure that Larga was dead and his body wasn't going to decay that much more in the next twelve hours. Besides, he had a date with Maura and wanted to get out of there as fast as he could. So Don had left the request with the DA's office and jumped in his car.

As he was making his way toward Hollywood and Maura's apartment, he suddenly pulled over and went into a Barnes and Noble bookstore. He walked past the espresso bar, where students seemed to sit for hours and hours, toward the cookbook section.

It didn't take him long to locate the works of Max Larga. They were all clumped together. *Sophisticated Cooking, More Sophisticated Cooking*, and the best-selling *Sophisticated Cooking Made Easy*. Don picked up a copy and studied it. Larga's face, smug and arrogant, his hair styled in a way to make him look hip, graced the covers of all three books. How did this guy get mixed up with Esteban Sola? It just didn't make any sense.

Don leafed through the book reading the recipes. There were fresh figs stuffed with foi gras, caviar blinis with white truffle oil, roast loin of pork with rosemary and grapes, and an entire section devoted to the proper decanting of red wine, as well as a list of recommended dishes and the wines that they complimented.

Don decided he could use a good cookbook.

Felicia opened her door.

"*Hola,* Roberto."

Bob was so happy to see her that all he could do was just stand there and grin.

"You want to come in?"

"Absolutely."

Bob entered, still grinning, and looked around her place. It was marvelous. In the living room alone, four walls painted four different colors fought for attention. There was a fuschia pink wall next to a chartreuse green next to a vibrant orange next to a deep purple. Paper flags depicting skeletons from *el Día de los Muertos* festooned the ceiling. Scented candles burned on various tables and shelves.

But it was the walls that really got Bob's attention. The walls were splattered floor to ceiling with various *milagros* and representations of Frida Kahlo and her work. There must've been a thousand of them.

"You must like Frida Kahlo."

Felicia smiled.

"You know of her?"

"Of course."

"She is my patron saint."

Bob was puzzled.

"She's a saint?"

"She's my saint."

"Your own personal saint?"

"She gives me power, Roberto."

With that, Felicia came up to Bob and wrapped her arms around him before planting a big wet kiss on his lips.

"Do you feel it?"

"Maybe, just a little."

Felicia kissed him again.

"Oh, yeah."

It was like some kind of Mayan vision. Lupe stood naked in front of him, her dark brown skin and soft breasts glowing, moist and luminous in the dim light of the Jacuzzi. She looked like a goddess. Esteban floated in the hot water, felt the tequila flowing through his veins, and gazed up at her. Mother Mexico.

She stood above him holding a terra-cotta bowl filled with fresh guacamole. An offering from a Mayan goddess. That's when it hit him. That's when he realized that he was in love.

"I made more."

Esteban dipped his finger into the bowl and tasted it.

"You make the best guacamole I have ever had."

"*¿Verdao?*"

"*Cierto.*"

Esteban couldn't help himself. He put his hand in the guacamole and smeared it on her belly. She didn't resist, recoil, or
react. She was nonjudgmental.

He took another handful and coated her breasts. He dug
his fingers into the bowl and fed her, feeling her hot tongue
sucking the avocado off his fingers. She moaned.

"I love guacamole."

Lupe lay down on the warm cement as Esteban began lick-
ing the thick green goo off her belly, working his way slowly up
to her breasts, until he was on top of her. He felt her underneath him, soft and strong. He felt the residual guacamole,
sticky between their bodies, causing them to stick and slide as
they moved. He felt the heat that was emanating from his skin.
It was like the midday sun over the *zócalo*.

Martin hit the brakes. Fuck, that light changed fast. Were the
yellows getting shorter? It fucking seemed like it. He looked at
the floor and saw that Amado's arm had slid out from under
the seat. The plastic had come unwrapped and a couple of the
fingers were exposed. *No way I'm touching that.*

He looked around and saw a Burger King. The jolly orange-
and-red sign sent a message to his brain. His synapses fired
rapidly, if chaotically, as his brain relayed an urgent message to
his stomach. His stomach received the message and, anticipat-
ing a meal, began to expand and growl.

The light changed but Martin didn't go. He had a sudden
attack of the munchies. His stomach was demanding some
kind of nourishment.

Some prick in an SUV honked Martin out of his catatonia.
Martin stomped on the gas and jerked his car into the Burger
King's drive-thru lane. He pulled up in front of the menu
board and contemplated the selections. He'd recently seen yet

another special on mad cow disease and had decided to swear off beef and other red meat. But variety was offered here. Little fried things, other fried things stuffed with stuff. Kid's meals, cookies, onion rings. A metallic voice demanded that he decide, but Martin kept his cool.

"Gimme a minute."

"Would you like a Value Meal?"

"I don't know. Let me look."

Where was the fucking fire? Martin studied the board. There was chicken, several different chicken things, and fish. A fish sandwich. Maybe just some fries. The voice came back.

"Sir, you're holding up the line."

Martin looked in his rearview and saw a couple of cars idling behind him. He ordered quickly, opting for some kind of ranch-chicken sandwich, fries, and a root beer. Why don't they sell alcohol? He could use a stiff one right now.

He pulled forward, got his meal, and drove off. They were fast. How did they cook it so fast? Even a microwave wasn't as fast as that.

Martin drove with one hand and reached into the hot bag with his other. As he pulled the sandwich out of the bag, the french fries spilled out all over the seat, the floor, and the arm. Oh, fuck, what next.

He devoured the sandwich.

A pot of vegetarian curry simmered on the stove. Don and Maura sat on the couch kissing. Maura broke from their embrace.

"I bought a gun today."

It took a moment for Don to switch gears and actually register what she'd said.

"What?"

"I bought a gun. A Colt."

"You don't need a gun."

"I want a gun."

Don couldn't argue with that. He'd spent years seeing the kind of damage, intentional and unintentional, that guns could produce, yet he still believed that people should have the right to keep and bear arms.

"Have you ever fired a handgun?"

Maura bit her lower lip and leaned toward him.

"I was hoping you'd show me."

Don smiled. He'd seen other detectives with their wives and girlfriends at the range. He'd start the tongues wagging in the precinct when they got a load of Maura.

"Whenever you want."

"I have to wait ten days."

"That's not too long."

"Seems like a long time to me. What do they have to check?"

"They can check your record in a few minutes. The ten-day thing is called a cooling-off period."

Maura gave him a quizzical look. Don tried to explain the law.

"For example, if you get fired and you're upset about it, they don't want you to be able to just go out, buy a gun, and come back and kill your boss. That's why it's called cooling off."

"But people do that all the time."

"Right. But those people already had guns. They didn't just go buy them that day."

"But I'm not upset. I just want my gun."

Don shrugged.

"You'll get your gun. You just have to wait a few days."

Maura sighed.

"It just doesn't seem fair."

Don wrapped his arms around her and kissed her forehead.

"Life's not always fair."

Nestled up against him she reached around and stroked his back, her hand finding its way to his belt and the handgun clipped to it. Maura felt a surge in her already-surging loins as she touched the gun. With her other hand she unzipped his trousers and reached in. Don's cock bolted out of his pants like a thoroughbred coming out of the gate.

Maura shifted, keeping one hand on his pistol and the other on his cock. She dropped to her knees and began sucking him.

It was Don's lucky day.

Bob opened his eyes. Frida Kahlo stared back at him. What was bothering her? Bob realized that he had his shoes on and his pants were crumpled around his ankles. He could hear Felicia in the kitchen cracking ice trays and dropping cubes into tumblers. He pulled up his pants and smiled. He couldn't believe how far he'd come in such a short time. It seemed like only yesterday he was bickering with Maura, working at a stupid job, spending all his time playing games on the computer. He had been a nerd. Even proud to be a nerd. Listening to nerd music, wearing nerd clothes, surfing the Internet, reading comic books from Japan.

He had been under the impression that he was cool. But when he thought about it . . . what had he been thinking?

If anyone had told him he'd find himself mixed up with dangerous gangsters, being interrogated by the cops, and making love to a smokin' hot Latina, well . . . honestly, who'd believe that?

But Bob now believed that there was a rhyme and a reason to the universe. He had been transformed. He was a new man.

There was a purpose to life. He just didn't know what it was. Yet.

Felicia came in carrying a couple of cocktails.

"*¿Y ahora?*"

"What?"

Felicia nodded toward the icon of Frida Kahlo.

"What do you think of my patron saint now?"

Bob sipped his cocktail and thought about it.

"She's only got one eyebrow."

Felicia looked at the picture.

"So?"

Bob put his cocktail down and leaned forward. He kissed Felicia tenderly on the cheek.

"She may be a saint, but you're a goddess."

The TV was still yammering when Amado woke up from his dreams. He couldn't tell if it was an American western dubbed into Spanish or an Italian western dubbed into Spanish. For all he knew it could be a Spanish western dubbed into Mexican. He was just glad it wasn't the *telenovela*. It was getting weird. The *telenovela* was beginning to haunt his dreams. But then the *telenovela* itself was like a dream. It had a fractured reality. People didn't really scheme and betray and seduce like that. Or did they?

Chingao. It was getting confusing. He pulled himself upright and clicked off the TV. He was thirsty. Dehydrated. He stood up and walked into the kitchen. He reached for the refrigerator and experienced a strange, floating pain. It didn't hurt. It was more of a pang, really. The ache of reaching with something that wasn't there anymore. Reaching and not reaching. Phantom sensations of touch. It was like his dreams. He had dreamed that he was the padre in the *telenovela* and that he'd fucked Gloria on the altar of the church. He could still smell her, still feel her warm body as it bucked and spasmed and knocked over the chalice, spilling wine and communion wafers all over the floor. It had seemed so real.

He opened the fridge and reached in for a *chela*. It took him a second before he realized that his arm was gone. The arm wrapped in plastic on a cookie sheet. The cookie sheet was still there. But the arm . . . *se fue*. He knew right away the who, what, where of the situation.

That *pendejo* Martin had taken his arm.

Martin sat in his car. He was parked on Santa Monica Boulevard, across the street from the West Hollywood police station, right smack in the middle of boys' town. He watched as muscular gay men in tight T-shirts walked their dogs, chatted, held hands, or went in and out of bars. Martin fired up the last bit of his joint and sucked in the smoke. It was just another layer. There was a gay community, a gay economy, a network of gays who all supported each other in their gayness. The gay layer. He saw a couple holding hands as they walked into a bookstore. Dressed in leather, with big motorcycle boots, and heavy chains hanging off their pants, they represented a layer within the layer. The gay S&M layer. Martin realized that there were hundreds of millions of layers to the city. He smiled to himself. How come no one else ever noticed this?

Martin finished the last speck of the joint and flicked what remained out the window. He looked across the street at the police station.

And then it hit him.

He couldn't just walk into the police station with the severed arm of a murderer. They'd arrest him.

Fuck.

He thought about running over and just, you know, tossing it in through the front door, but then he realized they'd have security cameras filming him. They'd eventually track him down, drag him in for questioning. And how do you explain that you just found a severed arm that was supposed to be in police custody?

Fuck.

Martin sat back in defeat. He was out of weed, out of ideas, out of luck. He thought that he should probably just put the arm back in the fridge and go back to business as usual. Taking orders from illiterates. Trying to explain the simplest possible business strategies to violent thugs who only knew how to rob, cheat, steal, and kill.

Fuck.

That was the last thing he wanted. He closed his eyes.

And then, like what happens many times in our lives, just when he felt completely defeated, just as the obstacles to his success appeared insurmountable, inspiration came in the form of a gay man walking his immaculately groomed schnauzer. Martin saw the man walk up to a blue mailbox on the corner and drop in a large envelope.

Fuck, yeah.

Martin quickly wrapped the arm up in the plastic, sealing a few french fries in with it, jumped out of his car, and jammed the arm into the mailbox.

17

NORBERTO, FRESHLY SHOWERED and dressed in newly pressed clothes, sat in his comfortable chair watching television. He had his shoes off, his feet up on an old cardboard box which once held a stolen computer, and sipped a cold beer. He realized he hadn't relaxed, hadn't had any sense of his normal life since Amado had showed up at his door without his arm. It had all gone totally loco. But now that everything was *resuelto,* he could get back to the simple pleasures he enjoyed. Driving over to Van Nuys or out to Venice to collect money for Esteban. Maybe going with Amado to drop a trunkload of narcotics at some storage unit in Glendale. Sometimes going to the East Side to sell some guns and eat some *carnitas.*

It was easy, undemanding. As long as you kept your cool and dealt with professionals like yourself, not a whole lot could fuck it up. And then there were the perks. Free drinks at numerous bars. No waiting in line at the clubs. And the women . . . *caramba*, man, the women were all over him. *¿Y por qué no?* He was a sharp dresser, young, *guapo,* skilled at the salsa, the samba, and the cumbia. He drove a nice car and always carried the cash and the drugs to keep the party rolling all night long.

On the one hand, Amado's getting into trouble like that had helped Norberto. He had proven his *cojones* with El Jefe. That was *muy importante.* But on the other hand, it had been a dangerous run. Any number of things could've fucked it all up and ruined everything. But, for the most part, it seemed to have worked out.

Norberto realized he needed to distance himself from Martin. That gringo was *peligroso.* Norberto considered telling Amado and Esteban about Martin's plan. Although he knew it was bad to be a rat, this was an exception, and could help him get in good with El Jefe even more. Besides, Martin annoyed him. If they had to have a gringo around, Norberto preferred Roberto. Roberto was *simpático.*

There was a loud knock on the door, and Norberto got up to answer it. It was Amado.

"Hola, ese. ¿Qué onda?"

Amado walked in and looked around.

"Vale pendejo, where's *mi brazo?"*

Norberto looked stunned.

"What?"

"My arm. Where's my fucking arm? *¿Dónde?"*

Norberto quickly grasped the seriousness of what was happening.

" *¡Hijo de puta!* I can't believe it, man."

"What?"

Norberto walked over and clicked the TV off. He looked at Amado.

"Martin talked to me about taking your arm and giving it to *las placas.* But I said no fucking way, man. It's loco. I didn't do it, man."

Norberto looked at Amado. He was waiting for Amado to say something, to react. But Amado didn't say anything. He pulled a gun from behind his back and shot Norberto twice in the heart.

———

When Bob told Felicia that he didn't have a place to live, she immediately insisted that he move in with her. Bob was flattered and more than a little surprised by her offer. Sure, they were experiencing a kind of strange and intense passion together, but still, didn't it go against the rules somehow? He reminded himself that there was a kind of destiny to everything that was happening. It was preordained that he would be with her. It was just happening so fast. Destiny had its foot on the gas.

He wasn't sure if he'd ever get used to the hundreds of Fridas staring at him, but then, it wasn't like he was Diego Rivera. He wasn't a cad or a playboy. Sure, maybe he liked to look at porn on the Internet, but . . . Maura looked at naked guys all day. So he figured they were kind of even.

For a brief moment he wondered if Felicia modeled herself after Frida Kahlo. That wouldn't be good. Women who go in for that kind of self-torture really need to see a shrink. He watched her as she painted her toenails a bright orange. She was beautiful, wearing just a T-shirt, her feet propped up on a tile-topped coffee table. He realized that his fears, his hesitation, were just what they were. Not real. They were feelings that he could easily overcome.

Bob took the Polaroid of Amado's tattoo out of his pocket and looked at it. He thought for a moment and then stuck the photograph on the wall, right next to a picture of Frida.

Felicia laughed.

"You like that tattoo?"

"Yes."

"It's funny."

"What?"

"You. In love with a tattoo."

Bob shrugged.

"It's like all these Fridas."

Felicia looked at the Polaroid.

"Amado told you that was me?"

"Yeah."

"I hope I'm prettier than that."

Bob looked at the Polaroid and then at Felicia. It was the first time he'd compared the two.

"I'm surprised he didn't get your hair right."

Felicia laughed.

"I'm surprised you think it's me."

Bob couldn't tell if she was joking or not.

"So you and Amado never . . . did . . . this?"

She smiled.

"Maybe in his dreams."

Bob was perplexed. Felicia noticed this and kissed him.

"If you want it to be me, it can be me. I don't mind."

"You're way better than any tattoo."

"I should hope so. Can a tattoo do this?"

She started kissing him passionately. Bob began to melt under the onslaught of tongue and saliva when suddenly he remembered that he still had to call Esteban. He broke from the embrace.

"Shit. I need to make a phone call."

She looked off toward the kitchen.

"The phone is by the stove."

"I need to use a pay phone."

Felicia's demeanor changed.

"Business. With Esteban, no?"

Bob nodded.

"I have to call him. Tell him what happened."

She was disappointed in him.

"I thought you were a normal guy."

"I am a normal guy."

"Roberto, if you're calling Esteban you are not a normal guy."

"I know it's not a normal thing, but I'm a normal guy doing things that normal guys don't normally do. Honestly, I don't know what else to do right now, but I won't do this forever. Not if it bothers you."

Felicia looked at him and smiled.

"Just be careful, okay? And get some limes at *la tienda*."

Amado looked at Norberto. Man, was that *pendejo* dead. A huge and seemingly endless pool of blood spread like a big evil pancake across the floor.

He wanted to drag Norberto's body out of the living room and stuff it in a closet or something, but he'd come to the sudden and exasperating realization that while it might just take one little trigger finger to whack someone, it took two hands to dispose of a body.

Amado went into the kitchen and opened the fridge. He half hoped that his arm would be in there, that Norberto had been lying. But there was nothing but some moldy take-out, some bottled salsa picante, and a half-dozen beers. He took out a cold Pacifica and went back into the living room. He knew Norberto and Martin had been up to something, he just didn't think it was anything so stupid as going to the police.

Amado heaved a sigh. Young people, they just act impulsively, they never think things through. Never look at all the angles. It's a mistake to be so impetuous. It's *estúpido*. He knew he'd have to call Esteban and warn him, but first he needed to think. Drink a cold beer and contemplate his next move.

Amado popped the tab on the can and flicked on the TV. He was careful not to step in any of Norberto's blood.

Bob stood on Third Street near the Guatamalteca Bakery. People, dozens of them, were lined up for *pupusas, conchas,* and whatever else they had in there. A middle-aged Mexican woman, wearing a bright blue sweater, was selling roast corn on the cob from a pot she pulled in a small red wagon. A couple of little kids trailed behind her, laughing and slapping at each other. Next to Bob, a man sold peeled mangoes on a stick. Bob realized he was hungry.

In the ensuing communication breakdown, Bob saw his succulent and sweet mango dredged in a mixture of salt and chili powder. Oh, well, when in Rome.

Bob bit into the mango and was surprised at how good it tasted with the bite of the salt and the heat of the chili. He reminded himself that he needed to be more open-minded. Los Angeles, city of the future and hope of the world, demanded it.

The pay phone rang and Bob jumped to pick it up.

"Roberto."

He told Esteban what had happened, how he'd dropped the arm off, how the police had picked him up and tried to scare him, how he'd stood up to them, outsmarted them, and gotten away with it. Esteban told Roberto that he was proud of him. He'd have the ten thousand in cash brought over to him in a few days. Right now, all Roberto had to do was keep going to work, keep playing up the upset over his breakup, be normal. Esteban would call him in a few weeks and talk about other opportunities.

Bob hung up and finished eating his mango. He decided he'd better learn to speak Spanish. *Rápido.*

Martin drove up Beachwood Canyon looking for a parking spot. The duplex he wanted to go to was a block behind him. There was never any parking on this fucking street. What had originally been a quiet neighborhood was now dense with hipsters, the wannabe writers, actors, and directors who piled into Hollywood to earn their fortunes. Five people might be able to live together in one house, but that meant their five cars were scattered all over the street. So Martin drove on, hoping that he had good parking karma.

Eventually he found three-fourths of a spot and pulled in, letting the back of his car stick out into a red zone. Normally, he wouldn't risk it. The tickets, the possibility of getting towed or, worse, booted, where some kind of medieval torture device is attached to the wheel of your car, kept him out of red zones. But he was out of pot, and tonight, of all nights, he needed some.

He turned the car off, set the handbrake, and unconsciously picked some loose french fries off the passenger seat and popped them in his mouth. They were cold and had a slightly metallic taste. He shuddered, wondering if they'd been the fries that were on Amado's arm. The taste began to expand and take on a life of its own in his mouth. Growing from a dull greasy taste into a harsh accusation of cannibalism. A flavor that said, You have crossed the line, you are going to hell.

He reached for the tin of Altoids, the curiously strong peppermints, that he kept in the side-door pocket of his car, popped two in his mouth, and chewed them up. The mints effectively vaporized any residual french fry taste in his mouth.

He got out of his car and began the long walk down the hill to his dealer's duplex. The mints coupled with the crisp night air made him feel awake, alert, and very alive.

———

Esteban drove quickly, not fast enough to draw the attention of the police. He couldn't remember how many successful criminals had been undone by stupid traffic stops, but it was a lot. And it was, above all else, embarrassing. Let the FBI, the DEA, or some special task force bring him down. That was acceptable. He could go into *la carcel* knowing that the United States government had spent millions of dollars and invested thousands of man-hours putting together a case. But some lone *maricón* pulling him over for speeding?

Still, he pressed his luck. Amado had called and told him it was *muy importante*. Get over to Norberto's *ahora*. Amado was not the kind of man who asked for help, so it must be *muy importante*.

It was annoying. He'd just talked to Roberto, and everything seemed to have gone smoothly. Roberto had done his part and had done it beautifully. He was strangely proud of Roberto. Like a father might be. And he had plans for him. Big plans. Roberto wasn't just smart, he had a vibe, an *onda*, about him that Esteban thought could help. Bob was a people person. Just what Esteban needed.

Maura wanted to smoke. She craved one of those stinky-ass clove cigarettes that French people were always puffing in discos. Yeah. She pushed her plate of vegetable curry and brown rice aside and looked across the table at Don, who was plowing through his dinner like a refugee.

"This is really good."

"You like it?"

"Yeah."

Don reached over and refilled her glass of wine before refilling his. A gentleman.

"Do you think this is a safe neighborhood?"

Don put his chopsticks down and considered her question.

"No more or less than any other. At the end of the day it's a big city."

She nodded.

"I don't feel safe living by myself. That's why I bought the gun."

Don smiled at her.

"You're amazing."

"Why do you say that?"

"I don't know. I guess when I think of someone who's a vegetarian I don't think of a gun owner."

"I just don't want to be a victim."

Don looked at her, curious.

"Did something happen to you?"

"Women get victimized. Society is set up that way."

"I don't think a gun will solve society's problems."

"It's not just a gun. It's, I don't know, it's empowerment."

"Empowerment? Just because you can shoot someone?"

Maura nodded.

"But it's more than just shooting someone. It's something else."

"What?"

"I don't know, but it's very sexy."

Maura began to unbutton her blouse. She wanted to show Don how empowered she felt. Then maybe he'd understand. She took her shirt off, exposing her chest to him.

"Give me your gun."

Don hesitated. He knew he shouldn't be doing this, but he couldn't help himself, he couldn't stop. Don slowly reached around and took his gun out of its holster. He checked to make sure the safety was on.

"Be careful."

Maura took the gun.

"It's not about being careful."

She pointed the gun at him.

"It's about being intimate."

Esteban parked in front of Norberto's apartment. He checked his gun, making sure it was fully loaded and ready to go. He also checked his spare clip. No use jamming a new clip in only to find out that it was empty as well. He'd learned that the hard way when a couple of Mexican police had tried to jump him in a cantina in Juarez. Fortunately, the bartender had been a friend of his and had a twelve-gauge shotgun behind the bar.

Esteban knocked on the door and Amado let him in.

Esteban looked around the room. He wasn't shocked to see Norberto lying dead in a pool of blood. He figured it was something like that.

"Who killed him?"

"*Yo.*"

That was surprising.

"*¿Por qué?*"

"He and Martin stole my arm."

It didn't take long for Esteban to piece together what might be occurring. He was used to power plays. He'd seen people plot against him and his crew for years.

"Where is it?"

"I don't know."

Amado pointed to Norberto.

"He said that Martin was going to give it to *las placas.*"

So that was the plan. Let the police do Martin's dirty work. Still, Esteban was surprised. He didn't think Norberto would do something like this. The guy just wasn't a rat. Esteban walked over, carefully so as not to step in the blood, and looked at Norberto.

"I can't bury him with one arm."

Esteban looked at Amado and chuckled.

"I think your days as a matador are over, my friend."

"*Lástima.*"

"What will become of you? You need two hands to drive a cab or bus dirty dishes off of tables."

"I've been thinking about a new job."

Esteban looked at him and discreetly began to reach for his gun. Amado raised his arm in the air to reassure him.

"No, amigo. I don't want your job. I want to be a writer of *telenovelas.*"

18

BOB WOKE UP. The sun glinted in through a gap in the bright orange curtains and splashed across his face. He felt good. Warm, snuggled, and safe. The only thing slightly alarming was the fact that his cock was as hard as a lead pipe. He looked over and saw Felicia snoring peacefully next to him. Miss Scarlet, in the bedroom, with the lead pipe.

He shifted carefully, he didn't want Felicia to see it, because she'd make him fuck her again and, frankly, he was exhausted. He'd had sex so many times since he met her, fifteen, sixteen, maybe more, that he felt deeply tired, drained. His left eye had picked up a strange twitch.

The first thing he noticed as he climbed out of bed were the scabs on his knees. They were large, red, and painful. As he slid out of bed and stood up, his back squeaked in pain. *Christ, I feel sixty.* Bob hobbled off to the bathroom. He had to go to work.

Don shaved quickly, cutting himself twice on the chin. He didn't normally chop his face up this way, but he couldn't keep his hand from shaking. He looked in the mirror. He realized that he didn't know the man who looked back at him. What was happening to him? Was it the job? The pressure finally getting to him? He'd heard that sometimes officers take unnecessary risks in their personal lives. They become adrenaline junkies. Danger addicts. Maybe that was it. Maybe he should go see the shrink. Then again, maybe it was some unexplored part of him that Maura was able to reach. Or maybe he was just being completely stupid.

At first he'd thought it was love. He'd thought he was the luckiest man in the world. Here was a beautiful, intelligent, and charming woman, and she just couldn't get enough of him. Who wouldn't love her? God, just look at her body. Just talk to her. But after last night, he wasn't so sure it was love. He didn't know what it was. Something pathological, maybe.

He could've stopped her. He realized that. At any time he could've broken out of it and said that it was too dangerous or he wasn't comfortable or it was crazy or whatever he needed to say to stop it. He could've. Hell, he should've.

And what if the gun had gone off? He'd be dead, but what would his colleagues say? He'd become a laughingstock in every police department in every city in the world for the rest of history. They'd name a special rule after him. They'd teach it at the police academy. Don's rule: "A gun is not a sex toy."

Martin rolled out of bed feeling energized. Nothing like a couple of bong hits and a valium to give you a solid night's rest. Martin skipped the coffee and went right back to the bong, packing it full of some awesome bud, the little golden hairs catching the light and gleaming like strips of neon. Martin needed to remain calm. He had to get some things accomplished today. He'd made a checklist before he went to bed.

One, call Esteban and tell him that he'd taken Amado's arm and incinerated it. It was just no good to leave evidence lying around. He'd get Esteban to stand up for him. Tell Amado that it was the smart thing to do. That way when the feds came swooping down on them, they'd think it was each other who ratted. Divide and conquer.

Two, swing by Norberto's and borrow a gun.

Three, find Bob and kill him.

Four, well, actually there wasn't a four. Martin figured that by the time he got Bob out to the woods and shot him, that would take up most of the day.

The water bubbled in the bong as he sucked in a solid hit. Yeah. He felt good. Proactive. He released the smoke in a great gray geyser. Yeah. He was taking control of his life. It was about time.

Maura lit some incense and got the chair ready for her first client. She hoped Larga wouldn't blow off this appointment. It wasn't unusual for people to miss an appointment; in fact, it happened all the time. It was unusual for them not to call, not to apologize and reschedule.

But today she would let it slide. She was in a fantastic mood. Awash with an inner joy, a deep glow, a sense of sexual satisfaction that, well, she'd never felt before. Sure, sex with Bob had been fun, exhausting sometimes, but fun. Sex with Don was a whole other beast. They had a level of intimacy that you just didn't normally find between two people. He had taken her to a place, a deep, almost sacred place, that she had never known existed. Sex with Don touched an inner part of her and filled her with, well, filled her with fulfillment.

It moved her.

Perhaps it was because she felt empowered. Maybe that's what brought her to this sacred sex spot. She was glad that Don had let her keep his gun, just until she got her own. She opened her purse and looked at it. She felt a hot sensation shoot up through her body. She closed the purse. Later. She had work to do.

Bob walked into United Pathology.

Morris was there, already on the computer, looking at a Web site about cannibalism.

"Good morning."

Morris looked up.

"Hey, Romeo, how's it going?"

"I'm tired."

Morris grinned at him.

"Oh, boo hoo. You're having too much fun in bed. I feel so bad for you, man."

"Maybe I need to eat more protein."

"Oysters, dude."

Bob nodded. Oysters were fine, but right now he needed a coffee.

"Would you mind if I sat at my desk?"

Morris moused out of the site.

"*No problema,* dude."

Bob sat down behind his desk. He was hoping that it would feel secure, normal. He didn't know why, but he had a strange desire for everything to be back to normal. This morning in bed with Felicia he had felt so good. But somehow, on the way to work, he'd gotten cold feet. Maybe he wasn't cut out to be an underworld figure or a Latin lover. Maybe he wasn't strong enough to be a Roberto, and that's why his parents had named him Bob.

But the desk wasn't comforting. It felt strange. It was somebody else's desk. You can never go home.

Morris was looking at Bob in a strange way.

"So, Bob? How's the new chick?"

"She's different, man."

Morris was confused.

"Like, how?"

"She's just different."

"Like is it, you know, cultural? Does she do nasty shit that white chicks won't do? Does she taste spicy?"

"It's not because she's Mexican. It's her personality."

"So, are you, like, still in love?"

"Yes."

"Cool."

Bob typed the name Frida Kahlo into the search engine and hit the go button.

"You're the only guy I know who's gone out with a Mexican, man."

Bob turned away from the computer and looked at Morris. "Would you mind going to Starbucks?"

Martin drove down Sunset toward downtown. He was on his way to Norberto's house to borrow a gun and tell him that the plan was unfolding, they needed to watch each other's backs now. But Martin had a queasy feeling in the pit of his stomach. The conversation he'd had with Esteban on the phone this morning kept rewinding in his brain. Esteban had seemed so . . . calm. Martin had listed the reasons, the logic, behind destroying Amado's arm. Esteban had agreed, promising he'd talk to Amado so that there'd be no hard feelings. He went so far as to congratulate Martin for a job well done, then telling him to come over for lunch, they had a lot of work to do.

Esteban told him that his new tunnel operation was working more efficiently than he'd ever imagined. He had dug a tunnel, three kilometers long, between a house in Zaragosa, a pueblo just outside of Juarez, and a deserted cattle ranch in Texas. Esteban had purchased the ranch by setting up a corporation in Delaware as his front. He now found himself with too much cash, and was seriously considering the Mazatlán investment.

Martin was surprised. He'd never been very enthusiastic about the tunnel. It just seemed too big. Too showy. Someone would rat them out. He had tried to dissuade Esteban from building it. But Esteban had, seemingly, forgiven the bad advice, and was ready to actually do something Martin wanted to do.

But it was uncharacteristic. Usually when Martin fucked up, Esteban was the first to point it out. The first to remind him that an MBA might get you a job on Wall Street but it doesn't amount to a pile of shit on the street.

Although Martin was tempted to make some excuse, phone in sick, whatever, he was intrigued by the idea of all that cash. Where was it? If he could find out where it was, then he could snatch it while the feds were taking Esteban into custody. Maybe he wouldn't even need to take over the crew. Maybe with enough money, say three or four million, he could just disappear. Vanish and let Norberto take the heat.

He pulled up in front of Norberto's apartment building and got out of the car. He'd have to figure out something to say to Norberto. Maybe tell him that he should be the leader of the crew. The family wouldn't accept a gringo, but they'd take him with open arms. Martin knew Norberto was gullible enough to fall for that.

He rang the doorbell. He knocked. A couple of punked-out Latino kids on skateboards cruised by. He knocked harder.

Norberto was probably out getting laid.

Martin walked around to the back, he knew where Norberto kept a key hidden. He found it, under the planter of a spiky barrel cactus, and let himself in.

"Norberto?"

Martin closed the door behind him. He was hit by the strong smell of cleaning fluids. Maybe the housekeeper, a sexy woman from Guatemala, had been there earlier. He walked through the living room to Norberto's bedroom.

Martin peeked in the bathroom and saw the glaringly white bathtub. Yeah. The housekeeper had been there.

Martin opened the door to the bedroom closet and pulled out a suitcase. He plopped the suitcase on the bed and took a quick inventory. Several handguns, all of them Glocks, boxes of ammunition, a couple ounces of weed, three vials of various pills, a half kilo of coke, and a couple of small cellophane packets held together by a rubber band.

Martin picked up a Glock, checked to make sure it was loaded. He then took the cellophane packets. He'd put these in Bob's pockets. Make it look like he was a heroin dealer. Another red herring for the police.

Martin left a quick note for Norberto. He simply wrote "Viva la Revolución." He was careful to lock the door behind him. Now came the hard part.

Amado sat at the little coffee shop and looked through the *LA Weekly* magazine. *Carajo,* there were a lot of screenwriting classes and workshops to choose from, and each one seemed like some kind of scam. Write a script in thirty days? Sell your script in a week? Learn the secret to getting your script through the Hollywood maze? The secret of the pitch? How to meet an agent? They were like diet ads. Fast formulas for sure-fire hits. Lose weight now! Ask me how!

All of the classes were taught by people who put their names on them like they were somehow important or famous. Amado had never heard of any of them.

He was looking for one in *español*, because the *telenovelas* were in *español*. But there didn't seem to be one. Still, all he wanted was to learn how to write, he could translate on his own.

Eventually he found one. It was the most expensive one, and, in Amado's experience, you got what you paid for. It had the added attraction of being only two days long. Surely he could learn how to write a script in two days.

Amado tore the ad out of the magazine.

Don got there as quick as he could. Flores had taken the message and hadn't mentioned anything to Don for about an hour. Then he took his feet off his desk, looked over from behind the sports page, and blandly told him that some mailman, actually a very butch lesbian mailman, had found an arm in a postbox. An arm that matched the description of the arm found on Carlos Vila's garage floor.

So Don jumped in his car and raced over to the West Hollywood PD.

The arm looked exactly like Larga's arm. Except this arm was wrapped in plastic and had several french fries clutched in its hand. It was so similar that Don double-checked with the evidence room at Parker Center. He called and found that the other arm, Larga's arm, was resting comfortably in its cooler.

Don told the West Hollywood detective, a nice-enough man named Lowenstein, that the arm was evidence in an organized crime case he was working, and he needed it. Lowenstein blandly informed Don that it was a West Hollywood case now. They'd send him information as it became available.

Don knew better than to argue. He'd talk to his boss about it later. Right now, things were getting complicated.

The computer was boring. It took what seemed like an hour for the stupid Web pages to load. And then half the time they would jam or the URL would be missing or changed or something. Besides, what was Bob looking for? Even he didn't know. He was just killing time.

Maybe that's what I've been doing, he thought. *I've been living my life, killing time, waiting for my Web page to load.*

Bob heard the door open.

"I hope you got plain. I don't like vanilla in the morning."

"Hello, Bob."

Bob looked up. Martin stood there.

"Hey, man, what's going on?"

"I need your help. Can you spare some time?"

Bob nodded. Thank God, he was so bored.

"Yeah. No problem."

Bob quickly scribbled a note. Martin looked around suspiciously, then leaned in close.

"I'll tell you about it in the car."

Amado was lucky. He'd called the screenwriting workshop and they had room for him. Not only did they have room, but the class was starting that afternoon. Amado went out and bought a college-ruled notebook and several mechanical pencils. He was ready.

He now found himself sitting in a small lecture hall at Occidental College in Eagle Rock with two dozen aspiring screenwriters. Amado looked around the classroom. Most of the other students were younger than him. Several had laptop computers glowing in front of them. There was the cute Korean girl with pink pigtails and a strapless sundress that revealed some artistic tattoos. There were several young men with thick eyeglasses and scruffy haircuts. These men, boys really, lounged around in a kind of superior slouch. Like they'd already written successful screenplays and were just at the class as a kind of goof. There were a couple of middle-aged women, dressed in black and looking intelligent with stylish eyeglasses and asymmetrical haircuts.

Amado was the lone one-armed Latino in the class.

A cell phone went off.

The teacher, a handsome, slender man who had written several megasuccessful teen comedies in the late '80s, entered the room. He was *simpático* and confident. He assured them that with hard work and his formula they would all be pulling down big bucks in Hollywood sooner than they thought.

Words of encouragement. What every writer loves to hear.

Amado paid close attention, taking detailed notes, as the teacher began to describe the elements of a three-act structure. Every now and then the muted clicking of laptop keys would annoy Amado. But he realized that he would have to get one. He was serious about this and needed to have all the stuff that serious writers used. Like a cool laptop. He would call his friend Alberto after class and see if any laptops had fallen off a truck out by LAX.

Amado listened as the teacher told the class how someone named Shakespeare had used the three-act structure. He wanted to interrupt the teacher and ask him where the commercials went in a *telenovela* script, but decided that this was probably something that the writers figured out after they had the story.

The teacher talked. The class laughed. Amado wrote it down.

Act one: get man up a tree. Act two: shake a stick at him. Act three: get him down.

How hard could that be?

Esteban picked at a salad. He really wanted some kind of chorizo-and-egg burrito, but Lupe was concerned that he was eating too much fatty food. So Esteban picked at a salad. Not that it wasn't *delicioso*. It had slices of grapefruit and avocado, red chili flakes, fresh *lechuga*.

But something was distracting Esteban. Martin had failed to show up for lunch. Which meant that he was up to something. *Jodido hinchapelotas gringo gorrón*. Nobody liked a rat.

Esteban would have to make some quick moves. Shuffle bank accounts. Move storage facilities. Wire funds to the Cayman Islands and then have it moved back to another account in California. He hated to do it. It was better to stay under the radar. You never knew when some *pendejo* at the IRS would suddenly get suspicious of all these transfers and start snooping around.

But if Martin had really turned on him, and it looked that way, he needed to protect himself.

It was going to be a long day.

Bob looked out the window as Martin drove along the Angeles Crest Highway. He watched the scrub of chaparral give way to pine forests as the road narrowed and snaked toward the top of Mount Whatever-it's-called. He turned around in his seat and saw the view of the Valley. He wondered where the fuck they were going.

"Where are we going?"

Martin turned and looked at him.

"The desert."

Bob nodded.

"Cool."

Bob wondered if there was something in the trunk that needed to be buried. Or maybe they were going to meet a private plane coming up from Mexico with a clandestine cargo. It annoyed Bob that Martin was so aloof. Was it because he was stoned all the time? Maybe. Stoners never talked much. Or they talked too much. Bob couldn't remember. Martin didn't say much. Bob thought that it was because Martin didn't like him. Bob had tried to tell Martin how smoothly his plan had gone. How the police didn't suspect a thing. How smart Martin had been to think of it in the first place.

Martin just told him to shut up.

Bob figured he still might be mad from the time Bob had punched him out. Bob figured it probably wouldn't be so good to bring that up, so . . . he kept quiet and enjoyed the view.

There was a beat inside Martin's head. He couldn't figure out if it was a Beastie Boys' track or just some kind of random percussion his brain had decided to obsessively repeat over and over again. It didn't bother him. He rode with it. Tapping it out on the steering wheel. It was better than listening to Bob brag about how fucking cool he was. *Yeah, you're slick Roberto. One cool fucking cat. Too bad your sad carcass is about to be dumped in the desert.*

Martin had never thought of himself as a killer. He had always lobbied against it as a solution to problems. But now . . . well, now it made a certain amount of sense. It was, after all, an effective business strategy. And any qualms he'd had in the past about pulling the trigger on someone, well, somehow they had vanished too.

For the first time in his life Martin had a tangible goal. It wasn't just the idea of an MBA, the promise of a good job with an important firm. It wasn't all smoke and mirrors. It was real. Esteban had millions of dollars stashed somewhere. Millions. Cash.

The cash was the goal.

Martin imagined himself sitting on some kind of chaise longue, underneath a ceiling of blossoming bougainvillea, sipping espresso and listening to the waves of some warm-water ocean crash against the beach. Maybe some topless chick, like in a painting by Gauguin, would sit with him on the chaise and roll a jumbo. A big fat fucking spliff.

Yeah. Cash money.

Bob, and his insipid questions, brought Martin out of his fantasy.

"When are we gonna get there?"

Martin wanted to tell him to shut up and enjoy the view because it was his last fucking ride. But he didn't, he tried to ignore him. Martin wished he could blow a joint right now. He turned to Bob.

"Can you roll?"

"Roll?"

Martin cringed. Why was this guy so stupid?

"A joint."

"No, man. Sorry."

Typical, worthless fuck.

"I was never good at it. They wouldn't burn evenly."

It doesn't matter. You're as good as dead.

"Whatever."

"People, the general public, the movie-going audience, they like murders. Murders are interesting and murderers are the most interesting of all. That's why so many TV shows and movies are about murders."

Amado sat listening to the teacher. If people only knew the truth. They wouldn't be so interested. Sure, the part leading up to it is kind of exciting, but after you've killed. *Carajo.* What a fucking mess.

The professor told the class to take a ten-minute break. Cliques immediately formed as like-minded souls asked each other to be writing partners or what agent they had.

Amado walked out into the hallway and plugged some coins in the soda machine. He was getting used to this one-armed thing. It wasn't going to be as bad as he'd thought. At first he hadn't thought he'd be able to wipe his ass again. Now he could do all kinds of stuff. Well, he couldn't move heavy objects like Norberto's big dead body, but he could do lots of other stuff.

The cute Korean girl with the pink pigtails came up to him.

"Hi. What's your name?"

"*Hola.* I am called Amado."

He extended his hand.

"And you?"

"Cindy."

Amado pushed a button and a lemon-lime soda fell to the bottom with a thunk.

"Can I buy you a soda? Cindy?"

She smiled at him and their eyes met. Amado could see that animal thing inside of her switch on as he looked into her eyes. It was strange, he realized, he hadn't thought about having sex in days. In fact, he was even a little shy about it, not knowing if he'd be any good with just one arm.

"No, thanks."

Amado noticed that her knees were shaking. He smiled at her. She stammered when she spoke.

"Can I ask you something?"

"Of course."

"Because you look like someone who's had a lot of life experience."

"What the professor was talking about? Life experiences."

"Yeah. Life experiences make you a better writer. You look like a person who's had some."

Amado smiled. *You don't know the half of it.*

"Sí. One or two."

Cindy looked at him, looked deep into his eyes.

"I haven't."

Amado sipped his lemon-lime soda and shrugged.

"You are young."

The other students started back into the lecture hall.

"How did you lose your arm?"

"Maybe I will tell you after class."

Don jimmied the door to Larga's house. A uniformed officer and several crime-scene investigators stood behind him. Don drew his revolver and entered the house.

"Mr. Larga?"

He listened for a second.

"This is the police. Mr. Larga?"

Don nodded, and the uniformed officer and some of the crime-scene guys entered. They moved quickly in pairs, covering each other as they entered one room after another.

"Bedroom, clear."

"Bathroom, clear."

"Kitchen, clear."

It was not a big house, and they were able to search and declare it clear of dead bodies, hostages, or intruders in about thirty-two seconds.

One of the crime-scene guys, a balding man with those eyeglasses that make your eyes look really big, and who enjoyed collecting bugs off corpses because forensic entomology was his hobby, came up to Don.

"Looks like this isn't a crime scene. We're going to pack it up."

"No problem."

"Call me when you find the rest of his body."

Don nodded. *Yeah, so you can pick the maggots out of his eyes. Like I want to see that?*

As uniformed officer tacked a notice to the front door, Don began to sift through Larga's mail.

It was nothing special. Bills. Letters. People usually dump their keys by the front door when they come in. Don didn't see any keys, which led him to believe that Larga was probably stuffed in the trunk of his car somewhere. He'd get the license plate number and put it out. It'd turn up eventually. Either a patrol unit would find it, or some neighbor would smell it. They always turn up.

Don kept sifting. He was trying to find something that might connect Larga to Carlos Vila or Esteban Sola or anybody. Somehow there was a connection. There had to be.

Time to go through the dead guy's dresser drawers.

By the time they finally reached the deserted nether regions of the Joshua Tree State Park, Martin was sick and tired of driving. He desperately needed a cold drink and a hot jumbo. He had pulled off the paved road and jounced down some pocked dirt trail for what seemed like a day. His car looking distinctly geishalike with all the finely powdered dirt covering it. Bob had actually fallen asleep during the drive, the poor guy complaining about how tired he was, how hungry he was. Martin got sick of hearing it, and stopped at a Burger King in one of the strange little podunk suburbs they had passed through.

Martin killed the engine and rolled a joint. He was careful to discard any seeds as he lovingly crumbled the dried leafy bits into the rolling paper.

Bob woke up.

"Where are we?"

Martin lit his joint.

"In the desert."

Martin took a strong pull of the reefer and handed it to Bob. Bob shook his head.

"No, thanks."

Martin shrugged.

"It's your funeral."

Bob got out of the car to stretch his legs. Martin took another hit. He watched Bob. It was kind of like he was watching a movie about Bob. As the THC hit his bloodstream Martin began to feel detached. Floaty. He was in the audience watching a movie about a skilled and daring hit man about to pull off yet another job. That was him. He was the star of this movie. There was Bob. He was the job. The victim-to-be.

But it was also strange. Martin felt like he was in the movie but he was also not in the movie. He was watching himself watch himself think of himself in a movie about a cool hit man. Fuck, this was good shit.

Martin got out of the car. He watched himself get out of the car and heard himself speak.

"Hey, Bob."

Martin pulled the Glock out of his jacket pocket and pointed it at Bob. Bob looked really surprised. Martin watched himself watching Bob's surprised expression.

"You look surprised, Bob."

"What're you doing, man?"

Martin thought that was a really stupid question. Just like all of Bob's questions.

"Do I have to make the obvious explicit?"

Bob nodded.

"Yeah."

"I'm pointing a gun at you."

"I see that. Why?"

Martin went around and popped open the trunk.

"Because I'm going to kill you."

Martin watched Bob's reaction. That would be a close-up in the movie. Bob's big reaction.

"I did everything like I was supposed to."

Martin wanted to laugh, but he watched himself not laughing and figured he'd better play it straight. This was a time to be serious.

"You did a great job."

Bob looked very sad.

"Did Esteban tell you to do this?"

"No. Esteban has his own problems to worry about."

Bob looked around quickly, like he was going to run.

"Don't try it."

"Why are you doing this?"

"It's all about goals, Bob. I have goals. This is one of the steps I must take to attain my goals."

Martin took a shovel out of the trunk. He handed it to Bob.

"Dig."

Bob took the shovel and hit Martin over the head with it. He hit him hard. Martin watched himself see himself get hit hard on the head with the shovel. He saw stars, actual particles of lightning-colored phosphorescence in his field of vision. He watched himself drop the gun and fall to the ground. Then he felt himself see himself hit the ground as blood erupted from a massive gash on his scalp.

Martin heard the car start up and drive off.

A fine layer of dust rose up in the air and slowly settled on him.

This, he realized, was not good.

Don pulled open the drawer to Larga's bedside table. People always put their most personal items there. Maybe because they spent so much time in bed, or because they did things in bed they didn't do in the kitchen. He looked in the drawer. Condoms, lubricants, a pamphlet about understanding conflict in relationships, some sleeping pills of some kind, loose change, a couple of business cards. There was usually a gun or pepper spray. Once he found a Taser. Those are wild.

One of the business cards caught Don's eye. He picked it up.

It was Maura's.

There was no sound but the steady drip from one of the showers in the locker room and the occasional gasp or moan from Cindy, the screenwriter with pink pigtails. Amado was on his knees. The hard tile floor didn't bother him at all, he was a man on a mission. Cindy stood over him, her legs slightly spread, her mouth open in surprise. He lifted Cindy's dress with his teeth as he pulled off her panties with his hand. He began to lick and nibble at her inner thighs, working his way between her legs. She tasted good.

She let her body relax, giving herself over fully to Amado and the experience. Amado unbuckled his pants, unleashing his hard cock. He picked her up with his one arm, entered her, and fucked her against a wall of lockers. He was surprised at how strong he felt. He felt really good.

Cindy, pinned against the lockers, was crying out in bursts of staccato moans and squeals. She was getting some life experience.

Now she had something to write about.

19

WHEN BOB TURNED onto the paved road he took a breath. He sucked in a deep gulp of oxygen and hit the gas. He realized he hadn't taken a breath since he had hit Martin with the shovel and taken off. That's what it seemed like, anyway.

Bob was pretty sure he hadn't killed Martin, but he'd hurt him, and he'd left him with a good twenty-mile walk through the desert. But he wasn't dead. Martin would be back. Bob would have to deal with him.

So Bob drove fast. He wanted to put as much time and space between himself and Martin as he could. He needed to figure out what to do. He tried to calm his mind, but it was on fire. Was Esteban behind this? Should he go back and finish Martin off? With what? Martin had the gun and the shovel. Bob thought maybe he could just run over him with the car. But what if it damaged the car? Then he'd be stranded in the desert.

Bob realized he needed a plan. To formulate a plan he needed to consult a professional. He decided he needed to trust his instincts.

Bob pulled over at a gas station, went to the pay phone, and punched in Esteban's number. He went inside and bought a bottle of Cherry Coke while he waited for Esteban to call him back.

When the phone rang, Bob couldn't contain himself.

"Martin tried to kill me."

Esteban remained calm on the other end.

"Roberto? Are you all right?"

"He was going to shoot me and leave me in the desert."

"Where is he now?"

"In the desert somewhere."

"Is he alive?"

"I think so."

"Did you shoot him?"

"I hit him with a shovel."

There was a pause.

"Good work, Roberto."

Bob didn't know what to say.

"What do I do now?"

Esteban's voice was soothing, reassuring.

"Tell me where you are and where you think Martin is. I will send some people to find him."

"What about me?"

"You should go home and wait for me to call."

That wasn't what Bob wanted to hear.

"He'll try to kill me again."

"Roberto. I will protect you. *¿Entiendes?*

Bob wasn't so sure, but what could he say?

"Okay."

"Now tell me where he is."

Amado sat at his kitchen table. His new laptop computer was beeping at him. Although he'd never used a computer before, Amado was surprised at how simple it was. He had loaded the screenwriting software in a couple of minutes.

The phone rang.

Amado looked at it. He didn't really want to be bothered right now, but it wasn't like he had dozens of amigos who'd just call up. And he had given his number to Cindy, in case she felt the desire for more life experience. So he answered it.

It was Esteban telling him Roberto's story.

Normally, Amado would've just said *Sí, está bien,* and he'd have been out the door. But now, what could he do? He could drive out in the desert, find Martin, and blast him. He'd be happy to. But he couldn't dig a hole or move a carcass. You can't rely on the vultures to dispose of it. They'd leave Martin's teeth, and he'd be identified through his dental records.

Besides, Amado was just sitting down to start writing his episode of the *telenovela.* He had it all planned in his mind. He had his new computer with the cool software. He had some cold *cerveza* in the fridge. And he'd had a *buena cogida* with Cindy earlier that afternoon.

The last thing he wanted to do was drive over the fucking hills and kill someone.

Amado suggested Esteban call the Ramirez brothers. They had been doing odd jobs, errands, small stuff for the crew. It was time to bring them up. Give them a mission. Sure, they were drug addicts with a touch of *caballero* about them, but they would jump at the chance to make their bones with Esteban.

Besides, Amado had work of his own.

Don drove over to Maura's office. He didn't know what to think. So Larga had Maura's card in a drawer. Was he a client? Were they friends? Was Maura involved in his disappearance somehow?

On one hand, he was glad that he had something to go on.

Otherwise it was looking random. No motive. No leads. Just some poor fucker with bad luck. Those sorts of cases were unsolvable.

As Don pulled into the parking lot by Maura's office he spotted Larga's car. He picked up his radio and called it in.

Don parked and walked over to Larga's car. He hated this part. If he'd had to bet, he would've wagered a thousand dollars on Larga's body being in the trunk. Don leaned close to the trunk and took an exploratory sniff.

The stench of rotting flesh did not assault Don's senses as he'd feared it would. He bent close to the trunk and sniffed again. It just smelled like a car. Don was relieved. It takes days to get the smell of a corpse out of your nose and mouth. You need to gargle with gin and eat raw onions and lemons. And still your brain remembers. The sensation of the smell lingers for weeks, sometimes longer. It's nasty.

Esteban hung up the phone. He was disappointed in Amado, but he understood. Amado couldn't do the things he once could. Esteban could no longer rely on Amado to take care of the necessary but unfortunate side of the business that required murder, mayhem, and an unflinching ability to inflict pain, suffering, and even more pain. Amado was now disabled. A gimp. He could use those special parking spots.

Esteban reluctantly dialed the Ramirez brothers.

It's not that they were incompetent. If you needed a bar smashed up, a car stolen, or some money collected from a deadbeat dealer, you couldn't ask for two more competent employees. The thing that gave Esteban pause was that the Ramirez brothers actually enjoyed their job. They were sociopaths and sadists.

He and Amado had, over the years, dished out death, torture, and punishment. But they'd never enjoyed it. It had never felt good. It had always been a real drag. *Bárbaro.* They'd felt bad about it, no matter how justified they were. *Los hermanos* Ramirez thought it was fun.

It gave Esteban the creeps.

But, he figured, if anyone deserved an afternoon with the Ramirez brothers, it was Martin.

Martin felt the sun slowly baking him. His body basting in its own sweat. He rolled over and felt his head. A crunchy crust of clotted blood had formed and stopped the bleeding. Still, judging from the number of flies buzzing around his wound, it wasn't good.

Martin slowly sat up. He was dizzy. His head throbbing like a motherfucker. But he wasn't dead. Not yet, anyway.

He sat there and took stock of his situation. There were, he realized, a number of variables. If Roberto had called Esteban and ratted him out, then Amado was on his way to kill him. If Roberto had thought Esteban was behind this, well, he'd just run for cover and they'd never see him again. Martin preferred the latter. But either way, he had to get back to civilization, and an emergency room, soon.

He got to his feet and saw that the Glock was on the ground a few feet away. He bent down to pick it up, feeling a little dizzy as he did. He noticed the shovel on the ground. A divot of his scalp, the wispy hairs sticking up, was still stuck to the shovel's blade.

Martin didn't want to think about it. Time to move.

Maura was surprised and happy to see Don.

"Hey, what're you doing here?"

She gave him a nice wet kiss, wrapping her arms around him as she did. Actually, the kiss could've led somewhere. It was one of those I've-got-the-time-and-the-interest kind of kisses. Don pulled back.

"Hey, I hate to do this. But I've got to ask you some questions."

Maura was concerned.

"You didn't get an infection or anything?"

"No. These are police questions."

Maura swallowed. Don was looking at her in a different way. A new way. He was studying her reactions. Even though she hadn't ever broken any laws or done anything bad, except for a little recreational drug use, Maura suddenly began to sweat.

"What's going on?"

"That's what I'm trying to determine. I'm hoping you can help."

"Of course I'll help."

Don looked at her and then pulled out a cookbook.

"Do you recognize this man?"

He showed her the picture of Larga on the cover.

"Yes. That's Max Larga. Although you know that, because his name's right there on the cover of the book."

Maura caught herself. *Why do I feel so nervous?*

"Do you know him?"

"Sure. He's a client."

Don nodded.

"This is important. When was the last time you saw him?"

Maura thought for a second.

"I can tell you exactly."

She went to her desk and pulled out her schedule book. Looking through it, she realized that she might need to take out an ad in one of the holistic newspapers. Business had been slack.

"He was supposed to come the other day, but he didn't show up."

Don wrote down the exact date and time.

"You sure he didn't show up?"

"Yeah. I was annoyed. He didn't even call."

"We found his car in the parking lot."

Maura blinked.

"That's weird."

Don nodded.

"Yes. Yes it is."

Bob turned on the car's radio. He hit the scan button, and station after station came into the car, blared a commercial, and then drifted off into a static void. Didn't anyone play music on the radio anymore? It was all talk. Somebody selling something. Even the news was selling something. Bob believed that people watched the news on TV or listened to the news on the radio so they could feel superior. They didn't want to be informed, they weren't interested in politics, half the time they didn't even vote. People watched the news so they could say, *I'm better than the poor fuckers fighting floodwaters in Iowa; I'm smarter than the guy driving wildly down the freeway to avoid arrest. My life is better, not because of the luck of being born in the First World, but because I am inherently superior to the hungry masses rioting in Botswana, robbing banks in Van Nuys, and selling their bodies on the streets of Bangkok.*

Bob's theory was that the news comforted people by showing them how horrifying the rest of life was. You couldn't help but feel safe and smug when confronted with the stupidity that raged outside your walls.

At least that's what Bob thought. So he didn't pay much attention to the news.

Finally, the radio landed on an AM station and stuck there. It was in Spanish. It was all talk. But Bob could tell from the passion and inflection in the speaker's voice that it was religious. A preacher speaking Spanish, imploring people to follow the word of God. Bob liked the cadence of the preaching. It was somehow reassuring.

Bob could not help but marvel at the fact that he was still alive. Twice in the last few days he'd been kidnapped and marked for death. Only each time he'd gained a reprieve. He had been lucky. He had cheated death.

There was a reason for it. He was sure of that. He didn't know what the reason was. It was somehow connected to Felicia. They were in love. Was it love that kept him alive, or some higher power? Maybe love was the higher power.

The preacher continued to spread the word of Jesus as Bob drove down from the mountains and into the Valley. Bob knew that he was on a path. He could feel it. He didn't know where it was heading, he couldn't foresee the twists and turns that he knew lay ahead. But he'd been trusting his instincts, relying on luck, and so far things were unfolding in miraculous ways.

There was a reason he was lucky.

As he drove toward Felicia's house, Bob was overcome by two distinct feelings. The first was a great sense of relief that traveled from the top of his head down to his sweaty toes, and made his blood pulse and his lungs suck in big heaps of air. He was alive. The sun was shining, the trees were waving in the wind. He could see the world in all its glory. The other feeling that tugged at him, and this urge was even more compelling than a feeling of general well-being and appreciation for the beauty of life and the surrounding world, was the sensation of being incredibly horny.

He couldn't wait to get home to Felicia.

Martin had walked about three miles when he saw a pickup truck heading toward him. He stopped in his tracks. His adrenal glands began to furiously pump adrenaline through his body. He was finding it difficult to stay upright. He clenched his teeth and fought back the urge to barf.

This was probably Amado. Martin knew he needed to stay calm, stay focused. He clenched the Glock tightly in his pocket. When Amado got close, really close, he'd whip that sucker out and just start blasting.

But it wasn't Amado. It was the park ranger.

The pickup stopped in a cloud of desert dust, and a lanky young man, his face looking like it had been hit with a blowtorch from all the acne and sunburn it had experienced, hopped out. The ranger had a concerned expression.

"Hey, mister, are you okay?"

Martin didn't know how to answer that question. It seemed so stupid that he felt like shooting the guy right then and there. *Just look at me,* he thought, *how could you ask that question?*

"I fell and hit my head."

It was probably better not to kill the ranger.

"Let me take a look at it."

The ranger walked close to Martin and looked at his scalp.

"I think I need to go to the hospital."

The ranger nodded.

"I'll say you do."

The ranger helped Martin into the passenger seat of the pickup. Martin suddenly felt weak. Like he was going to black out. The ranger hit the air conditioner and did a quick 180. The cold air dried the sweat on Martin's face, sending a chill through his body. It wasn't a bad chill, it was a good chill. It would be the chill of the hospital, the cold stinging burn of antiseptic and suture. The cold air of safety.

As the pickup left the trail and started off down the paved road toward town, Martin got another kind of chill. The chill you get when you see the Ramirez brothers go flying by in an SUV.

Ah, fuck. This was bad.

He became lightheaded. In fact, he felt his head detach from his neck and float. It would've drifted out the window if it had been open. A prickly sensation rushed through his arms, and then everything went black.

Martin passed out, his head lurching forward and hitting the dashboard. The ranger looked over, dismayed as the wound had opened and a soft trickle of blood was dripping on his pickup's interior.

The ranger grabbed a box of tissues and, taking out three or four, smushed them into the wound. The tissues stuck up, out of Martin's head. They waved in the air-conditioned breeze as they slowly turned red. Like a beautiful rose.

Maura had seen these interview rooms on TV shows. Drab, institutional, kinda grotty. But what you couldn't get from television was the smell. The sweet, gag-inducing perfume of fear and desperation. She was surprised. You'd think it wouldn't be so noticeable. But there it was. Unmistakable. Pure animal fear.

The smell didn't just nauseate her, it infected her. Soon her skin was covered in a cool, clammy sweat. Nerves jangled and on edge. The smell rising off her.

Why?

What had she done wrong? Why was Don being so weird with her? She wondered if this was what he was really like.

Don entered the room carrying a cup of hot tea for her.

"I'm really sorry about this."

Maura took the tea. She didn't feel like talking.

"It's just easier if we can run through the sequence of events again."

She sipped her tea.

"Are you okay?"

Maura thought about how to respond to that question. She decided no response would be the simplest.

Don gave her an earnest and loving look.

"Maybe bringing you in wasn't such a good idea. I'm really sorry."

She didn't give him anything in return.

"I'm just stuck. This is a big case for me and it's just getting weirder and weirder. The only clue I've got, the only lead whatsoever, is this connection between you and Mr. Larga."

Maura blinked. His honesty had helped her. Helped alleviate some of her fear. Now she was just pissed off.

Don doodled in his notebook.

Maura sipped her tea.

After a beat, Don tried again.

"Please?"

Maura didn't say anything. She kept her breathing regular. Her eyes remained soft, not showing any of the anger or emotion that was building up inside her, hot, gaseous, and continuously expanding like the lava dome of Krakatoa.

She watched as Don squirmed in his seat. Now he was sweating. She decided to speak.

"Do I need a lawyer?"

Hit with a Buick's worth of guilt he crumpled like a cheap, imported bumper.

"Oh, no. No, honey. Nothing like that. You're not under arrest. You're not even a suspect. I just . . . I just thought—I'm sorry. I've messed everything up."

She kept her poker face on, but she was enjoying this. She'd managed to turn the tables on Don. She could barbecue him if she wanted. She could get him to do anything.

"You're going to have to make this up to me."

Bob felt good. He rolled off Felicia, their bodies slippery from sweat, and lay on his back gasping for air. She rolled on her side and looked at him.

"Oh, Roberto."

Bob didn't know what to say, so he ran his hand down her body until he found her hand. He held it tightly.

Felicia let out a sigh and curled up next to him, drifting off to sleep. A contented purring sound rising from her throat. He felt her breasts pressing against his ribs, felt the weight of her leg as it rested on top of his. Her warmth. The rise and fall of her breathing. The blood flowing just under that soft brown skin. He wanted to stay here, in bed, with Felicia for more than a few weeks or months.

Bob's brain slammed on the brakes. He came to the shocking realization that he wanted to stay with Felicia for the rest of his life. He was in love.

He wanted to stay alive and enjoy this for as long as he could. Until something happened and the two of them tore each other's hearts out and went their separate ways. Although Bob held out a good deal of hope that you could actually have a long-term, mutually satisfying relationship that didn't end in heartbreak. Perhaps he was naive. But he didn't care.

It seemed like for the first time in his life he'd been lucky. All those times when the other guy got the girl, the job, the last copy of the collectible first-edition comic that he had spotted. Yeah, he was due for a little luck.

Still, luck runs out. You always hear that. Somebody's luck ran out. Bob realized he'd need more than just luck. It was time he took an active interest in his long-term survival. Particularly if he wanted to continue being employed in this new line of work.

He catalogued the various methods of self-defense. Learning to shoot a gun seemed obvious enough. But guns have drawbacks. They go off a little too quickly. You could shoot someone accidentally. You could get arrested for carrying them. Bob realized that guns had a negative vibe for him. He just wasn't a gun person.

He wasn't a knife person either. Too messy. Maybe he could learn kung fu or some equally deadly martial art. He'd discuss it with Esteban. Learn from the old pro. Stay alive.

Bob drifted off to sleep.

It took a few minutes for everything to come into focus. It was like a dream. Diffuse light glaring through the curtains. The hundreds of little holes in the ceiling tiles. You could count them. Across the room, some dark silhouette watching TV. The sounds of a baseball game.

Martin was groggy, disoriented. He had the pleasant sensation of being stoned on some kind of painkiller and the unpleasant sensation of having his arms and legs strapped down onto a bed. With some effort he lifted his head up.

He could see his hands, with little plastic tubes going into his arm. Something, water, food, drugs, were being fed directly into his body from above. He tried to move his arms again, this time seeing the thick nylon straps that secured him to the bed.

Now what?

As the room came more and more into focus, so did several extremely unpleasant physical sensations. His throat, for one, was parched. As though the membranes had shrunken and cracked like a dry lake bed. His head, where that fucker Roberto had clobbered him, hurt with a kind of insistent slicing pain. And, oh, this can't be happening, there was some kind of tube shoved up his penis and into his bladder. He was catheterized.

"Water."

Did he say that? If he had, he hadn't meant to. He'd wanted to keep quiet until he came to his senses.

"Water."

That was him. That croaking sound was coming out of his mouth.

"Thirsty?"

"Water."

The silhouette stood and came over to him. Martin could tell right away that it was some kind of law-enforcement person. The man held out a plastic cup. Martin lifted his head and grabbed the flexible straw with his lips. He slowly sucked the icy fluids down. Nothing. No drug, no sex, no fabulous food, nothing ever tasted so good.

"Don't drink it all."

The officer pulled the cup away. Martin laid his head back.

"Glad to see you're awake. We didn't know when you were going to snap out of it."

Martin didn't know what to say.

"We've got a lot of questions for you."

"What?"

"I'm the sheriff out here, and you're our mystery man."

The sheriff stood up and patted his beach ball of a beer gut.

"What were you doin' out there? Didya think you could sell heroin in the desert?"

Martin was confused, and then he remembered. The packets of smack he'd taken from Norberto. The ones he'd planned to stick in Roberto's pocket.

"Marijuana possession. Heroin possession with intent. Possession of an unlicensed firearm."

The sheriff gave him a sincere look.

"You want to tell me what you were doing out there?"

What Martin really wanted was time to think. He wanted to put his feet up, fire up a jumbo, and consider the various possibilities, scenarios, etc.

"You're looking at five to fifteen in Soledad."

He'd be what? fifty when he got out. What would his parents say?

"I want to make a deal."

It came out so quickly and so easily.

The sheriff smiled.

"You want to tell me who you bought this crap from?"

Martin blinked.

"I want to talk to someone from the FBI."

"Oh, you're a bigshot."

The sheriff sat back down on the bed, only this time he wasn't careful, and the catheter in Martin's penis shifted. Martin winced.

"Looks to me like you bought your drugs in California, you were trying to sell your drugs in California, and you are in California. That ain't what we call a federal problem. That's a state problem."

Why was he being so difficult?

"I want to make a deal."

"I heard that."

"I work for the Mexican mafia."

The sheriff stood up.

"That's a good one."

He started for the door. Martin didn't want him to leave. He didn't want to be left alone. The image of the Ramirez brothers in their car flashed back to him. He was suddenly scared. Very scared.

"You've got to protect me. They'll find me and kill me. You've got to protect me."

The sheriff stood in the doorway.

"I'm gonna get a cup of coffee, and when I come back, you're gonna tell me the truth."

Esteban hated going into places like this. A dark bar in East LA. If he was looking for trouble, he could find it here. He had asked Amado to come with him. But Amado said he was busy working on his *telenovela* script. Esteban was tired. He didn't want to argue. He knew that if he'd told Amado who he was going to see and where, he'd have come. But sometimes El Jefe's got to show his *huevos*. So Esteban stuck a fully loaded, semiautomatic, nine-millimeter handgun in his sports coat and went alone.

Theoretically he shouldn't have been nervous. The Ramirez brothers were his employees. They should be loyal, protective. But things were getting weird. Esteban didn't feel the bluster and confidence he normally carried with him. He was starting to look over his shoulder.

The Ramirez brothers, Tomás and Chino, were sitting in a back booth. They had a couple of long neck Pacificas in front of them, a little bowl of lime slices, and several thin white lines of crystal meth. They hung their heads when Esteban entered the bar.

"*¿Qué pasa, amigos?*"

Esteban sat with them. He nodded toward the bartender, a

man who'd spent the last twelve years in prison on a trumped-up manslaughter charge, for another round.

"*Lo siento, jefe.*"

Tomás then went into a long meandering story recounting their drive out to the desert and attempt to find Martin. Esteban wanted him to get to the point, but the crystal meth in Tomás's brain kept his story running through a mouse maze of incidental detail and collateral anecdotes.

Finally the story came to the end. They had seen Martin in the custody of a park ranger.

Esteban looked at them for a long time. Chino squirmed in the vinyl booth.

"Sorry, man."

Finally Esteban spoke.

"Where did they take him?"

Tomás and Chino exchanged a look.

"We don't know."

They started to say more, but Esteban silenced them with a look and pulled out a cell phone. He dialed a number, spoke rapidly into the phone, and then hung up. He turned and looked at the Ramirez brothers. Chino hesitated, then took a rolled dollar bill and snorted a line of speed.

The beers arrived.

Esteban squeezed some lime into his and sipped it. Tomás did a line of speed. He offered the rolled bill to Esteban.

"No. *Gracias.*"

The three men sat there, no one saying a word. Esteban was calm, *curado como un pepino,* while the two brothers were grinding their teeth, trying hard not to talk. Drinking their beers too quickly.

Esteban's cell phone rang.

"*Bueno.*"

He listened for a beat and then folded it shut.

"He is in the hospital. In Palm Springs."

Tomás and Chino exchanged looks. Finally, Chino spoke.

"You want us to go out there?"

Esteban nodded.

"Sí."

Tomás blinked.

"Now?"

"*Sí, ahora.*"

Chino quickly attempted to scrape the leftover meth into a pile, but he got some lime juice mixed up in it and it turned into a gluey lump. Tomás shrugged, and with some sheepish speedy grins, the two brothers left the bar.

Esteban sighed and took a long pull on his beer. It was good that Martin was in the hospital and so far away. It would give him time to make arrangements.

Amado was enjoying himself. Somehow, writing the script was like watching the show. Only this time Amado could have the characters do what he wanted them to do. What he thought they should really do. Like having Fernando kick the padre's ass for fucking Gloria. In Amado's version of the *telenovela,* the passions weren't hidden, they were worn on the sleeves. The characters shouted. They lived. They loved. They fought like maniacs.

If only the *chingado teléfono* would stop ringing and he could finish this sentence.

Amado had to admit he was curious. He wondered what the hell was going on. But he knew that Esteban could take care of himself. He just needed to remember how. Amado smiled to himself. Now maybe El Jefe would understand how much Amado had done for him. His efforts would be appreciated in hindsight. While Esteban had lounged around the pool or cruised the streets with his gringo, Amado had been working. Esteban had grown soft, while Amado had stayed hard and hungry. It would be good for El Jefe.

Amado struggled as he wrote, his one hand not able to type as fast as his brain thought or his characters spoke. But he stayed concentrated and, as the day wore on, the page count mounted.

He was interrupted by a knock at the door.

If it was Esteban he'd smack him. Tell him to look down and see if he had any *cojones* left. But it wasn't Esteban. It was Cindy, her pink pigtails mounted on top of her head like antennae.

20

BOB PULLED UP the gated drive to Esteban's house. He couldn't believe how nice it was. Palm trees and flowers, a manicured lawn. The house itself was an ornate Spanish colonial structure painted hacienda red with stark white trim. It was a big house. Impressive. A gardener was clipping the hedge while another swept up grass cuttings. They didn't use the gas-powered leaf blowers that swarmed around Los Angeles like a hive of angry wasps. People with money could afford to have their gardeners use a push broom.

It was peaceful. The sun glinted through the palm trees, a mosaic fountain gurgled by the front steps, birds chirped in the trees, and the soft and steady sound of a broom on asphalt took him to another time, another place.

Lupe opened the carved wooden doors to let Bob in. The interior was furnished in a kind of Mexican moderne style. Simple, light. The walls painted deep rich colors.

Bob was impressed.

Lupe turned to him.

"He'll be down in a minute. Would you like a drink?"

"A beer would be great."

"*Claro.* Just have a seat."

Lupe went off.

Bob stood and looked out the large windows at the Jacuzzi and the pool beyond it. The garden in the backyard was even more extensive than what he'd seen in the front. There were several jacaranda trees, a rose bed, and wild-looking clumps of Mexican sage and rosemary growing down the side of a hill.

Esteban entered the room and cleared his throat. Bob turned toward him.

"Roberto."

"Hi."

Esteban came up and gave Bob a big hug.

"I am glad to see you are alive."

"Me too."

Esteban was wearing an elegant tan-colored suit, with a white shirt and a purple floral tie. Bob thought he was dressed like some kind of Latin American factory owner. The clothes looked good on him. Bob felt a little awkward in his jeans, T-shirt, with a funky bowling shirt on the outside. Esteban looked at Bob with a serious expression.

"Roberto, the next time someone tries to kill you like that, you cannot let them live. *¿Entiendes?*"

Bob nodded.

Lupe entered, carrying a couple of beers on a tray. Esteban kissed her tenderly on the cheek.

"*Gracias, corazón.*"

Lupe smiled at Bob and left.

"I think I'm going to marry that woman."

Bob grinned.

"I've been thinking that about Felicia."

Esteban handed Bob a beer and smiled.

"*Qué bueno. ¡A su boda!*"

They clinked the bottles together.

Bob took a swig of the icy *cerveza*.

"What are we going to do about Martin?"

"It's taken care of."

Esteban sat down on the sofa; Bob followed his lead and took a seat opposite him.

"Why did he want to kill me?"

"Perhaps because you are loyal."

Bob thought about that. Martin didn't seem the type, but then what did Bob know about corporate politics? He'd always stayed under the radar, able to steal paper clips or goof around with impunity.

"He's trying to take over."

Bob was surprised.

"Really?"

"He gave Amado's arm to the police. He killed Norberto. He tried to kill you."

Bob was stunned.

"Norberto's dead?"

Esteban nodded.

"Listen, Roberto, there are many people who would like to see me dead as well. People who would like to take over my business. I think Martin was working with some of them. I am going to need your help."

"What can I do?"

Bob was afraid that Esteban would ask him to go kill a bunch of people. Bob knew that he could've killed Martin, that he should've killed Martin, but that was different. Self-defense. Bob was not so sure that he could go around whacking Esteban's enemies. It was too cold-blooded. Too calculated. It wasn't what Bob wanted to do. He could never be like Amado.

"I'm not a hit man."

Esteban laughed.

"I know, Roberto. I don't need a hit man, *sabes*? I need someone I can trust."

Esteban looked him in the eye.

"Can I trust you?"

Bob nodded.

"Absolutely."

Esteban slapped his knees and stood.

"*Vale,* we've got work to do, we don't have much time."

Martin lay in the hospital bed. He was feeling good. Very good now that he'd found the little plastic dial thing that controlled the Demerol dripping into his veins. He loved how the Demerol rolled into his brain like waves. Whoosh. It hit with a mild rush and then kind of receded until . . . whoosh. One after the other, taking him deeper and deeper into a dreamy kind of trance.

He wondered if he could overdose on it.

The fat sheriff sat on the bed eating a double cheeseburger and supersized fries from some fast-food joint. Martin had watched, curious and horrified, as the sheriff had dumped the fries into the bag, then sprinkled in two packets of salt before rolling the bag closed and vigorously shaking it like a giant oily maraca. The sound was not soothing. Martin hit the dial.

Big grease spots pocked the sides of the brightly colored bag, as the sheriff dipped his hands in and pulled out clumps of glistening fries. The sheriff was saying something, Martin wasn't sure what, but the sheriff's voice was irritating. Not the sound of it, but that kind of condescending cadence that authority figures liked to use when they were talking to you. The more he blabbed, the more Martin flicked the dial on the drip.

He wished he'd had this IV drip all the time. Someone annoys you, flick the dial. Traffic's backed up and there's only commercials on the fucking radio, dial this in. Yeah. A Demerol drip could greatly improve your quality of life.

Amado sat in bed, the covers tangled around him, and watched as Cindy read his script. He had to admit he was nervous. Giddy because he'd finished his first draft, and proud because he felt that he'd actually accomplished something. He couldn't remember a time in his life when he'd had an idea, sat down, and just done it. From start to finish. Sure, he'd been given orders and carried them out. Start by finding someone, finish by burying them in some field. But that was different. It didn't take a lot of brains to do something like that. It wasn't personal. He'd never gotten emotionally invested in the day-to-day business of organized crime. He'd been going along with it because it was easy and the money was good.

But it was an empty experience.

Amado found that having characters live and breathe through his imagination, putting raw emotions on blank paper, inventing a story that was compelling, a story that just had to be told, these things were fulfilling. He felt good about himself. It wasn't easy, but he loved writing.

He was also strangely nervous and giddy about Cindy. She was different from the women he was used to. For one, she was petite, small and slender, not the usual voluptuous Latina with a great heaving rack. He could easily cup Cindy's small breasts in the palm of his hand. She had just the faintest wisp of pubic hair. Her hips and ass were slightly flat, almost like a boy's. But Amado was crazy about her.

It dawned on him that maybe what he found so compelling and sexy about Cindy was not her body but her brain, her personality. She was smart and funny and unlike anyone he'd ever met before. She was interested in things: People, places, ideas, words. She was curious. And she wasn't afraid.

He watched as she paged through his script, her interest

and delight in everything. She was so beautiful, her pink pig-tails in post-sex disarray, her surprisingly strong body laying brazen and naked on top of the covers.

"Amado, I don't read Spanish."

Amado smiled.

"You want me to read it to you? To translate it?"

"Yeah."

She squirmed under the covers, like a little kid about to be tucked in.

Amado began to read.

Maura sat in an extremely uncomfortable chair next to Don's desk. She amused herself by leafing through a catalogue of law-enforcement equipment. Holsters, handcuffs, Tasers, pepper spray, Kevlar vests, all kinds of cool stuff. Even the different styles of shoes appealed to her. She was going to ask Don if you had to be a police officer to order from this catalogue, or if you could just be a normal citizen. It would be fun to dress up like a policewoman and handcuff Don to the bed. Maybe with these cool plastic cuffs; strong, light, and affordable. Perfect for civil unrest. And if Don felt uncomfortable about using firearms in bed, maybe this nightstick would be the ticket.

Don hung up the phone and turned to her.

"I've got a question for you."

"Yeah?"

"How well do you know your ex-boyfriend?"

Maura thought about it for a second. She knew Bob as well as you could know someone. They'd been intimate. They'd shared their hopes and dreams. But then they'd never been as intimate as she and Don had. It was a difficult question.

"Why?"

"Well, I've got two severed arms. One is unidentified. The

prints on it don't match any in our existing database. Although I'm sure if the body of a one-armed gangbanger showed up I'd find a match.

"The other belonged to Max Larga. Your ex, Bob, delivered Larga's arm. Larga was a client of yours. Larga was supposed to see you, but Bob came in and saw you instead. Yet Larga's car was parked by your office."

Maura stared at him, blankly.

"I don't follow."

"Let's assume that Larga wasn't involved in a crime, that he didn't have anything to do with the Mexican mafia."

"So what did Bob have to do with it?"

"That's what I want to know."

Maura shrugged.

"I honestly don't know. But I don't think Bob was mixed up with any mafia types. I mean, I can't imagine it."

Don fixed his serious, I've-got-bad-news expression on his face.

"You may not like this, but I'm starting to think that Bob had something to do with Larga's disappearance."

Maura burst out laughing.

"Cool."

"Cool?"

Maura tried to contain herself.

"It's just, well, it's just that if you knew Bob . . . it's unbelievable. If he really did, well, wouldn't that be cool?"

Don started to say something, then caught himself and heaved a sigh.

"Let's go try and find him."

Maura jumped up.

"Cool."

Bob and Esteban had just finished signing the last of the signature cards. The bank manager, a reedy-looking dude in a fancy suit, smiled at them.

"Thank you very much."

Esteban nodded.

"The money will be wired into this account by the end of business today."

"Excellent. And with a sum that large, might I suggest some investments that will not only protect it but allow it to compound and grow at a rate well above what you normally get with a savings program?"

Bob looked at Esteban.

"What do you think?"

Esteban smiled at Bob.

"Why don't you decide, Roberto? Take the man's card and talk to him about it tomorrow."

Bob had the manager's card in his hands before he could blink.

"Thanks."

"Call me anytime, Roberto. My home number is on the back."

Esteban stood. Bob followed his lead.

"I'll call you tomorrow."

The men all shook hands. Bob followed Esteban to the door. He spoke quietly to Esteban.

"I didn't know banks were so nice."

"You never opened an account with twenty million dollars."

The gunshot jolted Martin awake. It was followed by a couple of other gunshots, crashing sounds, some screaming. Martin tried to move his head, he wanted to see what was going on.

But he was just too stoned. He knew, deep in his brain somewhere, that he should probably be scared. But his face held a
dreamy Demerol grin, as if what he was watching was amusing.

A big blurry figure, it must be the sheriff, crossed the edge
of the bed firing a pistol. Man, was that thing loud. Martin
could feel his arms and legs twitching involuntarily with each
report. There were a lot of shots now, and Martin felt like he
was doing some kind of cool new dance. Like something the
kids on MTV might be doing. Strapped down an' twitchin'.

Martin felt his face get splattered with something wet. For a
second he thought it was his own blood, that he'd been shot.
But the liquid was clear and kept raining down in a constant
stream. Martin turned his head toward the flow of fluids, and
saw that his IV drip had taken a hit.

Bummer.

They met Amado at a Japanese noodle place downtown. Esteban watched as Bob used his chopsticks to scoop fat noodles
out of a gigantic bowl of soup and noisily slurp them down.
Amado sat across the table with some kind of punk-rock girl.
Cindy Kim. Esteban thought that was *un poco raro.* Doesn't
she have a last name? Even Selena had a last name.

Esteban liked udon, but realized that it was necessary to
tuck a napkin in under his chin to keep the soup from splashing all over his suit. He wished they were eating something a
little less wet.

Amado slid a manila envelope across the table to Esteban.

"I need a favor."

Esteban grinned. They always do. They always come back
and beg you for something. That's the best part of being powerful. They always come back.

"I asked a favor from you."

Amado looked down at his soup.

"I'm sorry, Esteban. I'm just trying to make a change."

Esteban carefully ate some of the pork floating in the soup. Couldn't they have gotten *media noches* somewhere?

"I will need a favor in return."

"I can't do what I used to do."

Amado held out his one arm to demonstrate.

"I need two arms."

"I haven't asked you to do anything yet."

Esteban could see that it pained Amado to even have to ask this favor. Although part of him wanted to make sure that Amado understood he was still the boss, another part of him genuinely cared about Amado.

"Amado, you know I will help you."

Bob chimed in.

"We're family."

Esteban looked at Bob. He must've seen that in a movie or something, but the mention of family touched both of the men at the table. Amado turned to Cindy.

"We've been through a lot together."

Cindy just smiled. Esteban liked her. There was something about her. She was different than the other women Amado had been with. It signaled to him that Amado had made a change.

"I know you've got friends at Telemundo."

It was true. Esteban knew everyone.

"*Cierto.*"

"I've written a script for a *telenovela.*"

This took Esteban by surprise.

"*¿Qué?*"

"I wrote a script."

Cindy interjected.

"It's really good, too."

Bob looked at Amado.

"That's cool."

Esteban was still trying to process the information.

"You wrote a script?"

"*Sí.* And I want to know if you could get someone at the Telemundo to read it."

"*¿Tu eres un escritor?*"

Amado shrugged.

"*Un guionista. Sí.*"

Cindy looked at Amado.

"*¿Guionista?* What's that?"

"Scriptwriter."

Esteban and Amado locked eyes.

"Of course I will help. *Seguro.*"

"*Gracias,* Esteban. *Muchas gracias.*"

"*De nada, amigo.*"

Esteban looked over at Bob, Amado followed his look.

"I have a few things to clear up and then I'm going back to Mexico for a while. Roberto is going to look after things."

Amado shot Esteban a look.

"Roberto?"

Esteban nodded.

"The favor I ask is that you watch out for him while I'm gone."

Bob nodded.

"I might need, you know, a mentor or something."

Amado smiled.

"I will always help Roberto. We are family."

Thick smoke swirled around the ventilator as the air conditioning blew into the room. The smell of cordite hung in the air and assaulted Martin's nose. It was stronger than any smelling salt and smacked him right out of his stupor. There were now lots of people in the room. Doctors, a few nurses, many police-men. One of the nurses was fixing the IV bag. That was a relief.

She said something to him about the dosage controller being damaged, but such technical terms didn't matter as long as the narcotics kept flowing. The sheriff, his arm being ban-daged by one of the doctors, turned to Martin.

"Do you recognize this man?"

Martin didn't see anybody.

"Who?"

"The dead guy on the floor."

Martin craned his neck. It was a horrible fucking mess. Bro-ken glass, splintered wood, crap everywhere, and there, sprawled in a pool of blood, was Tomás Ramirez, as dead as a doornail.

Martin nodded.

"Yeah."

Martin laid his head back down on the pillow.

The sheriff jumped up and screamed at Martin.

"Who the fuck is it? Huh? Gimme a name, asshole!"

The sheriff was, apparently, a little testy from the recent gun battle. He could use a nice, relaxing Demerol drip. But then, who couldn't?

Martin found the little dial and cranked it. *I don't need this aggravation.*

"Don't yell, man."

Martin watched as the sheriff's face went through a few color changes.

"I'm sorry I yelled."

Martin suddenly felt good. The warm waves of Demerol were back stronger and better than ever. But the situation had changed. He had credibility. A little juice.

"You didn't believe me. You thought I was just some loser drug dealer in the desert."

Several other policemen looked at the sheriff.

"I'm sorry. Okay?"

Martin didn't think it was okay.

"You didn't take me seriously. Why should I talk to you?"

"I'll take you seriously now."

"Too late."

The sheriff moved to smack Martin, but his wound or whatever it was suddenly caused him great pain. He moaned and collapsed in a chair.

"Who do you want me to call?"

Martin thought about that. *Call the president. Or better, call that rock star guy who's always doing things to help political prisoners. I'm a political prisoner.*

"I want to make a deal. I want immunity."

"Then you'd better tell me who you want to talk to."

Martin liked that. The sheriff wasn't important enough to talk to. Now everyone knew it. Martin was important. He was a big-deal criminal. A political prisoner. Soon there would be concerts at Dodger Stadium to raise money for his defense fund, to raise awareness of his plight.

"The dead guy's name is Tomás Ramirez. Call the LAPD. They'll know who to send."

Martin cranked the Demerol dial. He saw Dodger Stadium, filled with thousands of people, all of them wearing T-shirts with his picture on it. Freedom for Martin! Freedom! A band hit the stage amid flashing lasers and lots of smoke. The lead singer, his hair perfect, his sunglasses still on, pumped his fist in the air and started the chant. "Free Martin! Free Martin!"

Maybe they'd let him sing on their next CD.

Chino Ramirez tied his blue bandanna around his wrist as tight as he could, using his teeth and his good arm to pull it. He had lost some blood, but not too much. He got out of his car and hustled over to the pay phone as quickly as he could. He knew he had about twenty minutes to either ditch the car or get the hell out of town, before the genius policemen would look at the hospital parking-lot security camera's videotape and see him walk out and drive off.

He dialed a number, waited for the beep, then punched in the number of the pay phone where he was. He hung up the phone and looked at his watch.

Chino kept his eyes scanning the road for any signs of police activity. As he did, he fumbled around in his pockets until he pulled out a folded square of paper. He'd need something to cut the pain once the initial shock wore off. He wished he had nailed that fucking cop. Who knew that Martin would be guarded by some kind of psycho jarhead? They'd come in, stolen some threads to look like orderlies or whatever they were. Walked down the hall with a bucket and a mop. Nobody's ever going to bother a Latino with a bucket and a mop. You look like you belong.

They get to the room, pull their guns and move in real quick. Next thing they know some guy's got like twelve guns out and he's just emptying the clips at them. Chino didn't even get off a shot before he was back out the door and moving his ass as fast as he could down the hallway. He turned and saw Tomás take eight or nine hits before he went down. That's when he caught a ricochet in the wrist. Even though he was in a hospital and could've used a doctor, Chino *salió*. No point in hanging around for more pain.

The phone rang. Chino explained what had happened to Esteban.

Bob had watched Esteban as he talked on the phone with the producer from Telemundo. It seemed that Esteban had, once upon a time, arranged for some competitor of this guy to lose his green card and then just disappear. Now Esteban was calling in a favor.

So that was how it worked. People did favors for people and expected those favors to be returned someday. Everyone helps each other up the food chain.

Bob realized that he'd need a lot of favors from people, a lot of help. The banking end of it, moving money around, talking to investment bankers, that had all seemed pretty straightforward, pretty easy. The other part of it, laundering the money, moving it from the trunk of a car, letting it filter through a dummy corporation, a telemarketing business, the phony payroll of a nonexistent construction company, a chain of fish taco restaurants, and a boxing gym; that part seemed too complicated. Wouldn't it be easier to just declare it as money earned doing something in Mexico? Then you could pay the taxes, and call it a day. Esteban had already built up a phony reputation as a papaya farmer. Why not say the money was from papayas? Why not actually buy a papaya plantation?

Esteban made another call, this time to a friend who would manufacture a fake identity for Bob. He'd get a U.S. passport, driver's license, social security card, everything. Esteban turned to Bob and asked him what he wanted to be called. Bob liked the name Roberto, but didn't really know what to use for a last name. Esteban suggested 'Durán,' that way Roberto could say his name was 'Roberto Durán', like the boxer. Everyone would remember that.

Bob liked that. Maybe he'd go to the boxing gym and take some lessons.

Get in shape.

The third call Esteban made was not a good one. He was returning a page. Bob heard Esteban's voice fall, then become short, curt, explosive bursts of questions.

Esteban hung up and turned to Bob. They had work to do.

Don watched as the kid behind the counter cut some clumps of bright green grass and shoved them through a juicer. A liquid that looked more like an industrial cleaner than a health panacea leaked out into a funnel. How could she drink that stuff? Don had ordered something a little more, well, tasty. He'd gotten one of those giant fruit smoothies. The kind that give you repeated brain freezes and taste like Styrofoam by the time you get to the bottom of the massive cup. He watched as Maura knocked back the shot of wheatgrass juice in one gulp. He shuddered.

But then Maura did lots of things that made Don shudder. Like having sex while holding a loaded gun. What was up with that? She had told him it gave her power, it was her *axis mundi*, a talisman, a fetish object. Don just thought it was a loaded fucking gun that could accidentally go off. It wasn't fun. It wasn't sexy. It was scary. Like wheatgrass juice.

His cell phone rang, and much to Don's surprise he found Detective Flores on the other end. Flores told him about some guy who had turned up staggering around in the desert and was now in a hospital in Palm Springs. Don figured Flores was just too lazy to get in his car and drive out there, so he was dumping it on him. But when Flores mentioned that one of the Ramirez brothers had been killed trying to get to the guy, well, Don couldn't wait to go. Whatever was going on in Sola's crime crew, it was big. If Esteban had to send the Ramirez brothers all the way to Palm Springs to whack some guy, well, maybe this guy had something to say about it.

Don wanted to get to Palm Springs fast, before Esteban
sent someone else to finish what the Ramirez brothers had
started. In fact, he didn't even stop to drop Maura back at her
office. She was just going to have to park that sweet
wheatgrass-drinkin' ass in the car and ride out with him.
Which, as it turned out, was fine with her.

Bob entered the house and found Felicia standing on a ladder
painting flowers along the top of the wall. She turned and
looked at him. It was the kind of look that everyone hopes for
when they come home. Her face lit up, her eyes twinkled, a
laugh escaped from her body, and her smile was the best thing
Bob had ever seen in his life.

"*Hola, corazón.*"

"Hi, sweetie."

Bob came up to her and wrapped his arms around her
waist. He gently lifted her off the ladder and set her down so
he could look into her eyes and kiss her sweetly on the lips.

"I'm making *pozole.*"

Bob didn't know what to say. For a brief second he wondered
why, when it was like ninety degrees out, he was going to be having hot soup twice in one day, but that thought quickly passed.

"I have to go to Palm Springs."

"For how long?"

"Just for the night. I'll be back tomorrow."

Felicia's smiled turned into a pout.

"I don't like it, Roberto. *No me gusta.*"

Bob was afraid that she'd react this way. It's so hard to bal-
ance a career and a relationship these days.

"But Felicia, honey, it's my job."

"You should get another job. I don't want to make love to a
killer."

Bob laughed.

"I'm not a killer."

Felicia wasn't convinced.

"Isn't that what you do for Esteban?"

"No."

"No?"

"I haven't killed anyone. I mean, I hit a guy on the head with a shovel, but I kinda had to and it didn't kill him."

"Really? You're telling me the truth?"

"Yes. Absolutely. Do I look like a killer?"

Felicia laughed.

"Honestly, no. But that's what I thought made you a good killer, because you didn't look like one."

"I'm not a killer."

Bob could see the smile return to Felicia's face. But just as her grin was starting to light up the room, it shorted out.

"Then what do you do for Esteban?"

"Well. I don't know. I'm kinda new. Right now he just wants me to look after his money, keep the business running. I guess I'm an executive or something."

"An executive?"

"I guess that's what you'd call it."

Felicia bit her lip.

"Do you know how to manage?"

Bob grinned.

"I'm learning."

Amado sat in bed, just wearing an old cotton robe. He had his laptop on his lap, and he balanced a cold beer on a fat Spanish dictionary that lay in the middle of the bed. Cindy's beer was next to his. She sat on the other side of the bed wearing a tattered Fugazi T-shirt. She had her laptop open too.

Amado looked up from his work. He looked at Cindy and realized that for the first time in his life he felt content. He wasn't working in the fields, he wasn't stealing a car or hijacking a truck. He wasn't carting narcotics from a van to a storage unit somewhere. He didn't have to go hunt someone down and kill them. He didn't have to clean up any bone chips and guts. And best of all, nobody was going to try to kill him for sitting in bed wearing his robe and writing. He was safe. He was content.

Cindy didn't look up from her work. She was concentrating. Amado smiled to himself and got back to work.

The only sound was the clicker-clacking of laptop keys and the occasional soft belch.

They both had a lot to write about.

21

ON HAD TO think of something. He couldn't very well tell the sheriff that he had brought his girlfriend along for the ride. So he told him that Maura was an assistant district attorney. The sheriff bought that without blinking, perhaps because he was admiring Maura's cleavage, and proceeded to tell Don and Maura about his day.

He took them down to the morgue to identify Tomás Ramirez's body. Don didn't want Maura to see something so gruesome, but there she was, standing right next to him as the sheriff pulled the sheet back and showed how he'd hit Ramirez in the torso nine times. Each bullet hole was neatly circled with a red marking pen, not that you'd miss them; they were black, nasty-looking wounds. The sheriff was proud of his work, his only regret was that he hadn't dropped the second one, but that guy hightailed it out of there like a scared jackrabbit.

Don felt like asking about the twenty-four shell casings found on the hospital-room floor. If nine bullets went into Ramirez, where'd the other fifteen end up? Ramirez's gun had been fired once, a shot which had managed to hit the sheriff in the arm, and that shell had been found in the hallway.

Don watched as Maura asked the sheriff lots of questions about the kind of guns he used, how he liked them, and which gun had landed the most shots on target. For a vegetarian, she sure liked guns.

Don interrupted the impromptu gun seminar and asked the sheriff if he could see the suspect. He wanted to get his statement as soon as possible.

Esteban drove. Every now and then he'd look over and see Bob fidgeting, looking out the window. It reminded Esteban of himself when he was young. All the excitement, the nervous energy. The great people he'd met. Like everything in life there were some bad moments, some close calls. But, all in all, it had been a fun ride. They'd worked hard and played hard. Now, after twenty-some years of it, Esteban realized that he was tired. Tired of maintaining the tough-guy facade that used to come so naturally for him. Perhaps the money, the cars, the women, the lifestyle had softened him. Amado had warned him. Amado, despite all the money he'd socked away over the years, continued to live in a modest apartment in the barrio. He drove a dirty Ford Taurus. He ate at taco stands and drank in local bars. Amado had never gone far from his *trabajadores* roots. He was a *tipo*. A normal guy.

But then that enhanced Amado's *onda*. He was *misterioso*. A samurai. It gave him an edge. People thought of Amado as dangerous. They thought of Esteban as dangerous, too. But in a different way. Esteban was a shogun, a warlord, a businessman. It was not about who he was on the inside.

When he thought about it too much, he had to laugh. Being a gangster is such a superficial thing.

Bob rolled down the window and sucked in a big gulp of air.

"You okay, Roberto?"

"Yeah. I'm fine."

"Nervous?"

"Yeah."

"You'll be fine."

Bob didn't say anything for a minute.

"Esteban? Can I ask you something?"

"Claro."

"I wouldn't normally bring this up, but how much are you paying me?"

"You want to know what you are worth to me?"

Bob nodded.

"Sí. Exacto."

Esteban smiled.

"Muy bien, Roberto. *Tu hablas español."*

"I'm learning."

"Qué bueno."

Esteban had to grin.

"How much do you think you should make?"

Esteban watched as Bob thought about it.

"I'll be honest with you, Esteban, I don't know what the going rate is for . . . you know, whatever it is I do."

"You will make a lot of money Roberto. But I will give you some advice. If you take the money and spend it, the tax people will find you, the police will find you, the federales will find you. You can't go spend the money."

"So what do you do with the money?"

"You put it away. In a box in a bank, or in a business somewhere."

Bob nodded.

"That's why you own all those businesses."

Esteban nodded.

"Exacto."

They rode in silence for a minute.

"So, like, how much will I make?"

Esteban suddenly pulled the car off the main road and

turned down a dirt side road that went out straight into the middle of nowhere.

Martin rolled his head over to see what was going on. Man, did his head feel heavy; he might not be able to roll it back. He saw the fat sheriff lead a guy and some woman into the room. The guy was obviously some kind of detective. He had that air of importance, an earnestness that those fuckers always had. It went along with his fried-food-damaged tough-guy looks. In fact, the detective looked kind of like an actor from a TV show. The sports coat, the striped tie, the let's-get-down-to-business voice. He was saying something about how the woman was a district attorney or something. Wow. She had big tits for a lawyer.

Martin said something.

The woman with the big tits nodded. The detective put a small tape recorder on the bed and flicked it on.

Martin concentrated. *I need to tell them something.*

"Immunity. I want immunity from prosecution."

That came out well.

The woman nodded, her boobs heaving as she spoke. They looked real, too. Man, you could just get lost in them.

The detective turned off the tape recorder, or maybe he turned it on. It was hard to tell. He then turned to Martin and started asking questions.

"What is your full and legal name?"

As if that were somehow important? It dawned on Martin that this was going to be a long and tedious process. He couldn't just blab about how he knew this or that, there was a method to this, bureaucratic bullshit to adhere to. It was going to be dull, dull, dull. Impossibly dull.

Martin decided to make a game of it. Every time he

answered a question, he got to tweak his Demerol drip and give himself a little reward. Like a laboratory rat.

Martin gave his full legal name.

It felt good.

Bob was sweating. He loosened the tie on the suit that Esteban had lent him. Bob couldn't remember the last time he wore a suit, but man were they hot. He knew he shouldn't have asked about money. Nobody likes a pushy employee. Now here they were, bouncing down a dirt road in the middle of the fucking desert at night. The last time this happened, Martin had tried to kill him. Bob considered opening the door and jumping out, kind of like they do in the movies. He'd roll in the dirt, jump to his feet, and then sprint off across the rocky terrain. The night would become his friend. He'd disappear into its dark embrace.

He looked out the window and saw nothing but pain flying by in the glare of the headlights. Rocks, broken glass, cacti, and barbed-wire fences. He turned to Esteban.

"Where are we going?"

Esteban smiled at him.

"Don't be nervous."

"Well, I know this isn't the way to Palm Springs."

Esteban laughed.

"You need some practice, Roberto."

"I was just asking."

Esteban laughed some more.

"It never hurts to ask."

"You will get paid *mucho,* Roberto. Don't worry. If you need a number I will say two hundred thousand dollars a year."

Bob couldn't believe it.

"Really?"

"You will make much more, my friend."

Bob didn't know what to say. The most he'd ever made was the thirty-five grand a year he pulled down at the pathology lab, and he thought that was living large.

Esteban pulled the car to a stop and got out.

"*Vale*, Roberto."

Bob climbed out of the car and looked around. You sure could see a lot of stars at night in the desert. Behind him were the mountains, black now, just a couple of radio towers shining their little red warning lights from the peak. Off to the east he saw a distant glow. That must be Palm Springs.

Esteban popped open the trunk and took out a toolbox. Bob watched as he opened the toolbox. There were screwdrivers, a ratchet, a few wire cutters. Esteban lifted the top tray out to reveal a bottom section filled with rags. He carefully picked up one of the rags and handed it to Bob.

"Be careful."

The rag was surprisingly heavy. Bob knew instantly what he was holding. It was a gun. A big, serious gun.

"What's this for?"

Esteban was loading rounds of ammunition into a clip. He turned and looked at Bob.

"Emergencies."

Using the car's headlights, Bob studied the gun's mechanisms.

"Don't look. You need to learn to do this by feel."

Esteban handed Bob a clip and began to teach him how to load and unload the gun. Bob was surprised at how easy it was. No wonder little kids got their dad's guns and took them to school. A monkey could operate one of these.

"Try shooting."

"What should I shoot?"

"It doesn't matter. How about that tree?"

Bob thought Joshua trees were somehow special. He didn't want to shoot one.

"No. Something else?"

"Why not the tree?"

"That's a Joshua tree."

"Roberto? So what?"

"I just don't want to. Okay?"

Esteban sighed and pulled a bottle of windshield-wiper fluid out of the trunk. He walked about twenty feet away and balanced the bottle on a rock.

"*¿Mejor?*"

"Yes. *Sí.* Thank you."

Bob took aim at the bottle and squeezed the trigger. The gun jumped in his hand like an electrocuted cat.

"Did I hit it?"

"It's still there."

Bob tried again. And again. Esteban offered some advice. Relax. Breathe out, hold it, squeeze. It didn't seem to help.

"Maybe it's the gun."

Esteban calmly took the gun from him, turned, and blasted the bottle of windshield-wiper fluid. Bob could smell faint traces of ammonia in the air.

"I guess it's not the gun."

Esteban handed him the gun back.

"Don't worry, Roberto. Just do the best you can. Pull the trigger a lot. Maybe you'll get lucky. At the very least you'll make a lot of noise and scare people."

Bob looked at his feet. He felt humiliated, embarrassed.

"Do I still get the job?"

Esteban smiled at him.

"*Claro,* Roberto. You are the man."

"I should probably learn to shoot better. Maybe I can take some lessons."

Esteban closed the trunk and got back in the car.

"That's a good idea."

Maura couldn't believe how cool it all was. First she got to see a dead guy, all shot up and stiff in one of those giant steel refrigerators. Now she was interviewing the consigliere to the Mexican mob. At least that's what the guy was trying to say. He was a little out of it. He'd mumble on about bank accounts and businesses, switching to small personal details about how much lime you need to put in someone named Esteban's margarita. Esteban was the godfather. That's what Don had said. Then the guy would switch topics and start complaining bitterly about being stuck with fake breasts, while Esteban got the real ones. Maura didn't understand that. Did organized crime members have implants? Maybe it was some kind of criminal slang.

Maura thought Don looked very sexy in his role as police detective. He had an intensity, like he was really concentrating, as he listened to the disjointed diatribe. Sometimes he'd gently pull the information out of the guy, other times he'd ask questions that would make the perp cry. Like when Don asked the perp about his parents. Man, turn on the waterworks.

You'd think a member to the mob would suck it up, say nothing, be a hard-ass. But here was the perp, bawling like a baby. Perp. Maura liked saying that. Maura hoped Don would interview her in the hotel room later that night. They could make a little game of it.

Don pressed the perp for information about the other members of the crew. He answered with a rambling tirade— he seemed to get more and more out of it as the interview progressed—about someone named Roberto. How this Roberto was really dangerous. How Roberto looked meek and mild but was taking over everything. Blood was going to flow through the streets of Los Angeles and it was all because of Roberto.

She saw Don perk up as Martin told him how Roberto was behind all the severed arms showing up. Maura shuddered. Some cracked sociopath running wild in the streets, hacking off limbs and sending them to the police. It was crazy. Like something out of Batman. This Roberto had to be stopped.

Bob got out of the car and followed Esteban into the hospital. The gun was wedged into the back of his pants, his suit jacket covering it. It was big, hard, and not at all comfortable. *Maybe that's a good thing. This way I'll know it's there.*

Bob's nerves were getting all jangly, his breathing shallow and rapid. He was nervous. Not scared, he thought he'd be petrified, but it was more like a sensation in his muscles, a readiness. A tension. Like a steel trap ready to snap shut. It felt good. Exciting. He was jazzed, juiced, and ready.

Bob couldn't help but marvel at his transformation. A week ago he'd been a slacker cyber-surfer; today he had a new name, a tattoo on his arm, and a gun wedged down the crack of his ass. He was Roberto Durán. He was going to speak Spanish. He was going to help his boss kill a rat. Which, actually, when he thought about it, made him feel slightly queasy. But Esteban had assured him that the actual murdering part he would handle himself. Bob would stand lookout. Be ready for any contingencies should something go wrong with the plan.

Of course, as Bob saw it, Esteban didn't have much of a plan. They were going to walk in and act like criminal defense lawyers. Tell the guard on duty—there would surely be a guard after the Ramirez brothers fiasco—that they needed to speak to their client alone and then Esteban would hold a pillow over Martin's head until he stopped breathing. Esteban even pulled out an official-looking briefcase to add authenticity. Attention to detail. It was admirable.

Martin was feeling no pain. He'd answered a shitload of questions and now had an equal amount of Demerol coursing through his bloodstream. He was having trouble keeping his eyes open. Besides, it was annoying when they were open. The lights were too bright. What were they thinking? Were they shining them at him on purpose? When he did open his eyes the left one would drift off one way and the right one would drift another. It caused him to feel seasick. Or was that the drug?

If he tried really hard he could focus. Sometimes he'd focus on the question being asked. For example: How much cocaine was carried across the border each week? Martin didn't like that question. He tried to tell the detective about the coyotes. It was difficult at first. The lawyer with the massive knockers kept talking about Griffith Park. Martin had to be rude. He had to tell her to shut up and take off her top. She didn't like that. But Martin didn't care, he wanted to see her breasts. She gave him a snarly look instead and sat down on the other side of the room.

Martin grimaced, swallowed, and explained that people called coyotes, because coyotes are allegedly fast and wily, carried the stuff over the border. So the question, if it really was a question, should be rephrased. What the detective should ask is: How much coke can a coyote tote if a coyote could tote coke?

Say that fast five times.

He made the detective say it. As the detective was struggling with the tongue-twister, things got kind of weird. Martin had just given himself a generous blast of the drip, the big dripper he'd nicknamed it, when Esteban and that fucking Bob, sorry . . . Roberto, entered the room. Martin saw the detective and Maura both look like they'd just shit their pants. But no one was yelling, and it didn't seem like any guns were drawn. Martin couldn't understand how they got in. Wasn't that fat fuck standing guard?

Martin saw Esteban looking at him. He heard the detective rattling on about something. It was getting tense in the room. Maura was saying something to that fucker, Roberto. Everybody was trying to say something. They were all a bunch of fucking tough guys.

It was killing his buzz.

Martin rolled his hand over and wedged the Demerol drip dial between the strap on his arm and the raised metal thingy on the bed. He jammed it in there good, so it would stay open. He immediately felt warm and fuzzy all over. The waves began crashing in on his brain more frequently. Like there was a hurricane somewhere near Hawaii and the waves in California were picking up the beat. The slow and steady drip of the Demerol turned into a drizzle, then a shower, then a torrential thunderstorm. Let it rain, let it rain, let it rain. His buzz was back with a stinger.

Martin reminded himself to breathe.

He heard a loud crack. Maybe someone shot someone. Then another. Oh, yeah. Someone shot someone. Martin thought about opening his eyes, but it just didn't seem worth the effort.

And then he experienced something he'd never experienced before. He'd been close. He'd walked the razor's edge. But he'd never gone over until now.

He was too high.

———

Don was happy. He'd just loaded in a third microcassette. The guy was delirious, half of what he said was just bizarre, unusable, the other half was great stuff. Details about shipments, bank accounts, and the infrastructure of the crew's operations. If even a tenth of this information panned out, Esteban would be spending a long time behind bars and Don might get to run a task force or something. There's lots of overtime in task force operations. Overtime pay plus a raise.

Don looked over at Maura. She had been pouting ever since the guy had asked her to take off her shirt. Don couldn't blame her, it was rude of the guy, but Don didn't have time to comfort her. He wanted to get as much out of the guy as he could, and if that meant humoring him, repeating tongue-twisters or taking off your shirt . . . well? What's the harm in that? The end justifies the means.

Don heard the door open, he assumed it would be the sheriff, but when he looked up he was shocked to see Esteban Sola in the flesh. Esteban muttered something about being a lawyer and handed Don a business card as he asked for a consult with his client. Don had to admit it was convincing and if the sheriff were sitting in this room instead of him, he'd probably have left the guy alone with Esteban. Of course when he came back, the guy would be dead. But he wasn't the sheriff. He wasn't some flunky sent out to write a report. He was the lead detective on this particular case. A member of the LAPD's Criminal Intelligence Division. He had looked at surveillance photos of Esteban for two years, had listened to hours of wiretaps, and had debriefed dozens of informants. He knew that Esteban was not a lawyer.

But then Don noticed that Maura's ex-boyfriend, Bob, was with Esteban. He'd remembered feeling that there was something hinky about Bob when he had him down at Parker Center. Now he knew why. There was a connection. Larga, Maura, Bob, Esteban, this guy here in the hospital . . . it was all starting to make sense. Not make sense in the way of actually understanding what had happened or how these people were all connected. That would come later. But the fact that they were connected, that was a victory for Don.

He felt good.

Then he heard the gunshots.

Bob watched as Esteban, smooth and suave, asked the nurse for directions to Martin's room. She pointed toward the elevators and Esteban thanked her. Esteban didn't say a word to Bob. He was in character and Bob didn't want to break his concentration. He just wanted to watch the master at work.

They got off the elevator and walked down the corridor toward Martin's room. It was the last one. It was easy to see which room it was, a fat sheriff sat on a folding metal chair next to the door. The sheriff was reading *People* magazine. He looked up when he saw Esteban and Bob coming toward him.

"Can I help you folks?"

Esteban handed him a business card.

"I've been retained by the parents."

The sheriff looked him up and down.

"This is my associate."

Bob stuck his hand out and shook the sheriff's.

"Hi."

The sheriff seemed reassured by Bob's presence.

"They're interviewing him now."

"Who?"

"The LAPD."

Esteban put on a sad, resigned expression.

"He was read his rights?"

The sheriff smiled.

"You betcha. Did it myself."

"Perhaps I should go in and consult with him in private. It's his constitutional right."

The sheriff nodded. He hated lawyers.

"Well, we wouldn't want to upset the founding fathers, would we?"

The sheriff opened the door.

Bob followed Esteban into the room. He saw Martin lying on the bed looking pale and sweaty with a big bandage on his head where Bob had whacked him with the shovel. Bob jumped a little when he saw the detective from Parker Center there. What a coincidence.

But what really knocked the wind out of him was when he saw Maura sitting in the corner.

"Bob?"

"Maura?"

No one said anything for what seemed like a week. Martin mumbled something.

"Fuckin' Roberto."

That's what it sounded like. But it was hard to tell.

Bob could feel his tie getting extremely tight, like he was choking. But Esteban didn't miss a beat.

"I've been hired to represent that man there."

He pointed to Martin.

"I would like to speak to him in private."

Maura stood up.

"Bob? What are you doing here?"

"He is my paralegal assistant. He's here to take notes."

Bob nodded.

"I'm here to take notes."

He looked at Maura.

"What are *you* doing here?"

Maura smiled at Bob.

"I'm the assistant district attorney."

Bob blinked.

"You're not a lawyer."

"You're not a paralegal."

Esteban interrupted them.

"It's my client's constitutional right to have a conference with his attorney."

Don smirked.

"I know who you are, and if you think I'm leaving you alone with a federal witness, you're mistaken."

Esteban persisted.

"I'm sorry. I don't know what you are talking about. I have been retained to represent my client."

Bob watched as the detective stood up and got in Esteban's face. The detective wore a kind of victorious smirk on his face. Bob was waiting for Esteban to wipe it off.

"Do you think I'm stupid? Do you think I don't know who you are? Do you honestly think I believe any of this? You're done, my friend. Your goose is cooked."

The detective was convincing. Bob felt like caving. Admitting everything and throwing himself on the mercy of the court. He looked to Esteban. Esteban wasn't about to yield to the detective's tactics.

"I just want you to realize that, if you persist with this wild accusation, anything this man says will not be allowed in court. You are not affording him his rights."

Maura interrupted.

"Bob? What's going on?"

Bob shrugged.

"I needed a second job. It costs a lot to move out. Set up a new apartment."

Esteban looked at Bob.

"She's my ex-girlfriend."

Esteban nodded.

"I have heard so much about you."

Bob didn't like that.

"Not that much. I don't talk about you that much."

The detective smiled at them.

"I just want you to know one thing."

Esteban looked at him.

"What is that?"

Don leaned close to Esteban, you could tell from the way he delivered his line that he really got off on saying it.

"You're under arrest."

But before Esteban could reply, he was interrupted by two gunshots from the hallway. The detective pulled his pistol out and leveled it at the door. Esteban stepped back out of the way. He shot a quick glance over at Bob. The glance said, relax. Wait.

Bob stepped away from the door, out of the detective's line of fire. The door burst open and Chino Ramirez stepped in, his gun pointed right at the detective.

No one moved.

Chino looked over at Esteban and Bob, surprised to see them here. He looked back at the detective.

"Drop it."

"You drop it."

The detective was calm.

"I am a police officer and I'm asking you to drop your weapon."

"No."

Bob realized he was watching a real old-fashioned Mexican

standoff. Chino wasn't going to put down his gun, the detective sure as hell wasn't, and there was nothing anyone could do.

Bob, whose arms and knees were actually trembling, looked across the room at Maura. She had a strange look in her eye.

Chino's eyes stayed glued to the detective. One twitch and he was going to pull the trigger. The detective's face was calm, too relaxed, like he did this every day.

And then.

The blast was painfully loud in the small room. Bob flinched. Chino was gone, blown out the door by the shot. Bob watched as the detective, a quizzical expression on his face, turned toward Maura. Bob saw Maura standing there with a smoking gun in her hands and an excited smile on her face.

"Did I get him?"

The detective turned toward Esteban.

"Don't fucking move."

Esteban put his hands up in the air. Bob followed his lead.

"Did I get him?"

The detective looked out in the hallway.

"Yeah. You got him."

Maura squealed.

"Yes!"

Maura ran to the door to take a look. Bob heard Esteban whisper.

"*Tranquilo*, Roberto. *Tranquilo*."

He felt Esteban's hand reach around under his jacket and remove the handgun. Esteban then slipped the gun into the detective's jacket that was hanging on the chair.

Bob turned his attention to Martin, who hadn't said much of anything for a while. Martin's face was white. His lips a bright blueberry blue. He wasn't breathing. In fact, he was very very dead.

"Esteban."

Esteban followed Bob's look. He broke into a wry grin. "You see, Roberto, sometimes God smiles on us."

Chino got out of his car and walked in through the loading dock in the back of the hospital. He knew that the police might be watching the front doors, and that they'd definitely be watching the door to the guy's room.

Chino felt bad that he'd failed Esteban. Esteban had provided for him and his brother. Had helped them come to LA. Set them up. Given them false green cards and lots of work. He'd given them something outside the scruffy dirtball life they'd had extorting and murdering in Mexico. Of course, they did the same things, you just got paid a lot better for it in the States.

He was halfway to Juarez, listening to some kind of motivational speaker on the car radio, when he realized that the voice coming out of the dashboard was right. What's the point of running from obstacles? There's no growth in that. If he wanted to be successful in business, and in life, he needed to face his difficulties and overcome them.

Besides, that fat fucker had killed his brother.

Chino decided he'd have to shoot his way in, hopefully killing that fat guy with all the guns, whack the rat, and then shoot his way out. He'd have to overcome the obstacles that kept him from realizing his full potential.

It was all pretty straightforward. He took the stairs, opened the door, and there was the fat guy reading a *People* magazine. Chino took out his gun, stepped out of the stairwell and put two bullets into the fat guy's heart before he even looked up.

The real surprise came when Chino threw open the door to the room. He'd expected a cop or two in there. But it was a fucking fiesta. Esteban, some guy who was with Esteban, a cop, and some *chica con pechos grandes*.

Chino quickly realized that he could turn this difficult situation into an opportunity. It wasn't a single hit anymore. Now he'd have to kill the cop, the chick, and maybe the other guy. That's four hits. He'd also do Esteban the favor of getting him out of a jam. *Hombre,* that motivational speaker guy was so right. Running from problems is never the answer.

Chino took aim at the detective. He figured if he could squeeze a shot off and hit the guy in the head, well, then he wouldn't have the muscle control or coordination to shoot back. He'd be dead.

He had the detective's forehead lined up when he heard the shot.

It wasn't like the movies, where the guy who gets shot looks around and then realizes he's been hit. That's bullshit. There is no mistaking a burning hot piece of metal ripping through your body at high speed.

Chino felt himself roll backward, his legs not working anymore, and fall out of the room. He landed with a splat. He couldn't tell if he'd landed in the fat guy's blood or his own blood.

It didn't matter. He was dead.

22

AMADO DIDN'T KNOW how long they'd kept him waiting. He'd always worn a watch on his other arm and it just felt weird to wear one now. He didn't mind waiting. The lobby was nice. Very nice. Lots of magazines, lamps, and fancy telephones you could use for free. There were cushy sofas and funny-looking chairs with shiny metal legs and seats that looked like coffee-shop booths. A large potted ficus tree swayed as the air conditioner blasted cold, clean air into the room.

Above the sofa was a series of photos. It was the cast of the *telenovela*. They looked fantastic, bigger than life. Amado hoped he'd get to meet a couple of them.

A young woman with extremely long legs came into the lobby and handed him a tiny plastic bottle of mineral water from France. Amado smiled at her, he couldn't help admiring those legs, man, were they long.

"Gracias."

"De nada."

Amado wedged the bottle of water between his knees and carefully twisted the top off. He was about to take a sip when an anglo in a dark suit entered the lobby.

"You must be Amado."

Amado did a quick juggling act, trying to put the water on

the table, stand up, and shake hands all at once. He couldn't believe how nervous he suddenly was.

"*Sí.* Yes."

"I'm Stan. Thanks for coming down."

"No problem."

"Did they take care of you?"

Amado picked up his water.

"Yes. Thank you."

"Follow me."

Stan spun on his heel and started walking at a quick and important pace. He led Amado through a doorway and into a large open area. There were assistants in cubicles in the middle. Important offices on both sides. The atmosphere was hushed, serious, and very businesslike. Amado realized that he hadn't really known what to expect. But he hadn't expected something so corporate.

Stan was talking.

"I gotta tell you, normally we don't accept submissions without an agent. But you, sir, you've got friends in high places."

"I know some people."

"Well, we're glad you do, because that script blew our minds."

Amado blinked. Stan continued.

"It's like you're psychic."

Stan turned and they entered a conference room.

"Take a seat."

Amado, from years of habit, sat facing the door. He gave Stan a curious look.

"Did you like my script?"

Stan laughed.

"If I didn't like it, you wouldn't be sitting here."

Amado felt a rush of relief.

"Your script hit the nail on the head. It was inspirational."

"I like the show very much."

"That's obvious. But, frankly, the show is in trouble. Ratings are declining. We've been having a series of discussions, did some focus groups, deep market research, and want us to tweak the show in a slightly different direction."

Stan flopped into a chair and loosened his tie.

"We didn't know what that direction was until we read your script."

Amado was still processing the earlier information.

"I don't understand. People don't like the show?"

"It needs some edge."

"Edge?"

"You know, some street. Some barrio. Reality with a big *R*. The kind of stuff you write. Gritty. That's what the show needs. That's what we're looking for, and that's why I want to offer you a job."

"A job?"

"Yeah. You want to write for the show, right?"

"Cierto."

"Well, we want you to join our staff."

Amado couldn't believe his ears.

"When?"

Stan looked at him.

"Can you start today? We can close a deal right after lunch."

"I don't have an agent."

Stan looked at him.

"A writer as good as you should have an agent."

Amado shrugged.

"I'm just starting."

"Don't worry about it. I've got a friend in the Lit Department at ICM. She'll take care of you. In fact, let's conference her in now."

Stan hit a button on a star-shaped telephone sitting in the middle of the conference table.

"Lois? Get Allie Williams on the phone. Tell her it's important."

Stan looked up at Amado and smiled.

"You, my friend, are going to be a big star in this business."

Amado sipped his water as the assistant at ICM put Stan on hold. Stan looked at him.

"Can I ask you a personal question?"

"Sure."

"What happened to your arm?"

Don sat at his desk typing. There are clusterfucks and then there are clusterfucks. This, he realized, was the mother of all clusterfucks. The granddaddy of all fuckups. A Saddam Hussein supersized fuckup. And who was responsible for this royal fuckup?

He was.

Don checked his list. Two murders, the one that started this whole mess—Carlos Vila—and the sheriff in Palm Springs. The two police shootings, both ruled justifiable, of the Ramirez brothers. One death ruled an accidental drug overdose. One severed arm attributed to a missing, and presumed dead, cookbook author.

Make that three murders.

One severed arm belonging to an unknown individual.

Four.

No witnesses. No testimony. The only evidence seemingly useless. And, if the mumblings of a deranged drug addict were to be believed, it was all because of some new über-gangster named Roberto.

Don wouldn't admit it to his captain, he wouldn't tell Flores or any of the other detectives working in his division, but he was worried. For the first time in his entire police career Don was worried. Whoever this Roberto was, he must be something else. Some kind of criminal mastermind. He had fucked with the LAPD. Brazenly. And they didn't know the first thing about him.

Don had done his best to find out. He'd kept Esteban and Bob in custody, trying to crack them. Trying to get something. He lied. He told Esteban that Bob had cracked and spilled everything. Did Esteban want to return the favor? He told Bob that Esteban had broken down and implicated him in a string of murders. Bob had laughed in the detective's face.

There was no evidence to hold them. He couldn't even get them on simple gun possession charges. A couple of guns had mysteriously appeared in his jacket pockets, machinery wiped clean of finger prints, like a trick by Siegfried and Roy. He couldn't prove that Esteban or Bob had put them there. He couldn't prove that they had conspired to do anything. He couldn't prove shit.

What was he going to charge them with? Impersonating an attorney? Pretending to be a paralegal? What was that? That was bullshit. And bullshit rarely holds up in court.

Esteban and Bob had played it right, kept their mouths shut, hired a fancy lawyer and got out. The American legal system firing on all cylinders, working in all its crook-lovin' glory.

What a fucking mess.

Don hung his head. He'd already heard rumblings that he would be bounced out of the Criminal Intelligence unit and back over to Homicide. *Ugh. There is nothing worse than that. I'd rather be a traffic cop. Anything's better than looking at dead bodies all day. Especially in the summertime.*

But Don wasn't a quitter. He was down but not out. Even though it appeared that Esteban Sola had skipped the country, Don knew he'd be back and he vowed to bring him down. Esteban and this mystery man, Roberto. One of these days they'd slip up again and next time, he'd grab them by their balls and squeeze.

Which is more than he could say about his balls. Since he'd broken off the, well, he couldn't really call it a relationship—it was more of an unhealthy fling, a sick fuck—he'd reverted back to his old routine. He'd leave work and saunter through the downtown streets. Watching the people drain out of the area like it was some kind of old bathtub, until it was empty, just some scum and a few drips left.

He might grab a taco or a little bag of fresh fruit with chili and lime from a cart on Broadway. He couldn't afford to have appetizers or dinner at the wine bar so he always tried to eat something before he got there. Then he'd perch at the bar and let the vino tell him the truth. The version of the truth he wanted to hear.

Maura didn't mind the gray sweatsuit. She didn't mind the shouting of the instructor. She didn't mind the slow jog up and down the hills of Elysian Park. In fact, she was smiling. She couldn't help herself. Here she was, a cadet in the police academy. A year of training and she'd be out on the street. Working a beat.

It was a good change for her. She hadn't realized how burned out she'd gotten helping guys learn to jack off. Honestly, if they can't come by the skills naturally, they ought to just forget about it. No one's making you masturbate.

She jogged in formation with the other cadets, a mix of

men and women, Asians, Latinos, blacks, and Anglos of various ages. The youngest was an eighteen-year-old Chinese girl,
the oldest was a forty-two-year-old washed-up screenwriter.
All of them were committing themselves to change. It was
inspirational.

Maura thought about her life. She hadn't expected too
much out of it. An interesting job, if she was lucky. A
boyfriend. A couple of good vacations. Maybe get married and
have a kid.

She hadn't expected to be opened up and turned inside out
by life. She hadn't expected new passions, obsessions even, to
erupt out of her consciousness and explode fully formed into
her world. She never even knew such things existed.

Now that she'd had a taste of them, there was no turning
back.

Esteban felt his weight cause the hammock to swing gently side
to side. A breeze came off the ocean, smelling like very fresh
salt. Even though it was chilly in the shade of the palm-
thatched umbrella thing—was it called a *palapita?*—the sand
around him reflected the warmth of the sun.

He could hear the clear blue waves crashing against the
shore, *gaviotas* honking overhead, and the unmistakable sound
of ice clinking in salt-rimmed glasses.

Esteban shifted, the hammock bouncing, and turned
toward the sound. He squinted against the glare and saw Lupe,
looking *guapisima* in a fluorescent orange bikini, walking
toward him carrying a couple of drinks. Esteban saw a glint of
rainbow, the flash of a large diamond, flicker on her left hand.
He smiled. He was enjoying being married.

He took the drinks from her and tried to hold them steady

as she eased her way into the hammock with him. He could feel the little grains of sand that had stuck to her body as she pressed herself close to him.

They sipped their drinks in silence.

There was nothing to say.

Felicia rolled over and looked Bob in the eyes. Bob shifted, turning so he could meet her gaze.

"What's up?"

"I'm just looking at you."

Bob smiled.

"What do you see?"

"I see a good man. A man who is trying to do the right thing even when he doesn't always know what the right thing to do is."

Bob laughed and stroked her hair.

"I do try."

"I hope you always try, Roberto. The effort is more important than the results."

She kissed him.

"And I see something else, my sweet Roberto."

"What?"

"I see the father of my child."

Bob couldn't believe it.

"What?"

Felicia grinned.

"I'm pregnant."

Bob lay there, glazed with a strange kind of happiness. It was a new emotion. Electric and deep. A powerful completeness he'd never experienced.

"I don't know what to say."

"Are you happy?"

A tear jumped out of Bob's eye and ran down his cheek.

"Yeah. I'm . . ."

He choked on his words, turned and dove into her, holding tightly. She stroked his hair.

"I'm thinking if it's a girl, we name her Frida."

Bob lifted his head.

"And if it's a boy? Freddy?"

"No. Don't be silly. Freddy is not a good name for a boy."

"Not Roberto."

"Why not? Roberto is a lovely name."

"*Yo soy* Roberto."

Felicia laughed.

"There can only be one Roberto?"

"Yes."

"Do you have a name you like?"

Bob smiled.

"Diego."

Amado couldn't believe it. He had always thought that crime was the most lucrative job around. Well, investment bankers might make more, but then that's a kind of crime. Isn't it?

But when Stan and his agent had finished squabbling on the phone Amado just shook his head in amazement. Writing for television paid far better than he could ever imagine. He stopped off at a liquor store and bought a bottle of expensive French Champagne. He couldn't wait to tell Cindy the news.

23

ROBERTO CAME TO a stop with the rest of the traffic. He liked his new car, a metallic green Volkswagen Beetle. It looked like Kermit the Frog from *Sesame Street*. Friendly and cool, childish and groovy. Perfect for El Jefe's new consultant and second-in-command. Perfect for him.

He also liked that it had a small trunk. That meant he wouldn't be stuffing anyone in it anytime soon. The car had been Amado's idea. Why not go for a whole new image? The green bug and his slick new clothes—Felicia had decided he should wear khakis and guayaberas like Diego Rivera, sunglasses like that French actor who played the cool hit man in *The Professional*—everything about Roberto caught people off guard.

Members of La Eme wondered where he came from. How did he earn Esteban's trust? Had Roberto killed the other gringo? Just who was this dapper man in the froggy-colored car?

The word on the street was that Roberto was smart, fearless, and very ruthless. Amado backed up this story, telling everyone he knew how he'd been skimming some of Esteban's profit and that Roberto found him out and marked him for death. Only after Amado begged for his life and promised to quit the business did Roberto show mercy.

He only took Amado's arm.

This story spread quickly throughout the criminal sub-culture of Los Angeles and earned Roberto some serious respect.

It also afforded him some latitude. Roberto wasn't a man of violence. He didn't like all the kidnapping and killing. So, except in extreme cases, he put a stop to it. He wanted the crew to be run like a legitimate business. Like that hippie ice cream company where everyone has long hair and is happy all the time.

It took a little while to convince Esteban that this kind of strategy would work. But even Esteban had to admit that he was tired of running drugs and stealing cars, he'd much rather move into the legitimate business world. So he gave Roberto the authority to slowly begin the process of transforming a hard-core criminal enterprise into a legitimate and diversified holding company.

Roberto was surprised at how eager his employees were to make a change. It seemed that, deep down, they all wanted to work on the right side of the law. They were tired of living in constant fear of arrest, deportation, or worse, some kind of hostile takeover from a rival crew. After their initial suspicions that Roberto was some kind of highly skilled FBI agent, almost everyone in the organization came around to his way of thinking.

And why wouldn't they? Roberto was open, friendly, smart, and persuasive. He would stop in at the chop shop and take all the guys out to lunch. He would give the coyotes gifts for their kids. He instilled a pride of belonging in members of Esteban's crew.

For the more unpleasant work, still, sadly, a necessity, he hired a couple of bikers from the Mongols outlaw motorcyle club, earning their devotion when he paid for their rehab to cure a nasty crystal meth addiction.

He instituted a profit-sharing plan that gave everyone in the organization a big fat bonus. Roberto had even set up retirement plans for anyone who wanted to participate. That way your money would be laundered for you and you'd have something to live on when you decided to retire or got out of prison.

Roberto wasn't just respected, he was loved. Occasionally he would remember what it had been like to be Bob. But as time passed that was less and less often. He had been born a Bob. He had grown into a Roberto.

Roberto made his way toward the freeways, huge, slow-moving rivers of steel and glass. He popped a CD into the stereo. A stern yet reassuring voice came over the speakers and began to teach him how to conjugate verbs in *español.*

All around the city, the jacaranda trees were in full bloom. Fantastic explosions of purple, courtesy of Brazil, they dotted the landscape and reminded Roberto that he lived in a special place. A tropical place with palm trees and sunshine. A city where roses and cacti grew side by side and bright orange-and-purple birds of paradise sprang up out of cracks in the sidewalk.

The sun was beginning to make its way west, the light filtering through the jacaranda trees, splashing the city in gold and lavender. Roberto listened carefully to his CD. He repeated the words in Spanish. It was like a magical mantra.

The beautiful language of revolution.

Roberto loved this city. With its millions of people from hundreds of countries, speaking ninety different languages, Roberto felt truly at home. People came here to find transformation. They surrendered their past and looked for a future.

They lived *sin banderas,* without flags, they weren't Mexicans or Cambodians, Peruvians or Laotians, Salvadorans or Koreans, Africans or Americans, Pakistanis or Ecuadorians, Thai or Argentine; they were Angelenos.

Roberto was happy to be alive. He was happy he lived in Los Angeles, city of the future, hope of the world.

acknowledgments

This book would not have been possible without the enthusiasm, support, and assistance of Mary Evans, Elizabeth Beier, Kevin Jones, Tom Strickler, Brian Lipson, Christopher Donnelly, and Bill Weinstein.

The author would also like to thank: Steve Wilson, Juan Solá, Alberto Gieco, Corinne Farley, Jared Levine, Dan Jinks, Bruce Cohen, Adam Schroeder, Mark Sourian, Michael DeLuca, Gray Rembert, Spencer Baumgarten, Phil Raskin, Adrianna Alberghetti, and Denny Eichorn.